Mystery
at
Magpie
Lodge

BOOKS BY CLARE CHASE

Mystery at Magpie Lodge

CLARE CHASE

bookouture

Published by Bookouture in 2022

An imprint of Storyfire Ltd.
Carmelite House
50 Victoria Embankment
London EC4Y 0DZ

www.bookouture.com

ISBN: 978-1-80019-969-9
eBook ISBN: 978-1-80019-968-2

For Kate

PROLOGUE

The intruder had no need to pull on gloves – they were wearing them already. The weather had been below freezing for two days now, after what seemed like endless rain. Anyone looking on would be hard put to recognise them. They were dressed head to toe in black, their coat bulky, their woollen hat pulled down low. Unremarkable. Everyone was wrapped up against the bitter January weather.

They gripped the doorknob of Sycamore Cottage tightly to stop their hands from shaking, not from fear but anger, barely controlled. They turned it, slowly, experimentally. The cottage only had an old-fashioned deadlock and no one had turned the key to secure it. That was a bonus, though not entirely surprising when they thought about it.

In a moment they were stepping quietly into the tiled hall, exchanging their outdoor boots for the plimsolls they'd brought. Soft, unlikely to leave a mark. They closed the front door behind them and found themselves in near darkness. The curtains downstairs were drawn against the January evening and the ground floor was unlit. The faint glow of a landing light just reached the entrance hall, but they wouldn't be seen. They could tell the current occupant of the house, Emory Fulton, was already in the bath. The sound of water slopping as he changed position was perfectly audible.

Not long now. Emory wouldn't be prepared, even when he saw who'd come to call.

No one truly believed someone they knew was capable of murder, did they?

What an advantage that was.

1

A WEEK EARLIER

Eve Mallow was standing in the Dower House of Fairview Hall, surrounded by the villagers of Saxford St Peter. The place smelled of food, polish, woodsmoke and expensive perfume. The room was opulent: there was a Persian rug on the shiny wooden floor and the mantelpiece was home to a beautiful ormolu clock. But despite these old heirlooms and the antique mahogany furniture, the place didn't feel lived in; there wasn't a mark on any of the belongings.

The perfection gave the room an oppressive feel, but it wasn't just that which made the atmosphere tense. Eve's best friend Viv was standing to one side of her, holding forth about their hosts in her version of a whisper. Selina and Roger Fulton had thrown the Dower House open to raise money for a local nature reserve. It was an excellent cause but they'd committed the cardinal sin of not asking Viv to do the catering.

Viv was the creative genius behind Saxford's only teashop, Monty's. Its cakes were sublime, and since Viv had employed Eve to address the managerial side, it ran like clockwork. Eve had all but eradicated the last-minute panics associated with its catering service, and taken charge of its crafts area too. The

calm order she'd managed to establish gave her immense satisfaction.

She felt Viv was judging her for tucking into the Dower
House food quite so heartily, despite its unfortunate
background.

'Mass produced!' Viv held a florentine at arm's length as
though it might be laced with cyanide. 'And you know why,
don't you? It's because Roger Fulton' – she pulled a snooty face
– 'wanted to support Pepys Fine Foods, because the owner's a
bigwig contact of his on the board of the Blyworth and Villages
Charitable Trust.'

Luckily, the Fultons had a string quartet playing at one end
of their spacious drawing room, so no one was likely to hear
Viv's accusations. Eve only hoped there were no lip-readers
present. There were plenty of eyes on Viv, even if her words
were drowned out. Her current hair colour (cobalt blue) tended
to attract attention.

Eve shook her head. 'Power corrupts. But since he did
decide to order from Pepys, I thought I'd sacrifice myself and eat
the food anyway.'

Viv tutted as Eve took another florentine from a tray by one
of the sixteenth-century building's mullioned windows. The
tray sat on a highly polished table. Eve had seen Selina Fulton
glance at it anxiously as she passed and adjust the tray to make
sure it was fully on the soft mat that was protecting the wood
underneath. There were several children present. Eve was
waiting to see what happened if one of them put a sticky glass of
orange juice next to the tray...

Eve took care of her belongings too, but there was no point
in having nice things if you couldn't relax around them. But of
course, Selina's devotion to her possessions figured. She was the
co-owner of a very select interiors shop in the nearest town,
Blyworth. It was crazily expensive and too chic for words.

'I suppose it's good of them to throw their house open like

this,' Eve said, reining in her judgemental thoughts. 'And they are supporting an excellent cause.'

'Driven by Roger Fulton's desire to look good in front of his clients and the Trust's management,' Viv said darkly. 'I've heard he's hoping for a knighthood.'

The judgemental thoughts bounced back. 'Interesting.' Fulton was a lawyer with a practice in Blyworth. After observing him that day, Eve could certainly imagine him fundraising to boost his personal brand; she was sure he'd love being Sir Roger. He was all about appearances from what she'd seen. She'd watched his reaction as one of her fellow villagers entered the house and removed her coat. Underneath, the genial nonagenarian's outfit was revealed as a bed jacket (orange, two sizes too small), and a pair of pink and green floral leggings. Eve had just been admiring her chutzpah when she caught Roger Fulton's look of horror. A moment later he'd moulded his features into a false, welcoming smile.

Eve had been predisposed to judge him ever since. She felt he was false and overly conventional. It was instinctive to watch people and fathom out their characters, thanks to her true profession. As well as working part-time at the teashop, she wrote obituaries. She loved every aspect of the work. The gradual piecing together of the deceased's character was fascinating: the best sort of puzzle. But it was almost as enthralling to delve into the psyche of surviving friends and relatives. Reading between the lines to unpick their relationships with her subjects told a whole other story.

It was no surprise that she enjoyed social situations, where people-watching was officially sanctioned.

As Viv went off to air her grievances to her brother, Eve's attention was caught by one particular cameo in the crowded room. A young woman with cascading platinum-blonde hair was leaning against a tall bookcase in a shadowy corner, her head thrown back, laughing. She was Coco, Roger and Selina

Fulton's daughter. Eve had been introduced to her by her
mother on her way into the party. Well, introduced after a fash-
ion. Coco had been on her way to the drinks table to switch her
empty glass of Prosecco for a full one. She'd given Eve an
amused smile over her shoulder as her mother mentioned her
name. Self-assured, languid. She hadn't paused or changed
direction.

She must be in her late twenties, Eve guessed. She had the
figure of an A-list Hollywood actress, and a deliberate, almost
insolent informality that clashed with her parents' smooth
veneer, polite greetings and enquiries about local issues.

Eve guessed the man with Coco might be in his mid- to late-
fifties. He was rather heavily built, with grizzled hair and a
widow's peak. He was laughing too, his eyes sparkling, face
ruddy, what looked like a whisky in his hand. Like Coco, he
slouched against the bookcase, one elbow on a convenient shelf.

At that moment, Moira, the village storekeeper, appeared at
Eve's side. 'That's Coco Fulton, of course, Roger and Selina's
daughter.'

Eve turned and smiled. 'Ah, yes. We were introduced.'

Moira's face fell slightly. Conveying exclusive information
was her favourite pastime.

Eve took pity on her. 'I don't know the man she's talking to,
though.'

The storekeeper beamed. 'Oh! I assumed you'd be aware by
now – that's Emory Fulton, Roger's younger brother.'

Eve knew he'd arrived; Moira had broadcast the news in the
store. All the same, she was surprised. She'd have guessed the
man talking to Coco was older than their host. She wondered
what fortune had thrown at him. Or perhaps it was down to
lifestyle – he looked like a merry soul, and the whisky glass was
now empty.

'I don't imagine he's been into Monty's,' Moira went on.
'Not with the way things are.'

Eve shook her head. Moira had already explained that Emory Fulton had hit rock bottom, financially. Monty's wasn't expensive, but there were certainly cheaper ways of getting your calories.

The storekeeper sighed. 'Such a pity he's fallen on hard times after being so successful. But from what I've heard, with all the women, and the drink...' She shook her head with ill-disguised relish. 'A man reaps what he sows.' His exploits must have given her hours of pleasure as she passed on the details.

She'd given Eve the low-down, of course, some of which she'd known already. Emory had been a household name twenty years ago. Eve knew about the 'Haunted' series of books he'd written, from *Haunted England* and *Haunted Wales* to *Haunted Castles* and *Haunted Inns*. They'd all been bestsellers. For years he'd been a regular guest on television, talking about ghost-hunting and making contact with 'the other side'. He'd spoken about it as though it were similar to ringing Australia. But Eve didn't believe in ghosts.

Moira said his fame had led to extravagant living, putting a strain on his health and his pocket. Apparently he was back in Saxford because he had nowhere else to go. Roger and Selina Fulton had put him up on their land, in a separate building called Magpie Lodge. Originally, it had been 'The Lodge, Fairview Hall', but the chattering birds which gathered there had led to its atmospheric nickname. It sounded romantic, but Eve had never seen it up close.

She was drawn out of her thoughts by the sight of Selina Fulton, her lips tight, expression fixed, watching her daughter and Emory.

'Coco was away when he arrived,' Moira said, following her gaze, 'but they've been thick as thieves ever since she got home, I gather.' She shook her head. 'I'm not sure what sort of influence he'll be.'

Coco picked up their empty glasses and sauntered towards

the drinks station, her figure-hugging calf-length dress swishing. Eve saw Emory catch Selina's eye and raise an eyebrow. The look Selina gave in response shocked her: it was one of pure, ice-cold hatred.

A moment later, Emory pulled out a peacock-blue cloth-bound book from the case and opened it, a frown furrowing his brow.

In three quick strides, Selina had reached his side and snatched the book from his hands. She rammed it back into the case and marched away through an open door and down a corridor beyond. Eve lost track of her progress – there were too many people blocking her view – but within a minute she was visible through a leaded window, striding down the lawn despite the rain.

Emory Fulton remained where he was. He stroked the spine of the blue book, the frown still present, but just then one of Eve's neighbours came to join her and she was forced to look away.

It was half an hour before Eve became aware of Emory again. She was chatting to the vicar, who was laughing uproariously about his recent appearance in the village pantomime. (He'd played one of the ugly sisters in *Cinderella*, alongside Matt from the Cross Keys pub.)

As the vicar and Eve recovered themselves, the vicar's eyes watering, she could hear snippets of Emory's conversation with the middle-aged woman who was now standing opposite him. She was his polar opposite: immaculately turned out in a fawn dress and jacket.

'... no, you mustn't believe what you hear. Dear old Roger invited me to stay here at the Dower House, but reading between the lines I could tell that wouldn't suit Selina, which is very understandable. It would have cramped her, having me move in.' He grinned and gestured around the vast drawing room towards the corridor which led to the rest of the cavernous house. 'Three's a crowd – imagine four! And Magpie Lodge is excellent for my purposes. I don't mind about the lack of bathroom. I can always wash at the sink and there's an outdoor tap and WC too.' Emory's eyes twinkled in the light from the large open fire and his lips twitched. Eve guessed he'd be laughing as hard as the vicar if he let go.

The woman put her head on one side. She had her back to Eve, so it was hard to judge her response, but a soldierly man in a dark suit next to her stiffened. Eve sensed he was shocked.

Roger was passing and Eve heard him say hastily: 'I offered to get Emory somewhere in Blyworth but—'

His brother patted him on the shoulder, still grinning. 'But I wanted to stay nearby now I'm in the area, rather than be farmed out. It's gracious of you both to let me use the lodge.' He was fighting laughter again, but his gaze turned wintery when it fell on Selina, standing across the room.

As Eve excused herself, leaving the vicar in order to find the bathroom, she could feel the tension in the air.

The Fultons' cloakroom was decorated with floral blue and white toile-print wallpaper, the backdrop to a traditional white suite. *Tasteful.* It must have cost a packet. The gilt-framed circular mirror over the basin rounded the scheme off nicely. After washing her hands and availing herself of some of the Crabtree and Evelyn hand cream which rested on a side table, Eve unlocked the panelled door. She was on the point of crossing the threshold when she heard voices.

'That woman you were talking to is one of our top clients!' A woman's voice. Low. Angry. Was it Selina? Eve was pretty sure it was. 'She spends a small fortune on our interiors. What do you mean by making me look bad in front of her?'

Quiet laughter. It must be Emory, of course. 'For heaven's sake, take a joke, Selina. Your face was a picture, I must say.'

'And the man was a partner at Roger's firm.'

'Really?' Eve could tell he'd still got the giggles but his sister-in-law sounded anything but amused.

'I'm going to ask you to leave now, and if you don't, I'll ask Roger to throw you out.'

There was a long pause and when he answered, Emory's tone had changed. Eve guessed he was keeping a different emotion at bay now: anger. Hurt maybe. 'I want to be close to my family. Go ahead and ask Roger to throw me out if you don't mind me telling him what you're up to. Even today of all days, under his very nose.' There was a shake to his voice.

Eve jumped as a crash came from the room, accompanied by the sound of china clinking. What the heck was going on?

She'd been so taken up with their row that she was still standing in the cloakroom doorway. Catching her breath, she stepped out into the corridor and beyond a coat rack. She was only just in time. Selina strode out of the room where the argument had taken place, white-faced, her eyes wide.

A moment later, Emory followed her, rubbing his elbow, blinking.

Eve waited a minute before entering the room they'd occupied. It was a small box room lined with cupboards. The one on the far side had glass doors and china inside. Emory and Selina had both looked shocked, but Eve had the impression it was Emory who'd been shoved against the cupboard, and Selina who couldn't quite believe she'd done it.

2

Eve found it hard to shift her mind from the argument she'd overheard, but the Rice family was another source of intrigue at the Fulton's 'charity soirée'. Eve had seen Ada Rice in the village, but she didn't really mix. She lived at Fairview Hall, which, along with the Dower House and Magpie Lodge, had once been part of the same large estate, owned by a Fulton ancestor. Eve understood (mainly via Moira) that the Fulton family money had dwindled, forcing them to break up the estate. The Dower House would once have been set aside for a series of Fulton widows, who would vacate the hall on the death of their husbands, leaving their eldest sons to take over the family seat. It was a luxurious place to live by most people's standards and came with plenty of land. But Eve still wondered if Roger and Selina felt envious of the elegant and monied Ada Rice, who'd bought the Fulton's ancestral home.

Adding interest to their dynamic was the fact that Ada co-owned Selina's chi-chi interiors business.

As people shifted around the room, making a beeline for a new selection of cakes, Eve found herself in the same small group as Selina and Ada. Ada was distinguished-looking –

around sixty, Eve guessed, with a regal bearing, understated gold jewellery and perfectly applied, subtle make-up.

'What a hoot that Coco's finally got a university place!' Ada was saying.

Selina drew herself up. 'It's the first time she's applied.'

Ada nodded. 'Of course, I was forgetting. Good that she's got round to it. She's twenty-eight now, isn't she?'

Across the room, Coco had gone back into her huddle with Emory. They looked like a pair of conspiratorial teenagers, despite their ages.

'Just. Yes.' There was a momentary pause. 'She had to get the travel bug out of her system before settling down to study. And of course, time abroad is such a rich experience: other cultures, so many ways of life. And she did lots of sports: scuba diving and rock climbing.'

Ada cocked her head. 'And all that bartending. It will certainly stand her in good stead; she's highly qualified for pub work now, if nothing else.'

Heck. What must life be like at their store? Presumably the antagonism had developed over time and now they were stuck with each other. Eve silently thanked her lucky stars for her happy partnership with Viv.

'Still,' Selina said, her cheeks tinged red, 'she won't want for a top job with a Bathurst degree.' She'd played her trump card. Bathurst was a prestigious university in north London, up there with Oxbridge.

'That we can agree on. A first-class institution.' Ada laughed lightly and floated off to talk to another woman who'd been waiting at her elbow for a few moments. Long enough to hear her snide remarks about Coco.

Selina was quivering with irritation and in Eve's experience, fury inclined people to confide. Sure enough, she turned to Eve. 'Ada's son is a professor at Bathurst, in case you're wondering about her final remark. No gap years for him, and it's true, Coco has had a lot, but she's an entirely different personality. I'm sure she's got an extremely successful future ahead of her.' Eve's eyes lit on the girl and Emory again. 'As for Ada's son, he's here today, as a matter of fact, with his wife. They're staying at the hall for a while. He's on sabbatical.'

Selina indicated a man Eve guessed might be in his late thirties, with thick dark hair, a pristine white shirt and dark trousers. Next to him was a slender woman with high cheekbones and clear blue eyes. Her long red hair gleamed in the light from a chandelier. They were a handsome couple. Eve had met the woman before. She was a jeweller who'd recently approached Monty's in the hope that they'd stock her wares. Eve had taken over as gatekeeper for the crafts section thanks to her ability to say no, but her tactful assertiveness wasn't required on that occasion. The woman's work was beautiful. Eve kept quiet about their connection now. Selina was bound to clam up if she knew Eve and Ada's daughter-in-law were acquainted.

'I'm sure her son's very brilliant, of course!' Selina was saying. 'I'm not saying he's not. And if you talk to Ada, she'll no doubt tell you he's tipped to head up some exclusive society for Egyptologists. But you might be interested to know that the trustee chair who'll approve the appointment is his father-in-law. That beautiful wife of his is an asset in more ways than one. Her daddy's the vice chancellor at Bathurst too.' She paused. 'He's quite young as professors go. I'm not saying those facts are related – of course I'm not!' She laughed a brittle laugh and headed off to mingle with the great and the good of Saxford.

'Enjoying the party?' The query made Eve jump. She'd been staring after Selina, wondering if the event could get any more tense. Pepys' food wasn't really that bad, but Eve was getting indigestion.

She turned to find Emory standing next to her. His smile

was warm and the gentle amusement was back in his eyes. He must have calmed down after his row with Selina. 'It's... erm...' she hesitated, 'interesting so far.' Beyond him, Eve accidentally caught her hostess's gaze. Selina turned away instantly to chat to another guest, her shoulders rigid.

Eve realised Emory had followed her gaze and seen the mini-interaction.

'Was that Selina keeping an eye on me?' His tone was light, posture relaxed, but his expression had changed subtly. The amusement was fading. 'Don't take any notice. She's probably worried I'll use this event to tout for business.'

After their row, Eve guessed it was more likely that Selina was worried about what he might say, but she let it pass. 'Business?'

Emory nodded and grinned again. 'I'm freelance these days. Séances, that kind of thing. And I'm planning some ghost tours locally too. You might be interested.'

Perhaps he assumed she was a tourist, looking for entertainment. She still had her American accent, though she'd left Seattle when she was eighteen, travelling to London to study, encouraged by her British-born dad. She'd stuck around to raise a family. Her marriage was over, but her adult twins meant everything to her.

'So, tell me about you. You're visiting like me?'

Eve shook her head. 'I live here. I moved up from London a couple of years back. I'm in Elizabeth's Cottage now.'

It wasn't the grandest house in Saxford St Peter but it was easily the most famous. Back in the 1720s, the woman who lived there had become the village heroine by saving a servant boy from the gallows. His crime had been to steal a loaf of bread from his employers to feed his starving siblings. Elizabeth had hidden him in a tiny space under her house, then rowed him across the River Sax to safety – a striking act of bravery. Her grandson had renamed the cottage after her. She was part of village folklore now.

Emory's eyes lit up at her words. 'Elizabeth's Cottage! In that case, your house and lane will feature in the ghost tour I'm planning.'

'I guessed they might.' A hue and cry had been sent thundering after the poor cowering servant boy. Hearing echoes of their footfalls, late at night, was said to signify danger. It was how her road, Haunted Lane, had got its name. Eve had conjured up the sound of thudding feet several times now, often just before a death. But she knew the story. It made sense that it haunted her dreams when she was ill at ease.

'You still have the twice-yearly open house, I suppose? I remember those from when I was a child. I used to love visiting.' There was a sadness in Emory's eyes now. For some reason, it went right to Eve's heart; the thought of innocent times lost perhaps. It was something she could relate to. Life got so complicated.

'I do, yes. I had one just before Christmas.' It was tradition. The 'keeper' of Elizabeth's Cottage was expected to host the gatherings to raise money for children's charities, in memory of Elizabeth and the boy she'd saved. Visitors got to look round the house and see the cramped space where the boy had hidden in return for donations. There were always cakes aplenty too, supplied by Monty's, of course.

'Good for you. Did you know anyone when you moved here?'

'A few people that I'd met on a previous visit. There was no one I knew really well.'

'It must have been a shock to the system moving from London.' He sighed. 'It's what I've done, though it ought to be easier for me. I've come back to my family.' For a second his eyes went to Coco and then to his brother and sister-in-law. He looked sad but before she had time to work out what to say he was laughing again. 'Roger's such a stuffed shirt; I can't resist teasing him. Who could? But family is important.' He raised his glass to hers. 'Here's to the future. And I'd love you to come along on my ghost tour, to see what you think.' His cheeks flushed slightly. 'Perhaps you'd accept a percentage of the takings to whichever children's charities you're collecting for?'

The emotion was still there in Emory's eyes, and it rubbed off on her.

'That would be amazing, thank you.' It was especially generous, given his circumstances. Eve wondered what Emory's childhood had been like. Had he been the rebel of the family, comparing unfavourably to Roger? It seemed likely, given their careers and where they'd ended up.

Emory had just excused himself when Eve caught sight of Selina through one of the windows. What was she doing, nipping outside again with her fundraiser in full swing?

After the argument she'd overheard, Eve decided to get some air herself. What was it that Selina was doing 'under Roger's nose'? Officially, it was none of Eve's business, but the row and the violence of Selina's feelings had made her anxious. Finding out more was instinctive.

If anyone asked where she was headed, Eve had the perfect excuse for a stroll in the grounds. She'd eaten too many cakes and the room was stiflingly hot. She wove her way between the crowds, and down the same corridor she'd seen Selina use earlier. There must be a back door somewhere. At last she found it, off a side branch of the passage, and turned the black iron doorknob to let herself out.

It was a relief to get outside. Saxford was on the coast, but they were a little way inland here, on the other side of the River Sax from the main village. There was no invigorating sea breeze, but the rain had left the air feeling clean and the cold was bracing. The garden was beautiful too, even in winter, its stark trees forming patterns against the grey sky, with splashes of colour provided by red berries on the holly bushes.

Selina was nowhere to be seen, and Eve meandered down to the bottom of the garden, making a show of examining the plants in case anyone was watching. Beyond a collection of trees and shrubs, creating a border with the upper lawn, Eve spotted the back of an arbour and slowed her pace. Was that where Selina had hidden herself? Maybe she'd just come out for some quiet time.

But in that moment, Eve heard the soft murmur of voices.

'... can't be much longer. Roger's bound to come out here to look for me if he thinks I've gone AWOL. But I had to see you. I'm afraid our secret's out.'

'What?' A man's voice, sharp, shocked.

'Emory knows. Don't ask me how. He's already threatened to tell Roger if I try and push him away.' Her voice trailed off. 'He's still angry with me.'

'Hell.' The man paused. 'What do you mean "still angry with you"?'

'Never mind that now. I'd better get back inside. I just wanted to tell you.'

Heck. They'd spot her if she didn't move.

Eve ducked between a pair of viburnum bushes, her heart thudding so hard she felt Selina would hear her on her way past.

Selina walked up the garden alone, not looking back.

Eve stood still, drips from the viburnum's lush green leaves landing on her shoulders. After five more minutes – she timed them – a man appeared, walking up the lawn, just as Selina had. He wore an Arran jumper and tan cords. He turned to check over his shoulder before disappearing and, in that moment, Eve recognised him. A fellow Saxford St Peter villager who lived on Dark Lane. He was married, too.

Eve shivered as she finally dared to extricate herself from

the shrubbery. The situation was uncomfortably volatile. And why was Emory angry with Selina? It sounded as though it was she who'd made him feel unwelcome at the Dower House – refused to have him perhaps. That had probably hurt his feelings, for all his teasing about it. But what had made her act like that in the first place? Simple selfishness – a desire to protect her routine?

Eve shook her head. The way they'd quarrelled told her it was more than that.

3

Eve was working a shift in Monty's the Tuesday after the fundraiser when she next saw Emory Fulton. He arrived at the teashop in a thin damp overcoat, not cut out for the cold wet weather, which seemed to have settled permanently over Saxford. Eve wondered again about his relations with his family. She still wasn't sure what to make of him. He'd made mischief at the fundraiser, but she had a feeling he'd done it lightly, and that it had been aimed at his sister-in-law, even if it was causing his brother embarrassment too. Emory and Selina clearly had issues and it was hard to say who was at fault. She was cheating on Roger but Emory had had his wild days too. She didn't imagine he'd be above that kind of thing. Yet he was warm, and put an emphasis on the importance of family. That chimed with Eve's own views. And he'd offered to support the children's charities she collected for. That was what Eve loved about people – they were full of fascinating contradictions, and Emory more than most.

He gave her a cheery wave as she went to greet him. She was scheduled to be front of house that day. She liked the mix of admin and serving the customers. Viv often dragged her in to help with the baking these days, too. She'd trained her up.

'A table for two, please,' Emory said, as Eve took his sopping coat and hung it on the stand in the corner for him. She chose the side closest to the radiator and hoped it might have time to dry out. The teashop was lovely and warm, the colourful bunting in the steamed-up bay windows a cheerful contrast to the grey day outside.

'This is a lovely place,' Emory said, to a Cheshire Cat grin from Viv, who was within earshot, serving some other customers. 'It was very different when I was a child. Full of grubby doilies with a disapproving proprietor who hated her customers.'

Eve nodded as she pulled out a chair for him at a table close to Monty's crafts section. 'Viv – my boss – took it over with her husband years back now.' Viv had retreated into the kitchen. 'I'm afraid he died young, but she's done wonders with it, despite working single-handed.'

'No mean feat.' Emory settled himself and put the plastic bag he'd been carrying down next to his chair.

His table was decorated in standard Monty's style, with a cobalt-blue cloth (to match Viv's current hair colour), and a jam jar trimmed with matching ribbon. In it sat a bunch of snow-drops. The deep blue backdrop set off their white flowers and fresh green leaves perfectly. Eve handed Emory the menu.

'What would you recommend?'

She felt self-conscious. The prices varied a bit.

'I'm treating someone special.'

It was as though he'd read her mind. Maybe that was how he managed his séances. If he was excellent at guessing his clients' thoughts, he could gear his 'messages from beyond the grave' to fit their situation. Viv would tell her off for being cynical.

'In that case, the sloe-gin spice cakes are hard to beat. Good and warming in winter. So long as your friend doesn't mind the alcohol in them.'

Emory laughed. 'I notice you've decided I won't mind.'

That was hardly fair. 'I saw you have the odd drink at the fundraiser.'

He laughed again. 'Sloe-gin cakes it is, and a pot of tea with two cups, please. Whatever you've got that's strong and sustaining.'

By the time Eve came back with Emory's order, he'd been joined by Poppy Rice, the jeweller who'd asked Monty's to stock her wares. Eve put her into context now, with her new-found knowledge gained at the Fultons' fundraiser. She was Ada-up-at-the-hall's daughter-in-law, married to the woman's over-achieving son. As before, Eve was struck by her beautiful and distinctive appearance: high cheekbones, clear blue eyes and long red hair that fell in ringlets.

The woman looked up quickly and smiled at Eve. 'Nice to see you again.'

'You too.' They'd chatted when Poppy had first approached Monty's, but hardly at all at the fundraiser, where she'd been permanently attached to her husband's side. Eve remembered Selina hinting that their marriage had been convenient: her father was in a position of power at Bathurst, where Ada's son was a professor. She'd taken that with a pinch of salt; Selina had been point-scoring and to Eve, the couple had looked close. Poppy had been hanging on her husband's arm, not scoping the room for someone better to talk to.

But now, the woman looked anxious. She had the sort of expressive face that gave everything away: large eyes that were currently cast down and the sort of complexion that colours easily under stress. She was probably a similar age to Coco Fulton, but she had none of her cocksure arrogance.

Eve had the urge to cheer her up. 'We sold two pairs of your earrings yesterday. They're going down really well.'

A small smile lit her face, but it was gone in an instant.

As Eve served other tables, she kept noticing the pair. At one point Emory put a hand on Poppy's. She looked emotional and shook her head.

Eve heard snatches of her words as she passed them. 'Yes, of course, but I went in with my eyes open. You're sure you can manage?'

And then on another of Eve's flypasts: '... I know, I should have told you. And you're right of course, I've been meaning to, but it's not easy.' Poppy was shaking her head. A second later she added: 'You don't understand. Please, Emory, don't push me on this. I can't! Not now.'

Poppy sounded panicked and Eve wondered what they were talking about. It was desperately tempting to hang around for more details but it wouldn't do. Resolutely, she went to set a recently vacated table, and by the time she returned, the conversation had moved on. Poppy had her hand on Emory's sleeve and was leaning forward, a look of urgency in her eyes. Eve caught the words: '... something I wanted to tell you...'

But as she spoke, the old-fashioned bell over the teashop door jangled and Poppy's husband walked in. Ada Rice's son was dark-haired and broad-shouldered, and his perfectly cut coat, white shirt and dark trousers showed him off to best advantage. Eve spotted the appreciative glance Viv shot him from the kitchen doorway.

As he approached, Eve dredged up what she knew of him. He was young, but already a professor of some sort. A branch of history, wasn't it? Staying in Suffolk while he was on sabbatical.

'Here you are!' He strode across the room to greet Poppy. Eve caught her and Emory's looks: his shuttered, hers thwarted. Her sentence to Emory was left unfinished.

She half stood as her husband approached. 'Laurence.'

She raised her face and Eve was sure she'd intended to kiss

him but he left her standing there awkwardly as he turned to drag a chair from a vacant table.

'Someone mentioned you were in here.' He nodded at Emory. 'Mind if I join you?' There was a disconcerting mix of hostility and amusement in his eyes as he held out a hand. 'We hardly spoke at the fundraiser, but I know how *very* important you are to Poppy.' There was an edge to his words. He was obviously making a point. 'It would be nice to get to know you better.'

Eve found it hard to take her eyes off them. She turned for long enough to fetch him a menu, but she never got to hand it over. Poppy was gathering her things together.

'I was just about to leave, in fact, wasn't I, Emory?'

Emory's smile didn't meet his eyes. 'You were indeed.' Eve was impressed that he remained unruffled – outwardly at least. Internally, she could see there was something else going on. His fists were bunched. Eve was sure Laurence had been intent on breaking up the tête-à-tête from the start. His words were friendly enough but his tone said it all; you could cut the atmosphere with a knife. He stood up, already halfway to the door.

Poppy scrabbled awkwardly in her purse, half her attention on her husband, whose eyes were on the exit. 'You must let me—'

But Emory waved aside her efforts. 'Nonsense. If I can't treat my goddaughter now I'm back in Saxford it's a shame.'

There was still something grimly amused about Laurence's smile. 'I had no intention of cutting your tea short.'

Like heck.

Emory got up now and leaned in to kiss Poppy on both cheeks. 'It's been good to see you.' He clasped her hand and her eyes glistened.

'You too.'

Within seconds, Laurence led the way out of the teashop

again, rain blowing in as he opened the door. He paused outside
to put up a large black umbrella, but strode ahead before Poppy
could catch up, leaving her to dash after him. She'd forgotten to
say goodbye to Eve or Viv, and Eve wasn't surprised. Laurence
Rice had given her an adrenaline rush. What did he mean by
interrupting his wife's heart-to-heart with her godfather? And
why hadn't Poppy or Emory stood their ground?

Emory rose from his seat.

'Can I settle the bill now please?' He fetched his coat before
Eve could get to it and came up to the counter. A moment later
he'd paid and left her a small tip too. His eyes met hers. 'See you
soon, I hope. My first ghost tour's on Friday, if you'd like to
come along. I'd value your feedback when I tackle Haunted
Lane. Eight o'clock, starting on the village green, ending at
Fairview Hall. It's got an interesting history.'

'I'll be there.' Eve couldn't miss it – not after a request like
that. And in any case, she was curious – both to see him in
action and to hear more about the hall's history. Normally she'd
look online beforehand but on this occasion she decided not to.
She didn't believe in ghosts, but she enjoyed an eerie story as
much as the next person. Investigating in advance would steal
Emory's thunder.

Emory's eyes were on the green outside Monty's. As Eve
watched, Poppy disappeared into the village store which stood
opposite the teashop. Whatever she wanted, Laurence had
opted to wait outside. He was standing on the grass under his
umbrella as Emory reached Monty's door and set the bell
jangling again.

A minute later, Emory had followed Laurence across the
green. Viv joined Eve by the counter as she looked on. The two
men faced each other now. It was Emory doing the talking. His
stance was aggressive: his shoulders and head forward, making
Eve think of a bull.

Laurence met aggression with aggression, jabbing a finger at Emory's chest. Eve wished she could lip-read.

They clearly knew each other a lot better than they were admitting publicly. Eve was intrigued by the dynamic between all three of them. Emory was trying to persuade Poppy to do something, but she was pushing back hard. Poppy had wanted to confide in him – he was clearly a good listener – but Laurence's arrival had scuppered that. And Emory and Laurence were hostile towards each other, but only let rip when Poppy was out of the way.

What the heck was it all about? Was Laurence so controlling that he objected to Poppy spending time with another man, even if it was in full view of the village and he happened to be her godfather?

'Interesting,' Viv said.

'Very.' As they watched, Emory turned on his heel and tramped off, back towards the Old Toll Road out of the village. Poppy reappeared a moment later and she and Laurence got into a shiny navy Mercedes parked by the green.

'I'd give a lot to understand what's going on between them.' Eve explained what she'd heard in an undertone. Viv had seen the rest. 'But that's not all. When he arrived, Emory was carrying a plastic bag. The same one that's now stuffed into Poppy's tote. She bundled it in there the instant Laurence's back was turned. She didn't want him to see it.'

4

Eve was standing in her own road, Haunted Lane, with a small crowd of assorted villagers, listening to Emory Fulton tell the ghost story associated with her house.

'... imagine the boy's terror, as he ran to escape the men thundering after him. He'd have been small for his age – malnourished and overworked, poorly dressed, thin and shivering. When Elizabeth ushered him into her cottage, he was taking a gamble. Could he trust her? Think of having to make that split-second decision – to go with her, when she might give him up to the authorities? Or to carry on running, with what little strength he had left?

'He decided to trust her and it was the right call, but he wouldn't have known that. Minutes later he was hiding, shaking in the dark, the footsteps of his pursuers creaking heavily overhead. He'd have heard their fierce questions, the sound of them pulling open cupboards, moving furniture – knowing they'd gladly see him hanged if they could only sniff him out. Elizabeth's calm bravery and the brooms and mops she'd flung over the trapdoor were all that stood between him and the hangman's rope.'

Eve caught her breath. The hiding place always left her claustrophobic and terrified.

As she became conscious of her surroundings again she saw Moira had her hands over her mouth. Eve felt a mix of awe and irritation. *She'd* never had that effect on the storekeeper, despite reciting the same tale during her open-house sessions. If Emory's writing was as compelling as his storytelling, she could see why his books had sold. No wonder he'd been so sought after on TV talk shows.

The pauses Emory allowed between tales were effective too. He let the villagers' minds fill with what he was saying, conjuring up the scenes he'd created. In the evening darkness, Eve heard the eerie cry of a wading bird from the estuary out beyond the marshes. She shivered. After days of eternal rain, the temperature had plummeted. Puddles had frozen and frost twinkled in the light of Emory's lantern. Eve was snuggled into her chocolate-brown coat and matching boots, with her suede-effect gloves and a faux-fur hat for good measure. Gus, her beloved dachshund, had his coat on too: a stylish blue-and-green tartan number. But it wasn't just the conditions that were making her shiver. Eve wasn't immune to Emory's words, despite not believing in ghosts. His stories conjured up the past so clearly. Gus seemed affected too. Maybe he'd picked up on her emotions; he was huddled against her legs, his soulful brown eyes glinting in the low light. She bent to fuss him and a moment later, Emory did the same, making the dachshund the centre of attention.

'Animals feel the echoes of the past keenly,' Emory said, 'just like we do, only they're not too proud to show it.'

Eve was sure the comment was directed at her and bristled in spite of herself. 'I have a feeling Gus is part of Emory's marketing efforts,' she muttered to Viv, as the crowd moved on.

Her friend raised an eyebrow. 'You're such a cynic. Everyone knows there's something odd about Haunted Lane.

Even Simon.' Simon was Viv's brother, owner of the local stables and a serial entrepreneur with his feet firmly on the ground. 'And you've heard the footsteps.'

Eve should never have admitted to that. 'I've dreamed them when something in the village has put me on edge. I don't believe they're an omen of danger – they just feature in my nightmares when I sense something's wrong.'

'Yeah, right. You can't rationalise everything.'

But Eve usually found that she could.

The crowd moved off again, back along the lane in the direction of the village green. Ahead of them, frosted grass sparkled in the glow of the village's old-fashioned lamps. The leafless oaks stood majestic, and beyond them the edifice of St Peter's Church rose, mysterious and imposing.

At the top of Haunted Lane, Emory held his lantern high and turned right, towards the Old Toll Road, leading them over the River Sax, away from the main village. He was like the Pied Piper of Hamelin, Eve thought; everyone followed, spellbound, over the dark water below them.

Emory had already taken them round the parts of the village nearest the sea, pausing to tell dark tales on Dark Lane and stories of the ghost dog Black Shuck outside the ruins of the old church. He'd included legends Eve had never heard before too, one relating to a long-dead ferryman at the estuary end of Ferry Lane, another to the grisly murder of a smuggler down by Blind Eye Wood. Eve wondered what else he had up his sleeve, and how much he'd invented from scratch. Whatever the truth, the party was lapping it up, though Eve bet she wasn't the only sceptic. Viv was rubbing her gloved hands, her eyes wide with excitement and expectation. Moira looked deadly serious, frowning into the darkness as though something might leap out at her. But over to their right, Laurence Rice had an amused smile on his lips. His superior expression took away from his dark good looks. Heck, maybe Eve looked just as smug and disapproving. She rearranged her features into an eager smile; after all, she was enjoying herself.

'What's up with you?' Viv hissed as they walked along the road, sporadic houses to their left, marshland and mudflats to their right.

Eve turned and raised an eyebrow.

'You're grinning into the dark and it's giving me the creeps.'

'Sorry.' She must have overdone it.

Emory was walking slowly. Every so often he glanced back at the party, as though to check they were all still together. The move reminded her of Gus, but it also increased the sense of eeriness and tension. It was as though he expected something terrible to befall them. It was uncomfortable to admit how much of an effect it had on her.

She noticed one woman in the party hesitate outside a cottage to their left, which was in darkness. Emory paused too, and stared at the place intently. In the lantern light, Eve could just pick out its traditional red-tiled roof and the brick arches over its windows.

'This place...' Emory's words trailed off.

'What is it?' The woman who'd paused sounded breathless.

'I've no official tale to tell, but there's something: a story waiting to be discovered if I could access it.' He shook his head. 'It's so often the way. I walk past a house and a feeling overtakes me. There might be a loved one on the other side, wanting to pass on a message. I always have the urge to knock on the door, to tell the owner. But of course, I don't do it. It would be creepy to have someone say that out of the blue.'

The face of the woman who'd paused was eager now, her lips parted before she spoke. 'But that's our house!'

Emory immediately stepped back and stood up straighter. He was no longer staring at the cottage. 'Forgive me, I had no idea. Please forget I said anything.'

Eve was torn between disapproval for what he was doing

and a grudging admiration for his skill. She didn't believe him for a minute; he'd known full well – guessed the situation when the woman paused.

'Oh no.' The woman walked towards him. 'Don't apologise. I'm interested. I'd like to know more.'

But as she spoke, a younger woman stepped closer to her. 'Mum, I think Mr Fulton's right. You don't know what you're dredging up. It's best to leave it.'

Eve watched Emory's face. It only fell a fraction. He probably still thought he was in with a chance.

'It's entirely your choice,' he said quietly. 'It's interesting, of course, but I'm an outsider. It's different for me.'

The older woman looked torn. 'What would you do if you visited us?'

Emory shrugged slowly. 'It would depend on what you wanted. Sometimes I just walk around a person's house and tell them what I sense, but of course a séance tends to be more satisfactory. They answer more questions.'

Eve imagined they were more expensive too...

The younger woman had her hand on her mother's sleeve. Eve found she was holding her breath.

'Let's talk about it, Mum, and then decide.'

At last, the older woman nodded, just as Emory said, 'Of course. That's a good idea.'

Always best to accept a fait accompli with good grace.

Laurence Rice stepped forward now, his superior smile still in place. 'I'll take you up on a séance.' His words sounded like a challenge. Eve was sure he didn't believe in ghosts or an afterlife. She'd seen the way he'd looked when Emory was telling his spooky tales.

'At your mother's place, Laurence?' Emory smiled. 'That will be interesting. I might make contact with my family ghosts as well as yours.'

Eve imagined it would feel weird for him, plying his trade at

Fairview Hall. It might be irritating to see a man like Laurence living there in such luxury too.

Eve watched Poppy now. She was standing huddled next to Laurence, her arm tightly tucked round his.

'I'm not sure...' She peered up at her husband. 'Why would you do that? You don't even... And I don't feel—' It seemed to Eve that she clung to him all the more tightly. Her eyes were wide.

Laurence turned to her, a look of weary resignation on his face. 'It'll be fun, Poppy.' He shifted slightly: an impatient twitch of his arm so that his wife had to loosen her grip. 'Something new to try.' The combative gleam was back in his eye as he spoke again. 'Tomorrow night, Emory? I'll call you.'

Emory's eyes were knowing. Eve sensed he'd relish anything the academic could throw at him. He was ready for the fight, just as he had been outside the village store.

Emory's methods that evening had left her feeling conflicted. It wasn't right to manipulate people like that. But Laurence's attitude altered the scales again; she was more on Emory's side than his.

Emory turned to the group. The mother and daughter whose house he'd picked out were still debating the idea of a séance in heated whispers.

'Let's carry on now,' he said. Gus agreed with him. He was straining at his leash, though back towards home, not in the direction they were going. 'The tour's almost over, but I've saved something interesting for last. A personal story about Fairview Hall.' He turned to Laurence. 'A foretaste of any contribution my ancestors might make tomorrow night.'

As he turned to lead the way, Eve saw Laurence roll his eyes.

Viv and Eve found themselves close to Moira, who was positively twitching. 'Well, of course, I know the old tales about

Roger and Emory's great-grandfather. You must have heard them!'

Incredibly, Eve hadn't, despite occupying the same village as Moira for over two years. To be fair, she tended to focus on the most up-to-date gossip.

Moira rushed on before they had the chance to reply. 'I honestly can't believe *that's* the story that Emory's going to tell.' She was quite breathless with excitement. 'I mean, what about Roger and Selina? I wonder if they know Emory's plans. What with their clients and Roger's place on the charitable trust, it's the last thing they'd—'

Emory turned round again at that point. Eve didn't think he'd heard – he'd been chatting to one of the party – but Moira shut her mouth tight, like a frog which had caught a fly.

5

The cottages on the left had petered out now, and the ghost tour party was passing woodland. Emory took a narrow track through the trees, which Eve knew was a back route to the hall. Most of the trees were bare, but their branches were dense. It felt as though the woods on either side were closing in. Emory gained speed, walking ahead of the group. The pool of lantern light drew the rest of them forward. Without meaning to, Eve jogged a little to catch up. She saw Moira glance quickly over her shoulder, her eyes wide. It seemed the surroundings were enough to distract her from gossiping about Emory's great-grandfather.

Eve was relieved. She was itching to know but she'd rather hear it from Emory, after his compelling delivery in Haunted Lane. He might have an eye for the main chance, but she had to hand it to him, he was an excellent showman.

A minute later they met a grand driveway to their right, lined with densely packed poplars. To their left stood the inner gates to the hall, their stone posts topped with lion finials, and, directly opposite them, the track continued. If they followed it, it would curve round to the right and bring them to the Dower

House where the fundraiser had taken place. Eve had walked that route with Gus once.

'Here we are.' Emory lowered his lantern and smiled at the group.

There were lights on downstairs in the hall. An image of Ada Rice filled Eve's head: rigidly smart and cuttingly dismissive. She found herself hoping she wouldn't look out of her grand windows and see the tour party. Eve felt like she was trespassing. The hall was Emory's ancestral home, and they were standing on a public right of way, but Eve still felt shifty. If Moira was right, the Fultons wouldn't appreciate Emory including the hall in his tours, and she guessed Ada might agree.

'And now, to prove I tell the truth about the past, even if it reflects badly on my own family, I'll tell you the ghost story of Fairview Hall.

'Back in the 1920s, my great-grandfather, Eustace Fulton, lived here with his wife. I think you'll agree he ought to have been very happy. They had the whole estate and more wealth than many people could imagine. My great-grandmother Estelle was a beauty. They had five children, and everything they could wish for.' He paused. 'Lots of servants. Oh yes, plenty of those.'

Next to her, Eve heard a sharp intake of breath. Moira.

'Some of you might have heard whispers of the tale I'm going to tell.' Emory's eyes met the storekeeper's. 'The ghosts that haunt the hall, and the woods we're standing in, are of two maidservants – Dorothea Landon and Mildred Kirby. Their tales aren't told so often these days. Dorothea's family emigrated to America, and Mildred's died out. And my family... my family have no interest in telling this particular story.' His eyes glinted.

'Poor Dorothea is said to wander the attic corridor of the hall late at night. Pacing, always pacing and wringing her hands. Echoes of the past. She was anxious when she died. Pregnant and unmarried. She must have wondered what the future held. Did she have any hope that the baby's father would help her?

Provide for her? Give her some protection? Or did she always know she was on her own – abandoned to her fate?

'But many believe it was worse than that. Lots of women in her situation were dismissed, with no thought as to how they'd cope. But Dorothea never got that far. She was found drowned in a bath on the servants' floor. It's ironic. People thought the Fultons were generous to install a proper bath up there. But maybe – just maybe – that generosity came in handy for my great-grandfather, Eustace.

'Of course, I can't comment. I wasn't there. The facts are these: Dorothea smelled of alcohol when her body was found, and she was an unmarried mother-to-be. Not easy in those days. The death was ruled suicide. People speculated that Eustace was the father, but no one could prove it, and no one challenged the verdict.'

'Surely you could contact Dorothea through one of your séances and ask her for the truth?' Laurence Rice smiled and Eve felt hypocritical. She ought to have applauded his challenge – after all, she was a sceptic too. Instead, she felt a spark of dislike. He was unkind and Emory's story about Dorothea sounded all too believable.

'I've tried to reach both women, but I've never succeeded,' Emory said. 'Perhaps they don't trust a Fulton.'

Moira was nodding.

'The maid who haunts these woods, Mildred, was found strangled just over to your right.'

The whole group started slightly and turned, as though the body might still be there.

'She'd been stepping out with a young man in the village and when it was found that she too was pregnant he was hanged for her murder. He always protested his innocence. He might have been lying. Once again there was talk of a possible relationship between Mildred and Eustace. Once again, the investigation never looked at the family.'

Eve shivered and Gus glanced up at her impatiently. He was probably wondering when they could go back to Elizabeth's Cottage and some central heating. As for Eve, the story had shocked her. Emory was casting himself as an outsider, the family renegade, willing to face painful truths. It was all part of the show, but she sensed he minded and that speaking truth to power was important to him. Things had changed – of course they had – but too many people still fell under the wheels of the rich and influential.

But was Emory only concerned with justice? Telling such a personal story would ensure the tour party gossiped about the event later. Eve bet Emory would have people queueing for his next ghost walk. She suspected both motivations were at play. She knew he cared about people. He'd promised twenty per cent of his takings for the children's charities she supported, which was more than generous, especially considering his strait-ened circumstances. But the drive to earn a decent wage must be powerful too. He'd want to get back to living on his own terms – especially if Selina had made it clear she saw him as a burden.

Moira had been right, though: Selina and Roger wouldn't like him dredging up such a shocking story. They were both obsessed with appearances. But she sensed that hadn't occurred to Emory. He was caught up in his performance and his ideals.

'This is the end of the tour.' Emory's voice was low. 'I'll leave you now. My route takes me down the main drive, towards Magpie Lodge. Of course, you're welcome to walk back to the main road with me, if you'd prefer the comfort of the lantern, rather than travelling by moonlight.' He grinned.

Everyone except Laurence and Poppy Rice followed him towards the lodge. Eve needed to anyway; he'd asked her to pause there so he could hand over his donation.

After a few minutes, Eve caught sight of the lodge on her left, but she couldn't distinguish the details. She was curious about it, after Emory's description. How many places these days had no bathroom and an outdoor toilet? She'd seen the lodge's outline amongst the trees before, as she'd driven past towards Blyworth, but she'd never had a proper look. Other routes were better for dog walking.

'This is home for me,' Emory said, 'so I'll bid you goodnight. If you turn right at the end of the drive the old Thorington Road will take you back towards the village.'

'You carry on,' Eve said to Viv and Moira. 'Emory's just going to work out the donation money.'

'Are you sure, Eve dear?' Moira asked.

'Very. Thank you.'

Viv rolled her eyes. 'Eve doesn't believe in ghosts, Moira, you know that. It's a point of principle so we'd better do as she says or she'll go all fierce.'

As they headed off together, Eve heard Moira say: 'All the same, it's very dark.'

It was true. And Eve knew serious crimes occurred in idyllic villages; Saxford had had its share. But as Emory had said, the main road was close at hand, and it wasn't so very late. Her route wouldn't be deserted.

'How did you enjoy the tour?' Emory asked, bending down to stroke Gus's ears.

He was such a consummate performer that Eve felt he must be confident of praise, so when he looked up with a hint of anxiety in his eyes it took her by surprise. That and the fuss he was making of Gus made her warm to him again.

'It was spellbinding.'

His face lit up. He was such an odd mix: confident yet vulnerable, clever yet short-sighted, principled, yet happy to manipulate his punters.

She smiled back. 'You guessed the house on the Old Toll Road belonged to the woman who hesitated outside, right?'

There was a twinkle in his eye now. 'It seems I got the prickles about the place just as she paused.'

'Yes it does. How extraordinary.'

He laughed.

Eve's theory that he managed his séances by observing his clients closely seemed all the more convincing. He must be just as interested in human nature as she was. And it would be easy to gather gossip about people's circumstances in a village like Saxford. Moira would willingly act as his unpaid assistant, albeit unknowingly.

Emory paused. He was still smiling unashamedly but his eyes were intent as they met hers. 'I do what I do to make people happy. If I leave them feeling better, with more closure than they had before, it's a job well done.'

'Even if you haven't really contacted their dead relatives?'

'I can't make you believe.' He was calmly matter-of-fact, his expression still friendly.

Eve found herself trusting his good intentions, despite her other doubts. But in his shoes, she wouldn't risk that sort of intervention. In her experience, almost everything had unforeseen consequences.

'I'll get the money for the charities.' He walked towards the lodge.

'You're sure you're happy to donate?'

'Absolutely.' He paused, looking over his shoulder. 'I might not do it every time—'

'Of course not. Everyone has to make a living.'

'At least I've got a roof over my head. Of sorts.' He held the lantern up and the lodge was revealed in more detail.

Eve was puzzled. 'Is it clad in something?'

'Black corrugated metal. An emergency measure to stop further weathering. I'll just get your money from the prepayments I took. Do you want to come inside?'

Eve was intensely curious, but he might not have prepared

for visitors, and it was time she got home. Gus was tugging on his leash again. He'd probably have a sense-of-humour failure if she spun things out. Regretfully, she shook her head. 'It's fine. I'd love to see inside another day, if you don't mind.'

He chuckled. 'Of course. It's full of "character". I could have gone off to some soulless place in Blyworth. Roger offered to find me somewhere, but what's the point of coming home if you're kept at arm's length?'

Selina had tried to push him away, Roger was probably relieved, but had looked for a compromise, and Emory had dug his heels in – that was the impression Eve got. But the finer details had probably passed most people by. She imagined Roger and Selina's friends were shocked that they'd allow him to live in such circumstances.

She followed him up the path as he headed for the front door and caught him cursing. In a second, she saw the reason behind it. Someone had forced a window next to the entrance. The metal cladding was scratched and the wood of the frame just inside had splintered.

'Oh no. Is there anything I can do? Have you got coverage so you can call the police?' The mobile networks varied but all were patchy round there.

Emory nodded, his furrowed brow accentuated by the lantern light. 'I'll sort it. Don't worry. Just let me get your money. You can go and get warm then.'

Eve wondered if it would still be there, given the forced window, but a moment later he reappeared with a proportion of the takings. 'Thank you so much.'

'A pleasure.' He smiled, though she could tell from his eyes that his mind was no longer on her. She wasn't surprised – she was distracted too. Who would break in and not steal the cash Emory had just given her? And why would a burglar pick such a run-down place?

'There was a lone magpie outside the lodge at breakfast

time this morning.' Emory broke into her thoughts. 'And later on there were three, just sitting there.' He shuddered and looked up at the stark, dark trees overhead.

The old counting rhyme filtered through Eve's head. 'One for sorrow seems about right, what with the break-in, but three for a girl?'

Emory shook his head. 'That's not the version I know.'

6

It was two days before Eve saw Emory Fulton again but the break-in drifted into her mind several times in between. On Saturday morning, she sat in the dining room at Elizabeth's Cottage with Gus snuggled against her feet. Logs crackled in the fireplace, flames leaping up the blackened chimney flue. Warmth filled the space as Eve sipped her tea and ate her buttered toast, topped with her dad's favourite marmalade: dark, with plenty of peel. She found it helped her concentrate.

Who could have broken into Magpie Lodge? Kids maybe? Its cladding might hold the place together but it seemed the window had been easy enough to force.

'But would kids run around looking for trouble when the weather's so cold, Gus?' His soulful eyes met hers as she peeked under the table. 'I doubt it.' She went back to her toast. The lodge was out of the way. The intruder must have walked some distance to reach it, unless they'd driven – or ridden a bike, not something she'd fancy in the ice.

And surely if it had been any standard thief, they'd have made off with the takings from the ghost tour.

Emory's reaction had struck her as odd too. She'd have

expected him to be upset or angry, but instead it looked as though he'd been thinking furiously. She'd seen it in the furrow of his brow. It was as though he was processing information to add to a puzzle he'd been working on. What did it mean?

As her mind wrestled with the question, she remembered what he'd said about the magpies outside the lodge the day before. There'd been one in the morning and three later on. One for sorrow and three for a girl, Eve had said, but he'd told her he knew another version of the fortune-telling rhyme.

That was one mystery she could solve now. She keyed 'one for sorrow nursery rhyme' into the search engine on her phone. The familiar words spooled through her head as she thumb-typed. *One for sorrow, two for joy, three for a girl, four for a boy.*

But on Wikipedia she found the alternative wording Emory must have been thinking of: *One for sorrow, two for mirth, three for a funeral and four for birth...*

Eve took a sustaining sip of tea. Magpies flocked together all the time; the rhyme meant nothing. But inside her, unease was building. It showed the way Emory's mind was working. Perhaps it wasn't just the magpies which were putting him on edge. Once again, she thought of the way he'd threatened his sister-in-law.

As Eve took the last mouthful of her coffee on Sunday morning, she found her thoughts on Emory again: from his relations with his sister-in-law, to the weird dynamic between him, his goddaughter Poppy, and Laurence Rice. And then back to the break-in. Had it been personal? A random thief made no sense.

At last, she got up from the table, which forced Gus, who'd been using her slipper socks as a pillow, to shift too. He shot her an accusatory look.

'I'm sorry, but my feet are multipurpose. It's time to get moving if we're going to church.'

Eve didn't always go. She wasn't a true believer, but Reverend Jim Thackeray welcomed people of all faiths and none. On top of that, he was one of her favourite people in the village. He always looked so hopeful when he invited her along, his eyes appealing, that it was hard to deny him. Gus liked Jim too, and sometimes enjoyed 'singing' along to the hymns. Eve was still trying to master self-assured nonchalance in response.

An hour and a half later the morning service was drawing to a close. As usual, Gus had performed – on this occasion he'd been especially vocal to 'Hills of the North Rejoice'. Eve had had to endure Moira's pointed glances from the pew in front.

'Dear me, he really is *very* enthusiastic, isn't he?' she said as they stood to shuffle towards the nave.

Viv patted Eve's arm as she ground her teeth. 'There, there. She'll have to put on her "I adore all God's creatures" face in a minute. She's always got it ready when Jim's chatting with the congregation.'

It was true. Moira had an RSPCA collection box in the village store and pointed to that as proof of how much she loved animals.

Eve bent to pet Gus. She was always concerned he might pick up on Moira's disapproval, though from the beatific look in his eyes, perhaps not. From her crouched position she glanced up and saw Roger and Selina Fulton, talking to another couple. They were all noticeably in their Sunday best. Roger had a long dark woollen overcoat, a quality rust-coloured scarf, dark trousers and highly polished shoes. Selina wore a fitted plum-coloured coat, with a rose-pink skirt and high-heeled shoes visible underneath. Pearls at the neck too, Eve noted. Everything according to convention.

Standing up and scanning the scene, Eve saw Selina's business partner Ada Rice was there as well, and Laurence and Poppy were with her.

Emory must have visited them the night before, Eve remembered, to perform the séance. She wondered how it had gone. The thought made her stomach tense; she bet it had been awkward. Laurence had clearly wanted to catch Emory out, and Poppy had been nervous. Eve remembered her anxious eyes and the way she'd gripped Laurence's arm. She'd been dead against the idea. Maybe she felt protective towards Emory; he was her godfather after all, but was that enough to explain it?

Eve shifted her focus back to the present. Ada was engaged in polite chit-chat with the other parishioners, her smile gracious. She had the air of someone who would attend church for form's sake, just like the Fultons. Poor Jim. He'd confided in her that few of the villagers truly believed, but he remained optimistic. Viv was one of his stalwarts, along with the gang from the Cross Keys pub.

Eve was interested to see that both Emory and Coco Fulton had come along for the service too. Coco had managed to drape herself dramatically over a pew. She must be kneeling on the seat in the rear row; she was facing the chatting parishioners, her arms resting on the pew back, head cocked sideways, face like thunder. Eve saw her glance in the direction of her parents and the Rices but no one took any notice. Maybe that was why she was so grumpy; Eve was sure she loved being the centre of attention.

At that moment one of Eve's neighbours touched her elbow and she turned to catch up with their news.

It must have been ten minutes later when Gus started to get restless, letting out a short, sharp bark. She nodded, excused herself and waved to Viv. 'It's time we were off. I'll see you later.' Monty's opened after lunch on Sundays and Eve was due to work a session.

In seconds, she was pushing on the heavy oak door. She tied her coat belt tightly as she exited the porch, glad of her faux fur hat. Gus shot into the churchyard as though he'd been captive for months. Eve was dashing after him when she was startled by the sudden movement of birds, a group of them taking off into the air just beyond the church. Magpies – their wingbeats noisy. Eve shivered, then told herself off. There were at least eight of them. She couldn't remember what eight was meant to signify but she doubted it was anything alarming.

All the same, she paused. What had made them take fright like that?

As she stood there uncertainly, Gus looked up at her, tired resignation in his eyes. Quietly she bent down and attached his leash. She couldn't have said why later, but she felt compelled to go and take a look.

She picked her way round the church, taking care to avoid the plants and gravestones. As she turned to walk past the end of the building, she heard voices. A moment later she'd tucked herself behind a buttress, so she could peer round.

Emory was talking to Selina Fulton. And judging by the reaction of the birds, their conversation and maybe even their actions had turned violent.

The buttress provided good cover, but Eve wasn't too worried about being seen; the pair's words were heated enough to distract them from their surroundings.

'... none of your business!' Selina spat.

'It's family. Blood's thicker than water. I've every right to say what I think.' Emory was leaning forward, his normally genial face red with anger.

'Don't you dare! You'll upset everything. The damage you'll cause. We don't need this from you. Who the hell would listen to your advice anyway? It's not as though you've made a success of your life. Not like Roger and I have.'

'"Roger and I"! What a joke that united front is.'

Eve thought of the married neighbour Selina had been with in the arbour at the Dower House. Their panicked conversation. Emory had already threatened to tell his brother if Selina pushed him away. Was he giving her an ultimatum now, tell

Roger or be outed? *We don't need this from you...* Eve imagined
Selina enjoyed the status quo and her respected position in the
community. She'd lose all that and her nice house if her affair
became public. And what did she mean about advice? Had
Emory been holding forth about how they might fix their
marriage?

Eve looked down at Gus, put her finger to her lips, then
ruffled his fur and led him back round the church's walls again.
As she reached the area outside the porch, Viv was emerging
onto the gritted path.

'Thought you'd gone. Wait a moment. You've got that look
in your eye. What is it?'

'Hush.' Eve strode towards the lychgate, Gus trotting
eagerly beside her. 'I'll tell you this afternoon.'

Viv rolled her eyes. 'Spoilsport.'

The rest of that day was taken up with her shift at Monty's,
where she filled Viv in on her illicit snooping, followed by
supper at home, then drinks at the Cross Keys. It was the
birthday of Jo Falconer, the pub's cook, and fireworks were
being laid on at eleven. The assembled crowds duly oohed and
aahed as the jewel-like colours lit the night sky. Showers of
sparks were reflected in the estuary beyond the pub's garden.

Eve was tired but happy when she finally made it to bed
that night, but an hour later she awoke again, her heart hammering. She thought she'd heard thudding footfalls down in
Haunted Lane. A sign of danger... Visions of the hue and cry
back in the 1700s filled her head. But it was ridiculous of
course. She knew why she'd imagined them. After the tensions
she'd witnessed and all that talk about one for sorrow and three
for a funeral it wasn't surprising. More omens. But a moment
later she heard Gus whine as he came upstairs. She opened her
door and bent to cuddle him.

'There's nothing there.' To prove it to herself she opened the curtains. Maybe she'd set him on edge too, by sneaking around in the churchyard. She shouldn't have listened in. It was none of her business.

It was a long time before she slept, despite the comforting beams which reached over her head like protective arms, and the fresh hot-water bottle she'd filled to thaw her cold feet.

The next morning, memories of the footfalls filled her head. When her mobile rang she felt sick, her heart rate ramping up.

The number on the screen told her it was Robin, her secret lover.

The fact felt fun and ridiculous in equal measure. He was Saxford St Peter's gardener, but his past was shrouded in mystery for most of the villagers. He'd once been Robert Kelly, a detective inspector down in London. Uncovering high-level police corruption had put him in danger from colleagues and criminals alike. He'd gone underground and made a career out of his hobby, though he still helped the police secretly.

He avoided social occasions where people might ask awkward questions. Saxford's residents were merciless in their probing and no one would let it rest if their relationship became public. It was their reason for keeping it on the down-low. Eve didn't want to have to lie to everyone.

'Robin? Is everything all right?' Adrenaline was already affecting her; she felt breathless.

'*I'm afraid not. Emory Fulton's been found dead. The police are treating it as murder.*'

7

The news of Emory's death was fresh and Robin had hardly any details. It made the information all the more stark and hard to accept. Numb shock took hold, but after she rang off, it was gradually replaced by sadness. Like everyone, his character had been a rich mixture, but her gut told her his heart had been in the right place. He'd been there for his niece, in contrast to her parents, who seemed to treat her with wariness – and for his goddaughter too. Poppy had wanted to confide in him. It was only Laurence who'd stopped her.

Slowly, questions about Emory coalesced; every interaction and oddity Eve had witnessed since she'd met him filled her head.

Robin had got his information from the local police, through a man called Greg Boles, a detective sergeant who happened to be married to Robin's cousin. Apart from Eve, only he and the vicar knew Robin's true background. Greg's updates were entirely against the rules, but Robin was discreet and they both benefited. Greg enjoyed sharing ideas with a like-minded outsider. His boss, DI Nigel Palmer, fell short of ideal. Lazy, blinkered and bigoted were Eve's top adjectives for him. She could think of plenty more, none of them flattering. As for Robin, despite his love of gardening, he missed his old work. Having some involvement made him come alive.

Eve sympathised with Greg; she didn't get on with Palmer either. She'd written the obituaries of several murder victims now, each time interviewing the same people as the police. She'd played a crucial part in their past investigations, which irritated the inspector no end.

It would likely be the same with Emory. Robin said he'd call again as soon as he had more news. She was hoping she'd hear from him before she left to work that morning's shift at Monty's. In the meantime, she opened her laptop to pitch for Emory's obituary. His family had been informed, apparently, so she was clear to go ahead.

She was determined to get the work. There was a lot more she wanted to find out about Emory. Her mind went back to their conversation outside Magpie Lodge on Friday night. *I can't make you believe.* Had he really thought he could contact the dead? Sense spirits? She wanted to know. And after seeing the tensions between him and Selina, she felt the urgency of finding out who'd killed him too. She had inside information. It wasn't something she could pass on to the police; it would be wrong to risk Selina and Roger's marriage without knowing more. That meant she needed to get involved herself. Writing his obituary would mean interviewing his contacts. She might manage to draw out vital information.

She worded her email to *Icon* magazine carefully. They leaped on her pitches for current celebrities, but Emory might be a harder sell. She emphasised his recent ghost tours and séances. Hopefully the Rices would tell her about theirs.

She settled down on one of the matching couches in her sitting room, a fire crackling in the inglenook fireplace. She had time to do some initial research before heading to Monty's and it would help to focus on a task. Dwelling on a life cut short was too painful. It was somehow worse in a case like Emory's, when the deceased was in a state of flux, with unfinished business. He hadn't got his wish to integrate back into his family. It must have been a nasty shock when he discovered Selina's affair – it wasn't calculated to help his efforts.

Opening her laptop, she created two spreadsheets, one for the obituary she hoped she'd be able to write and one devoted to the murder investigation. She started with the basic facts. Her Google searches added details to what she already knew and provided clues to the gaps in Emory's story. After a string of bestsellers in his 'Haunted' series, it looked as though he'd run out of material. From the same period she found photos of him staggering out of smart London clubs – in each case with a glamorous woman on his arm. Eve guessed fame had gone to his head and his focus had switched from the spiritual to something more earthly.

He'd looked like he was going to seed, but then, as now, there'd been something compelling about him. He'd had the sort of face that made you look: not handsome but charismatic, with a mischievous smile and twinkling dark eyes.

Up for anything.

Too much so, from what the papers said. He'd gone over the top and burned through all the cash he had. Meanwhile, the time spent partying meant less time for researching new books.

So, twenty years back, the writing contracts had dried up, and fifteen years ago, the chat-show appearances had done the same. For a while, Eve sensed he'd remained popular with TV audiences thanks to his lingering aura of celebrity and renegade behaviour. But ultimately he'd disgraced himself on set, turning up too drunk to hide it. Even if the audiences hadn't stopped loving him, the presenters and producers had.

After that, his career was a patchwork. He'd given talks for a while, but was rarely asked twice, turning up wasted or not at all. Then he'd worked in bars, told fortunes and conducted séances at house parties. That had gone on for ten years but then it seemed as though Emory had pulled himself together. She found a record of him doing more regular talks at mainstream venues – theatres, art centres and the like. But in the last year, things had gone wrong again. He'd embarked on a new project, investing in a large country mansion: the most haunted house in Cambridgeshire, according to the papers. He'd planned to turn it into a hotel, with himself as host. Eve could imagine that being a success, but within months of the purchase the place had been repossessed. Eve wondered how Emory could possibly have saved enough money to buy it in the first place. He'd clearly managed to get a loan, but he'd have needed a good chunk of capital as a deposit. The newspaper reports put the price at a couple of million.

After the collapse of that venture Emory had resurfaced in Saxford St Peter. Whatever had happened it looked as though he'd lost everything. He was fifty-one when he'd died. The same age as her.

Five minutes before she was due to leave for the teashop, Robin called again. She set off to work her shift with the extraordinary details he'd shared racing through her mind.

8

At Monty's, Eve joined Viv in the kitchen, leaving Tammy, a regular student helper, serving along with a new recruit, Lars. Eve was still unsure about the blond twenty-four-year-old. He was wildly good-looking and charismatic, and a huge hit with many of the female customers (and some of the males). He was well aware of his charms, but oddly, it didn't make him arrogant. There was something endearing about the pleased excitement he felt at his popularity, but it meant he was scattier about the work than he might be. Plus his stop in Suffolk was part of his travels around Europe. He *said* he was intending to stay in the area for six months, but Eve wondered if he'd stick it out. Saxford wasn't exactly party central. On the upside, he had a soft spot for Tammy. That might make a difference. Viv had been throwing them together at every opportunity, even messing with the schedules Eve had created, which left her twitching.

'She's a bit young for him,' Eve had said when they'd discussed the issue.

'Eve, she's twenty.'

'A young twenty.'

'But sensible,' Viv had replied confidently.

Eve was missing Angie, a former regular who was doing office work now she'd finished her studies. The Blyworth and Villages Charitable Trust had taken her on.

'I can't believe the news. It's so awful.' Viv wiped her glistening eyes with the back of her hand. 'I wish I hadn't just walked off like that at the end of the ghost tour. I was too busy making snide remarks about your level-headedness to thank him properly. And we didn't talk in church yesterday.'

'I know. I can't believe it either.' Eve felt tears threaten and took a deep breath.

'Do you feel up to making a batch of the spiced apple cakes? I'll do some of the ginger chocolates.'

Eve tugged on a hairnet and her apron. It was a lot cleaner than Viv's – she took it home so she could wash it as often as she liked.

A moment later, Eve was peeling apples. It was therapeutic – something simple, grounding and familiar after the awful news.

'So, what have you heard?' Viv was chopping crystallised ginger.

Eve had known she'd want gossip. As usual, she'd have to claim she'd heard it on the grapevine. As Eve's closest friend, Viv was one of the very few people who knew she and Robin were close, but she had no idea he was a former policeman. Jim Thackeray had simply convinced her that Robin had good reason to keep his past a secret and she mustn't ask.

Eve marshalled her thoughts. 'That Emory was drowned in a bath at a place called Sycamore Cottage.'

Viv caught her breath. 'I'd heard the same, but I wasn't sure it was true. Isn't that Brenda Goody's place? What on earth was he doing there?'

'Washing himself.'

'Smart alec.'

A fresh wave of sadness engulfed Eve. 'Actually, he was probably enjoying a lovely soak and feeling warm for once.' It must have made a pleasant change from Magpie Lodge; Eve could imagine him relishing it. She removed the core from the apple she was working on. 'Apparently, Brenda was the Fultons' childminder, back in the day.' She was still trying to place her. 'I don't think we've met.'

'You'd know her if you saw her. Plump, smiley.' Viv glanced over her shoulder and frowned. 'I'd forgotten she'd looked after Roger and Emory though. Blimey, she's not a suspect, is she?' Then she slapped her forehead. 'I'm not thinking straight. She can't be. I saw her at Jo's fireworks do; I'm pretty certain she was around all evening. Doesn't she have a lodger though?'

Eve would have to tread carefully. She'd heard all about Brenda's 'paying guest' from Robin, but she might seem too well informed if she admitted it. 'Possibly. I just heard the house was empty for the evening. Maybe the lodger was at the Cross Keys too.' He had been, according to Robin, though the police hadn't checked alibis yet. 'You wouldn't recognise him?'

Viv shook her head. 'Not had the pleasure.' She was sieving flour. 'So I guess Brenda invited Emory to use her facilities while she was out, thanks to the lack of bathroom at Magpie Lodge. You'd think Roger and Selina would have offered him theirs, wouldn't you?'

'Maybe not, given the way he and Selina fought at the fundraiser.' Eve had filled Viv in on what she'd overheard that day. She bet his friendship with Coco made Selina and Roger anxious too. They'd see Emory as a bad influence and, given his past, perhaps she couldn't blame them. But Emory had taken the time to talk to his niece. She had a hunch he'd listened to her, and that he'd cared. 'If I'd been Emory, I might have chosen Brenda's place out of pride.'

'Fair point. Any other intel floating around?'

Eve had finished coring the apples and set some water to

boil while she diced them, ready to par-cook. 'Gossip about comings and goings yesterday, while Emory was at Sycamore Cottage.'

Her friend turned to her, spilling caster sugar on the floor. Eve winced and Viv tutted. 'Don't be strict, this is serious. What do you know?'

'A neighbour saw Emory arrive at around eight, if the rumour mill's correct. He was whistling, so it attracted their attention. Then, around fifteen minutes later, they heard the front door slam hard and the sound of birds flapping into the air.' It made Eve think of the magpies she'd seen at the church. 'The neighbour was watching TV by that time, so they didn't look, but they're under the impression someone left the house. They assumed it was Emory going again, but unless he went back and forth like a yoyo, it wasn't.'

'So it looks like he had a visitor?' Viv said. 'I wonder if the police think it was the killer.' She was breaking eggs into her cake mix.

'I haven't heard.' The pathologist had estimated the time of death as between eight and ten the previous evening, and Emory's phone had fallen into the bath, cutting his call at nine thirty-five. It was an old-fashioned model and, not being water-proof, it pinpointed the time nicely. He'd been listening to a pre-recorded horoscope line, but Viv would definitely smell a rat if she went into that much detail. 'Someone said Emory died quite a bit later. I suppose it's possible the mystery visitor only pretended to leave, or sneaked back in, ready to ambush him.' Either way, there'd been no signs of forced entry at the cottage. Eve was surprised Emory hadn't locked up after himself, given the break-in at the lodge and his worries over the magpie omens. It must mean something. 'What about you?' She glanced over at Viv. 'Have you heard anything?'

Viv looked pleased with herself. 'I had a customer in who lives up beyond Fairview Hall. She says she walked past the lodge yesterday afternoon and Poppy Rice came out. Apparently she was in tears.'

'That's interesting.' A young woman with lots of questions to answer. They filled Eve's head now: what had been going on between Poppy and Emory at Monty's? What was in the bag he'd secretly given her? And what was behind Emory and Laurence's hostility? Once again, the séance at Fairview Hall crossed her mind.

'Do you think she might be guilty?' Viv asked.

Eve took a deep breath. 'It's too early to tell. I thought she seemed fond of Emory when they came here for tea, but she was on edge too – under pressure. She's definitely on the suspect list.'

'Who else looks possible, do you think?'

'Selina, for sure. Emory was a threat to her marriage, and her genteel existence at the Dower House. And he was making a great joke of bad-mouthing her in front of her and Roger's influential contacts at the soirée. He implied his lack of welcome at the Dower House was down to her meanness. But I shouldn't overlook Roger. One of the people listening in was a partner at his firm, according to Selina. And on Friday, Emory told half the village their great-grandfather was probably a sexual predator and a murderer.'

'I can see Roger wouldn't like that, but do you honestly think he'd kill over it?'

'I'd say he's less likely than his wife, but worth bearing in mind. Respectability is vital to him; he's got his charity position and potential knighthood to consider, as well as his clients. Having a reputation as a mean-spirited man with a killer in the family could easily put people off. He claims he offered to find Emory somewhere to stay in Blyworth, but even that sounds unfriendly, when he and Selina have so much space. And after all, the Dower House was Emory's family home growing up.'

'True. And if Roger was halfway decent, he'd have used us to do his catering.'

Eve smiled for the first time that morning. 'Nice to get your objective assessment.'

'He's a bad egg in my book. And you know how I hate bad eggs. Is that it?'

Eve shook her head and lowered her voice automatically, even though they were alone. 'Dale Buckingham has as big a motive as anyone.' She'd recognised Selina's married lover at once. He lived just up the road from Robin on Dark Lane.

Viv nodded. 'I always thought he looked too smooth to be trusted.'

'I'll need to talk to all of them.' Once again, Eve felt the urgency of the task. Selina and Roger were just the kind of suspects Palmer would ignore – well-to-do and influential. Yet Selina had already lost control once, shoving Emory violently when the house was full of guests.

She couldn't wait to hear more from Robin.

9

On her way home from Monty's, Eve stopped at the village store, ostensibly to pick up some milk and cheese, but really to catch up on the latest gossip. Moira was the perfect conduit and she'd had all morning to gather details.

The old-fashioned bell jangled over the door as Eve entered. The small store was empty so she had all Moira's attention.

'Ah, Eve dear. What a tragedy.' She sighed heavily. 'I'm so sorry. Emory really was very charming, despite his chequered past. And of course, you stayed on to talk to him after the ghost tour; so generous of him to donate to your good causes.' She leaned forward expectantly, her lipstick gleaming in the overhead light. 'Did you gather anything significant?'

'I'm afraid not.' Eve wasn't going to mention the magpie rhyme or the break-in. She preferred receiving information to giving it out. Gossiping with Viv was different. Giving Moira details was the equivalent of standing on the village green with a megaphone. If *Icon* accepted her pitch she'd be after interviewees imminently. She couldn't expect them to talk if she was a known gossip. As it was, they often trusted her with a lot, including details they didn't want to put their names to.

Moira looked disappointed. 'You've heard he was in Brenda Goody's bath, I suppose?' Eve nodded and the storekeeper shook her head. 'I must say, it's a scandal that his brother wasn't letting him use theirs.' She sighed. 'Previously I'd assumed the bad blood from their great-grandfather had bypassed Roger and found its way to Emory and Coco. But now – well – people are gossiping about Roger's behaviour and I can't help but agree.'

Moira tended to follow public opinion.

'What made you think the bad blood had gone to Emory and Coco?' It was typical that she believed in the concept and that it had been occupying her thoughts.

'Well,' Moira said breathlessly, 'Emory was very wild for a long time, as I told you.' She leaned forward and lowered her voice. 'I've heard he dabbled in drugs! And the women... Still, young men will sow their wild oats.'

Eve gritted her teeth. Moira was always more forgiving towards men.

'But the Fultons have had an awful time with Coco too,' she went on. 'She was precocious. She looked adult by the time she was thirteen and I'm afraid she acted like it too. Very worldly-wise. And she spent years travelling and having fun when her parents wanted her to attend university. They must have breathed a sigh of relief when she got her place at Bathurst. It shows she's got brains.' She shook her head. 'I expect they'll be more relaxed now poor dear Emory's dead. I understand he was forming quite a bond with Coco. I must confess, I was worried he'd lead her astray. I tried to hint as much to Selina when she came in for a bottle of wine, but I think I was too subtle.'

Doubtful.

'Of course,' Moira added, 'a lot of people are comparing Emory's death to that of the maidservant, Dorothea Landon.

Can it possibly be a coincidence that they were both found drowned in the bath?'

Eve quelled her desire to say *almost certainly*.

'Some people think the death might be supernatural – Dorothea's spirit taking her revenge on the Fulton family. Of course, *I* don't believe anything like that.' She must have caught Eve's expression. 'But it's what people are saying.'

Eve had only been back at Elizabeth's Cottage for five minutes, thawing out by the radiator, when a knock at the door sent Gus into a frenzy.

Opening up, she found Detective Constable Olivia Dawkins on the doorstep.

'Come on in!' Eve was immediately embarrassed. She sounded like a hostess welcoming an old friend to a party, but she was so relieved it was the constable and not DI Palmer. Despite his seniority, he often turned up in person to tell Eve not to interfere. He was about as subtle as a rhino in a model village and had a terrible effect on her blood pressure.

DC Dawkins smiled and stepped inside. Gus greeted her with much tail wagging and random scampering around her ankles. Eve suspected his thoughts mirrored her own.

'We're talking to everyone who connected with Emory Fulton since he returned to Saxford,' Dawkins said. 'And we understand' – she blushed – 'that you and Mr Fulton had financial dealings, as well as social.'

Eve bet Palmer had put it like that. She took a deep breath. 'Emory kindly offered to donate a proportion of his takings from the Saxford ghost tour to the children's charities I support. He gave me thirty pounds in cash at the end of the tour. Twenty per cent. I waited outside Magpie Lodge while he fetched it.'

Dawkins flushed and loosened her scarf. 'It seems like a

generous proportion of his income. Did you have any written agreement about the money?'

Eve sighed and Gus gave the woman a disapproving look. 'I'm afraid not. He mentioned the idea casually at the fundraiser held by his brother and sister-in-law. But if Palmer – sorry, DI Palmer – wants to check, I've already transferred the money to the charities concerned and several of the villagers knew about his plan.'

'Of course.' Dawkins scribbled in her notepad with furious concentration.

Eve was gladder still that Palmer was absent. He'd probably accuse her of taking the money for services rendered, or being involved in some kind of weird micro-laundering scheme. Even now, he was vexing her by proxy. Eve's adrenaline was flowing nicely.

Dawkins proceeded to take down in great detail every interaction Eve had had with Emory: times, dates and the content of the conversations.

'Can you think of anyone who would have wanted him dead?' the constable asked at last.

Eve reviewed what she knew. Selina's lover and her secret conversations with Emory loomed large, but she couldn't bring herself to pass the information on. She didn't know the facts and she'd be risking the Fultons' marriage. She shook her head. It was time to see if she could get some information out of Dawkins.

'I presume you heard about the break-in at Magpie Lodge?' She wanted to know if they'd made progress on the investigation.

But Dawkins looked startled. 'No. Please, tell me about it.'

Eve was intrigued. The fact that Emory hadn't reported it was significant. It looked as though he'd decided to deal with the matter personally, or let it lie. It took her back to her original thought: that he knew or guessed something about the intruder.

She explained as much as she knew and Dawkins frowned as she noted it down.

'Thank you. This could be very helpful. The CSIs are working on the Lodge as well as Sycamore Cottage. They might find something significant.'

And Eve would hear about it if they did, thanks to Robin and Greg's friendship. She was glad she'd mentioned the incident.

Constable Dawkins was preparing to leave and Eve's mind turned to the article she hoped to write. 'I'd like to talk to Brenda Goody and her lodger for Emory's obituary,' she said aloud. She'd want to see them at the house, so she could get an idea of Emory's last hours. 'I guess it will be some time before your teams have finished at Sycamore Cottage.'

'I'd leave it until tomorrow.'

Eve nodded. And it was no good going straight to Roger and Selina. They'd be in shock right now, and presumably their police interviews would take a while; they'd been so much closer to Emory. In some ways, at least.

'I believe DI Palmer will have finished with Poppy Rice soon,' Dawkins said, then put her hand over her mouth. Her boss would hate her helping Eve.

Eve wasn't surprised Palmer had got to Poppy quickly after her tears outside Magpie Lodge the day of the murder. 'Thank you.'

Dawkins nodded and Eve got up to see her out.

10

After Dawkins left, Eve checked her emails and found she had one from Portia Coldwell at *Icon*. She'd managed to 'talk the editor' into accepting Emory's obituary, apparently. The thought of it being touch-and-go left Eve feeling fed up. She'd make sure her piece showed how complex and interesting he'd been. Portia emphasised that *Icon* wanted plenty of content about Emory's 'bad-boy' past, but Eve wouldn't let that influence her. She'd write the article as it should be written; it would be every bit as compelling as Portia wanted. For *Icon*, it was all about money, of course. They wanted current stars, or if not then something else to boost their value to the magazine. It was horrible, but the murder would act as clickbait as much as Emory's colourful past. The advertisers would love it.

At least she had the go-ahead. It would be full steam ahead with her investigations. As she took Gus for a restorative walk along the beach, she made plans for that afternoon. The sunlight looked beautiful, glinting on the waves, but they only managed five minutes before retreating. The warmth of Elizabeth's Cottage brought welcome relief but there was no point in getting used to it. A visit to Blyworth was in order.

As her fingers became functional again, she texted Angie, Monty's former student helper, to suggest an after-work drink. Thanks to her job at the Blyworth and Villages Charitable Trust, she probably knew Roger Fulton. It would be interesting to find out what she thought of him. But Eve had two missions before that.

She gave Gus a cuddle, made sure his water bowl was full and headed off in her Mini Clubman. She was armed with Poppy Rice's business address. Despite the size of Fairview Hall, she had a workshop in town and Eve's first task was to drop in there. It would be good form to call in advance or visit her at home but she'd dismissed the idea. Poppy was hiding something and she wouldn't relax in front of Laurence. And with advance warning, she'd have time to prepare, too. Eve wouldn't normally resort to such tactics, but the killing altered her approach. Emory had tried to pressure Poppy about something and she'd pushed back firmly. That could be her motive for murder. Eve needed to know what they were talking about and why Poppy had left Magpie Lodge in tears the previous day.

But when Eve reached the modern building where the jeweller had rented a workshop, she was told she hadn't come in. It wasn't entirely surprising, though Eve found it hard to imagine her at home, being comforted by Laurence. She must have picked up on his attitude towards Emory; it was obvious when he'd arranged the séance. In Poppy's place, Eve would have opted to go off by herself. The acres of wild beach and blasting wind could dull the senses, offering a numb sort of peace.

It was time to focus on her second mission. She turned on her heel and cut through a couple of alleyways to reach one of Blyworth's most exclusive shopping streets, filled with the half-timbered buildings the town was famous for. It was home to Rice and Fulton, Ada and Selina's posh interiors store. Eve remembered Ada's barbed conversation at the fundraiser and imagined her and Selina arguing over whose surname should come first. Though presumably things hadn't always been that tense between them. She couldn't imagine them going into partnership otherwise. Either way, it seemed Ada had won, just as she had with the house, occupying the hall on the Fultons' family estate.

Eve guessed Selina would be at home, under the circumstances, which suited her purposes. She wanted to ask Ada about the séance Emory had performed at the hall, but any loose talk about Selina would be welcome. Eve needed to know if she had the temperament to kill. She pushed the store's door open.

'Good afternoon,' Ada said, as a bing-bong bell announced Eve's arrival. She held out her hand. 'I believe we almost met at the Fultons' soirée.'

In the background, a second woman was busy with a feather duster, though the displays already looked spotless.

Eve was impressed by Ada's memory. They hadn't been properly introduced and there'd been a lot of people present. Her skill must stand her in good stead with her customers.

Eve introduced herself as they shook hands and explained about writing Emory's obituary. 'I don't suppose you knew him well?'

Ada gave a thin smile. 'Hardly at all. I could see he was ruffling feathers, though. I wonder who wanted him dead. Other than Roger and Selina, that is.'

Eve double took. 'You think they did?'

'Don't mind me, I speak as I find.' Her clipped voice and amused smile were reminiscent of Laurence. That and her words made Eve bristle. She took a deep breath. She needed to get past Ada's coldness; it was what she could tell her that counted.

'I suppose it must have been disruptive when Emory turned up.'

'No doubt. Selina didn't talk about him much but from what I understand he was trouble for years. Women, drink and debt. And poor Roger's so very conventional – in love with his position as a pillar of society. Selina's just as parochial, whether she realises it or not. So buttoned-up, but you never know what's lurking under the surface. It's a shame she wasn't here last night, or she'd have an alibi.' She laughed lightly.

'What was happening last night?'

'We have a Sunday evening private view every other month and I was running one yesterday. It's a chance to unwind over a glass of wine and get some individual advice on styling. I can add you to our mailing list.' Ada handed her a form.

Eve couldn't think of anything worse. She'd feel obliged to buy if she attended and she didn't want anyone else's advice. She was still rejoicing at having control since her ex, Ian, had walked out. She pasted on a smile and wrote her email address down anyway. 'Lovely, thanks.'

As she put Ada's pen down, she asked about the séance.

'I didn't sit in.' She raised her eyes to heaven. 'Not my cup of tea. But I know Laurence thought it was a hoot. Feel free to drop in at the hall if you'd like to know more. I'm sure he'll tell you all about it. Poppy was there too.'

'Thanks for your help. I'll do that.'

On her way out, she saw there was still a flyer about the previous night's event by the door. It had run from 7.30 until 10 p.m. Assuming Ada had been present throughout, there was no point in Eve adding her to the suspect list. She couldn't see her motive for killing Emory anyway, but it was best to be thorough.

Twenty minutes later, Eve and Angie were sitting in a cheerful bar on the main shopping street in Blyworth, with fairy lights around the steamed-up windows and radiators belting out a comforting heat. Eve still had her chocolate-brown coat on after the raw weather outside but felt able to ease out of it as they ordered. She chose a mocha and Angie a glass of red wine.

'So, how's life in the charitable sector?'

Angie laughed, strands of hair coming down from the bun she wore. 'An eye-opener. Let's just say Monty's most awkward customers were excellent training. I'd expected everyone to be selfless and noble, but there's an awful lot of politics. But the PA I work with is an old hand. She manages the lot of them without them realising it. I'm noting all her tricks and adding to my armoury.' She put her head on one side. 'The gossip's been rife today as you can imagine, what with the murder of Roger Fulton's brother.' She put a hand to her forehead. 'Pretty horrific. I never met Emory. Did you know him?'

Eve nodded. 'A little. We'd met a couple of times, and he'd been into Monty's.'

Angie shook her head. 'I'm sorry. It's so sad. Was he nice?'

Eve thought about the question. 'He was full of contradictions, but I warmed to him. He was friendly. Charismatic.' She glanced over her shoulder. 'He wound his sister-in-law up, though – and his brother, come to that.'

Angie grinned. 'He'd probably have got my vote then.'

Eve lowered her voice. 'You don't like Roger Fulton?'

'He's one of those people who're all nicey-nicey on the surface, but he's not genuine. Little things give him away. His smiles don't meet his eyes and he sucks up to whoever's wielding the most power in the room.' She shrugged. 'I've only sat in on the odd board meeting but it's obvious even to me. I've taken calls from him too, made diary arrangements, that kind of thing. He learned my name from the start and remembers it every time, but he uses it too much, if you know what I mean?' She gave an involuntary shudder. 'Smarmy. Are you going to write about his brother?'

Eve nodded. 'And look into his death. I saw a few odd things in the days leading up to his murder.'

Angie took a swig of her wine. 'I'm glad you're on the case. It sounds as though he needs a champion. Well, if you want information on his brother, I'm your woman! Do you think he might be the killer?'

Eve frowned. After her chat with Ada, the thought of Emory causing his brother trouble for decades made it seem all the more possible. But it felt wrong to poison Angie's mind when she had no proof. 'He might have a rock-solid alibi for all I know.' Her impatience for an update left her filled with pent-up tension.

'If it's any help, I'd say they had an "interesting" relationship.'

Maybe her mind was poisoned already. Eve leaned forward. 'Go on!'

'I overheard Roger having a row with the chair of the charity's board just before a meeting recently. They'd shut themselves away next door to the stationery cupboard and I was fetching markers for the whiteboard. The chair said everyone was gossiping about Roger's brother having to use his old childminder's bath. He thought the comments about Roger's meanness would put their donors off. This was just last week.'

'That's interesting.' Word must have got around quickly, but that was Saxford for you. 'What happened next?'

'Roger sounded injured. I was rooted to the spot by that time, as you can imagine. He claimed he'd invited Emory to use their bathroom, but Selina didn't like it. He said she thought he was dirty.' Angie gave a snort. 'Which he would be, given the lack of facilities at the lodge and her refusal to let him use theirs.'

But Eve was sure it had been an excuse. She couldn't imagine Emory not washing, even if it had been at a kitchen sink. He'd had his pride and a sense of self-worth. As for Roger, the fact that he hadn't put his foot down said it all. Eve could see how he might have let Selina have her way over the issue of accommodation; offering to find him a rental in Blyworth would have assuaged his guilt. But surely Roger could have forced the issue when it came to using their bathroom. It suggested he'd been just as keen as his wife to keep Emory at arm's length. They hadn't wanted him pottering in and out, becoming part of their lives.

'I'm curious about the lodge. Emory invited me in on Friday.' She explained the circumstances. 'But I said no. It seemed like an imposition when he hadn't been expecting me.' And now she'd never get to see inside.

'A friend of mine's been in,' Angie said, unexpectedly. 'She's saving up to go travelling. Doing all sorts of odds and bits, including some cleaning. Roger asked if I knew anyone who might tackle the place as a one-off job urgently, before his brother moved in. He was due to arrive in a couple of days and Roger said he was desperate so I mentioned her. He told me their regular cleaner didn't have time, but we wondered if he was too ashamed to show her the place.'

'It was filthy?'

'Not so much that, though my friend said there were loads of cobwebs in dark corners. It was the physical state of it; it was pretty much uninhabitable. They clad it a while back apparently, to keep the rain out, but not soon enough by the sound of things. My friend said there were damp patches, and bits of bare brick with plaster still falling off. She spent half her time looking at the ceiling, wondering if it would come down on her head.

'Roger kept telling her he'd offered to rent Emory somewhere smarter in town, but he'd refused. We just couldn't work out why they didn't have him at the Dower House.'

It would be what the whole village was thinking.

'There was a blackened old woodburner, but no central

heating,' Angie continued. 'And just a big old Belfast sink to wash in. You'd have to fill it from a kettle on the gas stove if you wanted hot water.'

'Wow. That does sound extreme.'

Angie nodded, then glanced down into her wine before raising her eyes sheepishly to Eve. 'I'm afraid I mentioned what she told me at work, on the back of other gossip that was circulating. And today I heard a couple of people speculating about the brothers' relationship after news of the murder broke. If the chair of the board was worried about damaging tittle-tattle before, it's nothing to what he must be feeling now. Roger was tipped to succeed him when he retires in the summer, but I'd say his chances are getting slimmer by the minute.'

11

That evening, on her way to Robin's, Eve went to knock at Dale Buckingham's door. The police had no reason to check his alibi for Emory's murder, but she had a plan to worm it out of him. It was his wife who answered. She was wearing an apron – getting ready for supper no doubt.

'I'm sorry to disturb you.' Eve smiled. 'We haven't met properly, but I know you by sight. I'm Eve. I work at the teashop.'

'Oh yes.' The woman's shoulders relaxed – probably as she realised Eve was local and wasn't likely to be selling anything.

Eve fished one of her own earrings out of her handbag. 'I just wondered if you'd dropped this at the Cross Keys last night. I didn't spot you there, but someone mentioned it might be yours – they'd seen you wearing something similar.'

The woman leaned forward and peered at it. 'No. No, that's not mine. We weren't at Jo's do, but thanks for asking.'

'No problem.' Eve slipped the earring back in her bag. 'It was a lovely evening.' She knew there'd been an open invitation to the whole village to attend, and Eve had certainly seen Dale's wife in the pub before. 'Did you have a clash?'

She nodded. 'We miss it most years. It's Dale's dad's

birthday and he's the sort who gathers the whole family together for special occasions. We all had to schlep down to a swanky restaurant in Ipswich, because it was central.' She sighed, grinned and lowered her voice. 'I'd have preferred the pub, to be honest, but what can you do?'

Eve nodded. 'Just one of those things.'

As she said goodbye, anger at Dale's behaviour welled up inside her. Faithless toad. All the same, it looked as though he was in the clear.

Twenty minutes later, Eve sat in Robin Yardley's cosy galley kitchen close to the fire he'd got going. The delay was thanks to the need for secrecy when they met. After leaving the Buckinghams' house, she'd overshot his cottage and entered Blind Eye Wood, the frozen leaves cracking underfoot, then approached via Robin's back garden. For a moment, the injustice of the situation struck her. Here she was, creeping around like Selina and Dale, even though she and Robin had nothing to be ashamed of. Anger at the selfish corrupt officers and their criminal contacts who'd driven him into hiding rose up inside her. She tried to dampen it down. There was nothing to be done.

Sparks jumped in the fire as Robin adjusted the position of the logs. Gus was sprawled extravagantly on the rug next to the hearth. He stretched now, his eyes half closed, back legs twitching.

The room smelled of woodsmoke, the mouth-watering chicken and mushroom pie Robin had cooked and the Merlot Eve was drinking.

She'd already passed on her thoughts on the suspects for Emory's murder. Selina came top of her list, but she'd explained her question marks over Roger, Poppy and Laurence Rice too. Poppy's last visit to Emory occupied her mind, together with Emory's attempts to pressure her into doing something, and the argument he'd had with Laurence on the village green.

The light from the fire was reflected in Robin's glass as he raised it to his lips. 'Greg was interested to hear about the break-in at Magpie Lodge,' he said, after taking a swig.

Eve nodded. 'It's curious that Emory didn't report it. My guess is he knew more about it than he said. Who was responsible perhaps, or what they were after. He looked as though he was assimilating the information when it happened – slotting it into some kind of context, if that makes any sense.'

He frowned. 'That might explain why he held back. We know a bit more about security there now. The Fultons told Greg there's only one key to the lodge. The spares got lost years ago and they never bothered cutting extras. They kept the key on a hook in their kitchen until Emory came, then handed it over to him. It was in his trouser pocket when his body was found, along with the key to Sycamore Cottage, Brenda Goody's place. As I said, there was no sign of forced entry there. Maybe he never bothered to lock up, or perhaps he let his killer in before he got into the bath. I'm assuming he didn't go to answer the door stark naked and dripping.'

'Especially not in these temperatures.' Eve sipped her wine and imagined the scene. 'Any word on a lover? If he let his killer stay it implies he was intimate with them.'

'He wasn't seeing anyone as far as his "nearest and dearest" were aware. And you know what Saxford's like. You'd probably have heard if he had a girl- or boyfriend.'

'True.' Eve had finished her pie now.

She wondered how it had been. Had Emory watched his killer come into the room without guessing their purpose? Or had he been lying there in the bath as she did herself, eyes closed, relaxing? She shuddered. She might not do that again for a few weeks. He'd probably been focused on the horoscope line he'd called, imagining he was alone in the house, appreciating the bath – a rare treat... The killer must have been surprised when they saw him holding his mobile. They wouldn't have heard him talking as they walked upstairs, so there'd have been no warning. They'd likely assumed Emory had an open line to a potential witness. It would have spurred them to act immediately.

She pulled herself back to the here and now. 'So the time of death was nine thirty-five, which fits with what the pathologist estimated?' Eve had most of the details he'd given her committed to memory now.

'That's right. The precise time depends on how long the water took to seep into the phone, but it was cracked at one end, so I'd guess it wasn't long. The pathologist won't narrow their window further, but unless the phone flew, Greg reckons it's nigh on impossible it slipped into the bath after Emory's death.'

Eve nodded. 'And although the killer could have hung around to drop it into the water once he was dead, remaining on the scene would rather defeat the object, if they were hoping to alibi themselves.'

'Quite.' Robin smiled for a moment, but then his expression turned grim. 'Emory had bruising on his legs. The killer must have grabbed his ankles and hauled them up while he flailed around until he gave up the struggle.'

Eve closed her eyes. It was too awful to contemplate. 'Could they tell anything more from the bruising?'

'Not much. His attacker won't be frail or petite, but that's about it. The tub was wide and deep, which gave them an advantage: less for Emory to hang on to for protection. They could have been male or female.' He took her hand and gave it a squeeze. 'I'm sorry. Are you okay?'

She took a deep breath and swallowed. 'Yes. Thank you. Has any new information come up since this morning?' Homing in on the facts would help. She could work out who to target for information as she did her interviews. She was determined to find evidence that would help catch Emory's killer.

'The alibis are interesting,' Robin said, reaching to top up

Eve's glass. By the fire, Gus had started to snore. 'Coco confirms she saw her parents at around ten past nine, when she came inside after a cigarette. Smoking's banned indoors. But she only exchanged a few words with them; after that, her ex turned up and they disappeared into Coco's rooms.'

'Rooms plural?' The family really did have a lot of space.

Robin grinned and nodded. 'Bedroom, en suite and sitting room. Greg says that's what Coco called it. Her father referred to it as her study.'

'Figures.'

He laughed. 'Anyway, her alibi's solid. Her ex corroborates her story and although I expect there was some rough and tumble in the bedroom, they used the computer too; logged into a couple of social media sites to snoop at mutual friends. The upshot is neither of them could have been at Sycamore Cottage when Emory died.'

'I can't see Coco's motive anyway. She and Emory were getting on like a house on fire at the fundraiser.'

Robin nodded. 'Better than her and her ex by the sound of it. Greg says the embers of the relationship aren't quite out but it's touch and go. They emerged from her rooms at eleven, by which time they were rowing. Roger and Selina were present at that point, but it doesn't follow that they stayed in the house while Coco was entertaining. They both claim they were home all evening but they admit they weren't in the same room. Roger says he was reading some papers in his study and Selina claims she put her feet up and watched television in the den. I'd guess either of them could have slipped out without the other noticing. And they might lie for each other anyway.'

Eve nodded. 'Despite Selina's affair, I can imagine her wanting to preserve the status quo. She's the sort to enjoy home comforts with a bit of excitement on the side, and he relies on his squeaky-clean reputation. Her motive is the most obvious, but they're both in the running.'

'And then there's Poppy Rice. Palmer's curious about her, just like you are.'

Eve shuddered. 'I don't like having anything in common with the detective inspector, but leaving Magpie Lodge in tears does look suspicious. All the same, Selina and Roger have clearer motives.'

'True, but there are other oddities about Poppy that Palmer's seized on. Emory Fulton bought her flowers after her visit. Got them himself from the village store – a large bouquet – and left them on the doorstep of the hall with a note.'

Moira's bouquets weren't cheap, especially in the middle of winter. Emory must have felt deeply guilty about something. If he was simply sorry for her, he'd have finished their conversation, not let her leave in tears. And it would have been hugs and sympathy that he offered, not flowers. What the heck had he done? 'I can see why that made Palmer curious.' Eve tried to keep the grudging note out of her voice.

Robin nodded. 'Greg says Emory's financial situation really was dire, so they're convinced the outlay on the flowers meant the grievance between them was significant.' Robin stepped carefully round the sleeping Gus to put another log on the fire. 'There's something else too. Laurence Rice has a rock-solid alibi; he arrived at his mother's private view at Rice and Fulton at around eight forty-five and stayed until the end at ten.'

Eve couldn't imagine him going in for that kind of thing.

Robin laughed. He must have read her incredulous expression. 'A case of family loyalty, I think.'

'And Poppy?'

He shook his head. 'She was home alone. She told the others she had a headache. And here's where it gets really interesting. Laurence said he called the hall's landline to check she was okay at half past nine and she confirmed that, but Greg says she sounded really flustered. It made them look more closely and records show the call lasted less than a minute. They questioned Poppy again this afternoon and she admitted she lied about picking up. She says she was at home but feeling ill, so she let the call go to the answerphone. Laurence didn't try her mobile.'

'That was very half-hearted of him.' She wasn't surprised. 'Did Poppy say why she lied?'

Robin leaned back in his chair. 'She just said she was frightened and it seemed the easiest option. She insists she didn't kill Emory.'

Which, of course, she would do. Eve closed her eyes. She wondered if Laurence had suggested she lie. She could imagine it. He'd be keen to avoid a scandal; it was the kind of thing Bathurst would be allergic to. But even if he had, that didn't prove she was innocent.

'What did Greg say about Brenda Goody and her lodger?'

Robin smiled now. 'Another interesting pair. I know Brenda a little. I do her garden. She's always warm and friendly but we don't chat about personal stuff.' He looked apologetic for not encouraging it. He never volunteered information about himself; it would be too easy to say something contradictory about his past. 'I've seen the lodger too,' he went on, 'but only briefly. Not enough to form a proper opinion.

'Anyway, Greg says he and Brenda spent the evening at the Cross Keys. Left Sycamore Cottage at seven. Dinner at seven thirty. Brenda's known Jo Falconer for years, so it was inevitable she'd stay on for the fireworks at eleven.'

'And if the killer knew that, they'd be confident of a wide window in which to commit the crime. It explains why Emory was relaxed about time too.' He must have been glad of a few hours in a warm, cosy house. 'So Brenda and the lodger have cast-iron alibis.'

'Probably.'

Eve felt a familiar spark of excitement inside her.

'The lodger, Kelvin Brady, admits that he left the pub "mid-evening", though he claims he can't remember when and Brenda's not sure either. They both say he was only gone for five minutes, but Greg's not convinced her timing's precise. Brenda admits to having a few sherries before she started on the wine, and Kelvin might be lying. He says he glimpsed a friend through the window and nipped out to speak with him.'

'So what's the hitch?'

'Conveniently, Brady claims he hadn't seen the friend in years and doesn't have an up-to-date mobile number for them. And apparently their name's John Smith.'

'Ah.'

'Quite. It's almost as though he wanted the story to sound invented. But the police don't have a motive for him, and Brenda Goody insists she'd have noticed if he'd been gone long enough to attack Emory.'

'I'll definitely want to talk to them both.'

He nodded. 'The final bit of intel from the police is that Emory died intestate, not that he had much to leave. There were the clothes at the lodge and around twenty quid in the bank. His brother will inherit, as his closest relative.'

'What about the royalties from his books?'

He shook his head. 'They're all out of print – they pre-dated the digital boom and eventually his publisher returned the rights.'

'Heck, Robin. It's so sad.'

'I'm afraid so. Where does all this leave you?'

'Selina Fulton is still my top suspect. She had the opportunity, and Emory was a threat. But his "jokey" comments and family ghost stories were damaging Roger, too. It was probably enough to ruin his chances of a knighthood and get him quietly dropped from the charity board he sits on. He could even have lost legal clients over it. And Emory had no money to move elsewhere; he looked set to remain a thorn in their sides long term.'

She frowned. 'But Poppy Rice is up there as well. She also had the opportunity and she lied to the police, though her motive's not clear. I need to know what went on at Magpie Lodge yesterday.' It was a shame she hadn't managed to get the jeweller on her own. 'As for Laurence and Kelvin, with their alibis they're in the clear, for now.'

Robin gave her a half smile and took her hand. 'But you won't rest until you understand why Emory and Laurence were enemies and why Kelvin gave such a lame excuse for leaving the Cross Keys?'

Eve smiled back. 'They're oddities in a situation where oddities might mean everything.'

12

On Tuesday morning, Eve woke early and organised the information she'd gathered the previous day. After marshalling details on the key players' alibis, she added a tab to the murder spreadsheet to set it all down.

Alibis for Emory's murder (Time of death: 9.35 p.m., Sunday 17 January)

Cast iron

Brenda Goody (Emory and Roger's old child minder) – no one disputes that she was in the Cross Keys from 7.30 p.m. until after 11.

Ada and Laurence Rice – both at Rice and Fulton's private view. (Ada all evening, Laurence from around 8.45 until after 10 p.m.)

Coco Fulton – busy with her ex-boyfriend, making out/internet surfing, then rowing.

Questionable

Roger and Selina Fulton – both claim they were at home at the Dower House all evening. Coco saw them at 9.10 p.m., but after that no one can confirm their presence. (They were in separate rooms.)

Kelvin Brady (Brenda Goody's lodger) – admits he slipped out of the Cross Keys 'mid-evening'. Claims it was only for five minutes, but no one's sure when he left or whether he really returned that quickly. (Brenda vouches for him, but she was tipsy. Can't produce a contact number for John Smith, the friend he claims he met.)

Entirely lacking

Poppy Rice – claims she was home alone at Fairview Hall, but after lying, now admits she didn't pick up when Laurence called her at 9.30 p.m. The call connected but went to the hall's answerphone. No one can vouch for her.

Based on opportunity, things didn't look good for Poppy. That and her suspicious behaviour made her a key contact. Eve made a couple of calls to arrange interviews later in the day and conducted some background research, leaving the way clear to focus on Poppy first as she headed out.

She decided to take Ada Rice at her word and drove up to the Fairview estate to visit the hall. Once again, she opted to call without warning, in the hope of honest answers, rather than carefully rehearsed platitudes. If Poppy was alone, Eve would dig to find out what had happened between her and Emory on the day of his murder, but she needed to tread carefully and gain her trust first. It was useful that they'd met through Monty's but it might take more than that to get Poppy to relax.

Eve remembered the woman's troubled look as she'd talked to Emory in the teashop. It might be best to open with questions about the séance; Eve wanted to understand how Emory worked and the topic ought to be more neutral.

She sighed as she parked her car on Ada Rice's grand drive. Her plans were all very well, but it was more likely that Laurence would be present, with or without Poppy. He was the one using the hall as an office. She was curious about him too, but he had a roomful of people who could testify he was nowhere near Sycamore Cottage when Emory was killed. Poppy took priority. Eve would have to think on her feet and angle for a private chat with her.

The hall was intimidating. The stone lions on the gateposts seemed to stare down at her imperiously as she walked between them. Up ahead, the regimented sash windows spanning three floors looked dark, blank and unfriendly. Eve's mind ran back to Dorothea and Mildred, the two women who'd died unnatural deaths in Emory's great-grandfather's day: one in the bath and one in the woods. Mildred's boyfriend had hanged for her murder. Images of the scene spooled through Eve's head, however hard she tried to suppress them. His fear, horror and protestations. What if he'd been innocent? She bet no one had wanted to accuse the lord of the manor.

The driveway and walk up the steps to the hall's front door felt long. She rang the bell but it took a couple of minutes before anyone answered. At last she heard movement inside and a moment later she was face to face with Poppy Rice. The jeweller looked pale and drawn, her eyes still red-rimmed.

'Hello, Poppy. I'm so sorry to bother you at a time like this.'

The young woman blinked. 'Is it about my jewellery?'

'Not today. I wanted to talk to you about Emory.'

Her eyes widened.

'I only work part-time at Monty's. My real profession is

obituary writing and I've been commissioned to cover Emory's life. I know you were close and I'd love to talk to you about him.'

'Oh.' She bit her lip, her gaze on the floor tiles. 'We had a lot of journalists here yesterday. We couldn't really tell them anything.'

It made sense that they'd call. The hall was close to the lodge and they'd probably got wind of Poppy's emotional outburst the day Emory died. Viv had heard about it on the grapevine and gossip spread like wildfire in Saxford. The reporters would only have to stop for a warming drink at the Cross Keys and chat to the locals.

What's more, Poppy was beautiful. Her photograph would sell papers and encourage clicks. Eve bet the hacks had wanted to go to town. Readers would be clamouring to know what had gone on between Emory and this beauty. Eve could only assume Ada or Laurence had managed to repel them the day before. She'd glanced over the online coverage and not seen their faces or any quotes.

'I'm not keen on talking to anyone.' Poppy's voice quavered.

'I wouldn't want to either, if I'd been pressed for gossip and scandal,' Eve said. 'But I promise you that's not what I'm after. The article will appear in *Icon* and focus on Emory, not anyone else.'

'Will you need photographs?' It was clear Poppy still didn't trust her and of course, Laurence and Ada would hate to be caught up in a scandal too.

Eve shook her head. 'Absolutely not. As I said, the article's about Emory; I'm not aiming to make life awkward for any of his contacts or promote gossip. I just need to speak to the people he was close to and those he worked for so I can get to know him better. I'd love to ask you about him as a person, and about the séance he performed.'

'Perhaps it might be all right, then.'

Eve's pulse quickened. She might get some answers. But as

Poppy stood back to let her into the hall, Laurence appeared, walking out of the shadows.

Poppy closed the gap between them. She slipped her arm through his and he flinched slightly, withdrawing just a little at the show of affection. It was the second time Eve had seen him react like that. Originally, she'd thought that they were a close-knit couple. Now she wondered if the relationship was off balance. He'd attempted to control Poppy's interactions with Emory, and she seemed anxious and clingy.

Laurence smiled at Eve, like a co-conspirator. 'The séance became a bone of contention, I'm afraid. I was all for it, but Poppy wasn't at all keen. My mother said you might call. Why don't you come in and I'll explain?'

Eve was sure Laurence thought she'd be on his side. His arrogance made her want to oppose him automatically, but that was irrational. She tried to dial down her irritation.

Eve followed the pair into an elegant drawing room where Laurence invited her to sit in a Georgian button-back chair.

'You were on the ghost walk, weren't you?' Laurence said, as he and Poppy sat too. 'You probably realised I asked Emory to visit because I'm a sceptic.' He glanced at Poppy. 'And of course, Poppy shares my views.'

There was no 'of course' about it as far as Eve was concerned. In Poppy's place, she would have been irritated to have someone else speaking for her. She waited for Poppy to comment but she said nothing.

'I hardly think it's anything to write home about,' Laurence went on. 'Surely most people feel the same? I was curious to see his methods. I'm an academic. I like to know more.'

She might not like Laurence, but Eve's approach was the same. She wanted to understand how things worked. People in particular. Viv was always telling her off for not having more faith. All the same, she wouldn't have invited Emory to conduct a séance under false pretences, just to make a fool of him.

'I can see what you're thinking,' Laurence went on, 'but I was just interested, that's all. I knew Emory would have some tricks up his sleeve. I wanted to understand how he convinced people. He was certainly a showman.' The last words were added grudgingly and echoed her own thoughts.

'I agree.' She couldn't overlook the edge to Laurence's voice, as though he was controlling his feelings. That wasn't borne of analytical, academic interest. It fitted with the way they'd interacted on the village green.

'He was my godfather,' Poppy put in, 'and I thought it was cruel to ask him when we don't really believe. I still don't understand why you of all people would want to taunt him,' she added, turning to her husband.

What did she mean, 'of all people'? Eve couldn't imagine. As far as she could see, Laurence was just the sort to relish belittling anyone who came to hand.

The academic shot Poppy a sharp look but seemed to relax when it was clear she'd said her piece. 'I don't think he was under any illusions. He knew the score.'

Poppy bit her lip. 'I felt bad about it.'

'You were being irrational. Letting your emotions get the better of you, as usual.' Laurence shook his head. 'His two-bit show was part of who he was. Besides, I'm sure he was glad of the money. He was clearly desperate.'

Eve's adrenaline ramped up. He was behaving like a pig and it frustrated her to see Poppy let him get away with it. Then guilt at her own impatience took over. He was a bully. If he'd been like this for years he'd probably crushed Poppy's spirit. It was disconcerting and worrying to see the way she clung to him. Eve wondered if she had any kind of support network. Laurence had dragged her away with him while he completed his sabbatical. Any friends she had were likely back in London, and if he was as horrible to them as he was to her they might keep their distance.

But however foul Laurence was, Eve needed to stay focused. Poppy had lied to the police to give herself an alibi and fallen out with Emory just hours before his death.

'Odd choice of godparent, I always thought,' Laurence was saying. 'I can't imagine what your mother was thinking of. I know your father agrees with me.' He smiled. 'We often think alike.'

That must be cosy, down at Bathurst.

Poppy bit her lip. 'But Dad realises I was fond of Emory, and that Mum was too.' After a moment, she added in a small voice, 'That matters to him.'

'Has he called you since Emory died?'

Poppy flushed. 'He sent me a text. He's dealing with that international delegation.'

Instead of responding, Laurence turned to Eve, his tone dismissive. 'For my part, the séance was interesting, though much as I'd expected. I don't mind telling you about it. I'm sure we weren't the only sceptics he dealt with.' He frowned. 'He insisted on us sitting in a darkened room, of course. Low lights, silence, holding hands, waiting for the spirits to come to him. Clichéd stuff.' He looked at Poppy. 'And you helped direct him, though I suppose you had no idea you were doing it. Whatever you say, you were nervous. The atmospherics were laughable, but they worked on you like a charm, didn't they? When we held hands, you were trembling. He'd have noticed too. Then naturally he claimed to have made contact with your mother. He sensed you were susceptible and he knew you both; his prior knowledge gave him a massive head start.'

Poppy's flush deepened. She opened her mouth to speak but then changed her mind.

'There's no need to be embarrassed,' Laurence said after a moment, his tone weary. 'I expect there are countless women who would have reacted just the same.'

Sexist jerk. It was as though he was back in the nineteenth century, assuming women would need smelling salts to deal with a bit of subdued lighting. There was more to this, Eve was sure. Trembling was an extreme reaction.

'In any case,' Laurence went on, 'having claimed to have reached Poppy's mother "on the other side", what gem do you think Emory came up with? Something specific? Where to find the family treasure? The real identity of cousin what's-its-name's father? No! He said Poppy's mother was still there and that she was thinking of her. She'd support her whatever she did.' His eyes met Eve's. 'The message could hardly have been more generic. It was obvious he'd made the whole thing up. It's only fair that your readers find out about the real Emory.'

Poppy had her hands to her cheeks now and had turned away, letting her hair fall forward so it hid her expression. Laurence was being appallingly cruel about a man she'd just lost. It would be enough to explain her reaction, but Eve wondered if there was more to it than that. Her hunch was that Poppy secretly believed in Emory's powers. That was a far better explanation for her trembling hands during the séance. But if so, what had she been afraid of?

Eve shook her head. Poppy certainly had secrets. Could she have worried that the event might lead to some kind of revelation? If she assumed Emory would enter a trance-like state, she might imagine he'd speak without filtering the content.

So much of this was speculation. She needed evidence: proof that Poppy had believed in Emory's powers, and keys to the secrets she was keeping. It was time to put her plan into action.

'Poppy, I'd love to ask you about Emory in more detail, if I may, as he was your godfather. I wondered if I could buy you a drink at the teashop. I can give you a lift. It feels wrong to focus on everyday things at a time like this, but I can show you our latest display in the crafts section at the same time. The colours might suggest which pieces you'd like us to stock next.'

It was the only excuse she could think of to get the woman alone. When Poppy met her eyes, Eve could see she'd been quietly crying behind her veil of glorious red hair.

Laurence stepped forward. 'I really doubt Poppy feels well enough to—'

But his wife cut him off. *No, that's all right.' She took a deep breath. 'I think it will help to get out.'

Poppy still sounded hesitant, but she walked towards the door and Eve joined her. Laurence followed them, and as Eve drove away, she could see him peering at them through a window. It was clear he would have spoiled her plans if he'd been able.

13

Eve had to give Viv a hard stare at the teashop. She'd followed her and Poppy into the crafts section to talk business, which was fair enough, but she continued to hover nearby after Eve had ordered their teas. At last, an alarm went off and she clutched her cobalt-blue hair and dashed into the kitchen.

'Thanks for talking to me,' Eve said, as she poured them each a cup of Assam. 'I could see how close you and Emory were when you came here together last week.' Poppy blinked at Eve's words; tears threatened again. 'I'm so sorry about what happened to him.'

Poppy nodded. 'Thank you.'

Eve leaned forward. 'It must have been nice to find he'd be staying in Saxford at the same time as you. Did you manage to see much of each other?'

She closed her eyes for a moment. 'You've probably already heard I was with him on Sunday afternoon. I've become the talk of the village.' She was fiddling with the handle of her cup now, her eyes not on Eve's. 'The police were quick to get in touch. Someone saw me outside Magpie Lodge.' She slumped forward suddenly, her head in her hands. 'The detective inspector—' She stopped abruptly and when she spoke again she'd lowered her voice to a whisper. 'The detective inspector thought I might have been having an affair with Emory.'

Eve couldn't suppress an eye-roll. She could see how close they'd been, and that there was something strange about the relations between her, Laurence and Emory, but every instinct told her Palmer was wrong.

'I know the detective inspector; he's not an easy man.' She spoke in an undertone. 'You'd hardly meet Emory here if he was your secret lover.' Did Palmer have no brain at all? Besides, Poppy had looked anxious when Laurence walked in, not guilty.

Poppy took a deep breath. 'I ought to have pointed that out, only he put me on the spot and my mind went blank.' That was Palmer all over. Talk about counterproductive. 'Anyway, you're right, and the police couldn't be more wrong. I loved Emory like an uncle; I used to turn to him as though he were family. I lost my mother to cancer, and I suppose...' She was crying again and broke off to wipe her eyes with a tissue. 'I suppose I looked on him as a link to her.'

Suddenly the quiet tears became a torrent. Eve felt terrible for taking her through all this in front of the other villagers, but the outpouring had come as a surprise. Thank goodness Viv had given them a table near the back of the teashop. Poppy's long hair hid her face, and with that and the general hubbub, she didn't think anyone else had noticed.

Except Viv, of course. Eve could see her loitering just inside the kitchen door.

Eve reached for a packet of tissues from her bag and put it on the table in front of Poppy. 'I'm so sorry.'

'It's okay. It's a relief to let it out.' She took a shuddering breath and pulled a tissue from the packet. 'As Laurence mentioned, Emory was my mother's choice as godfather. They became friends years ago in London; he was her go-to person if she needed someone neutral to talk to.'

Eve hesitated. Her next question was delicate. She wanted to know if Poppy secretly believed in Emory's powers. Was it possible she was keeping secrets and had felt threatened by the prospect of the séance? Scared of what might come out? Eve had no idea what sort of relationship Poppy had had with her mother. Her violent crying suggested they were close, but the tears could also be the result of shame and regret. 'You say Emory felt like a link to your mum. Had he ever tried to reach her for you before? Prior to Saturday night, I mean?'

She blinked. 'No. No, he hadn't.' Her tone was flat; heavy and with a hint of surprise and regret. Would she have been keener if they'd had a session in private? Did she wish she'd asked him now? 'But he knew her so well, you see. He felt like a strong link without any of that.' After a moment, she added, 'I don't honestly buy into all that spiritualist stuff.'

Eve nodded, though she wasn't sure she believed her; she'd cast her eyes down as she'd uttered her last sentence. 'Was your mum's death recent?'

She shook her head as she blew her nose. 'It's been three years now, almost exactly.'

'Anniversaries are hard.' It helped if you could share your grief, but she couldn't imagine Laurence being sympathetic. As for Poppy's father, Eve had the impression there was some closeness between them, but she doubted they spent much time together. He sounded too bound up with work. He probably spoke to Laurence more often, as a colleague.

Poppy took a deep breath, but she was back in control. Her shoulders rose and fell, but her breathing was calmer.

Eve leaned forward. 'I was surprised when Laurence said you didn't believe in Emory's gift, back at the hall. You looked so anxious at the idea of a séance when we were on the ghost walk that I assumed you'd attended one before and it had left an impression. Or,' she paused a moment, watching Poppy look down into her lap, 'that you were worried about what might happen at the one on Saturday.'

'Why would I worry?' The words came out sharply.

Eve felt she'd struck a nerve. Somewhere, just under the surface, the answer she was looking for was lurking.

'It must be a very odd prospect, getting in touch with a relative beyond the grave. One you were probably very close to. Who knew you better than anyone, perhaps – shared your secrets.'

Poppy opened her mouth. 'At the time I—' But then she stopped. After a deep breath, she said: 'I'm sure it would be, if you genuinely believed contact could be made.' She shook her head. 'That was never on the agenda.'

So near and yet so far. Eve felt frustration bubble up inside her. 'But you were nervous beforehand and trembling during the séance.'

Poppy still looked crumpled, her shoulders forward as if she was curling in on herself. She seemed so forlorn. Eve's feelings wavered once again, from frustration to sympathy.

'I wish I could tell you that Emory was excellent at his job and brought me closure and solace, but I can't,' she said at last. 'And Laurence isn't always very kind.' That was a massive understatement. 'I knew how awful he'd be to Emory if he came. And to me too. That's why I was tense.'

'Was it as bad as you imagined?'

Poppy wasn't meeting her eyes again. 'We got through it.'

'And what about the message Emory passed on: that your mum was still there and would support you whatever you did?'

The tears were back. 'Just standard patter, like Laurence said.'

'Poppy, I wonder if I could ask about your final meeting at Magpie Lodge on Sunday. When I write my obituaries I try to follow my subject from cradle to grave and speaking to someone who was close to Emory and interacted with him on the day he died would bring his story full circle. What did you talk about?'

It was a pushy question, and more direct than Eve would be with a standard interviewee, but Emory's was no standard obituary.

'The séance brought Mum's death back. I went to see Emory on Sunday to talk about it. Opening up to him was almost as good as being with her.'

'But he let you leave in tears...' What Poppy said simply didn't ring true.

She closed her eyes. 'I just dashed off. I was emotional and I wanted some air. I wish I hadn't left like that now – I should have stayed until...' She paused for a moment. Eve was sure she was reliving the events of that afternoon – events she had no intention of sharing. 'Until I'd calmed down.' She shook her head slowly. 'Emory was known as the rough one, the black sheep, but he was worth a thousand of Roger. It was just that he did some stupid things sometimes.' She paused and the look in her eyes was bleak. 'Appallingly stupid.' She was holding her teacup hard, her knuckles white, but at last she took a deep breath. 'Deep down, though, I think he wanted the best for everyone.' She shook her head. 'He just wasn't remotely clear-sighted about it.'

'Could you give me an example of that? It's useful to illustrate what I write with anecdotes.'

Poppy bit her lip; she was breathing quickly again.

'I can emphasise how good-hearted he was, if that's your overall impression.' Eve said gently. 'I won't even quote you if you'd rather not.'

There was a pause as Poppy sipped her tea. Eve felt she was playing for time, but in that moment, a flash of inspiration came to her. Emory had secretly passed a package to Poppy, right there in Monty's. What was it she'd said to him? Something about having gone into something with her eyes open. And then she'd asked him if he was sure he could manage. It stirred a memory. Eve had uttered similar words when she'd stood outside Magpie Lodge, ready to accept a share of Emory's takings. She'd wanted to be sure he could afford to pay her...

Suddenly, Eve had an idea about what Emory might have been handing over. And why. But the situation was sensitive.

'Poppy, did you lend Emory money to help him buy his haunted manor hotel?'

The woman went pale and sat back in her chair. 'What makes you think that?'

'I saw the hotel was repossessed, so I knew he must have had a mortgage, but he'd have needed a chunk of capital too, to use as a deposit. I was wondering how he'd managed to save enough. And I saw him give you a bag at Monty's. I wasn't meaning to snoop, but it's impossible not to hear people's conversations as you wait tables. You were asking him if he could manage, and telling him you'd gone into the arrangement knowing the possible consequences.'

Poppy's eyes widened. Eve was convinced she'd guessed correctly, and that Poppy was frightened.

'I won't put that in the obituary.' Eve met her eye. 'You have my word.' But it would account for Poppy's comment just now. Emory had done some appallingly stupid things. Like losing the money Poppy had lent him. She wondered how much she'd lost. And was her faith in Emory's good intentions really undimmed? Eve knew Poppy wasn't above lying; she needed to get her to open up, so she could judge her on her demeanour, not just her words.

She was crying again now. 'He really mucked up. He took a financial gamble with the funds I supplied, thinking he could pay me back with interest. I saw it as an investment, but it went wrong. The business didn't take off as quickly as he'd hoped, and the place was repossessed and sold off cut-price. The bank recouped their losses but there was very little left over. He gave me what he could straight away, but he had other debts too – for building work and interiors.' Her head was in her hands again. 'He was giving me the shortfall by degrees. Laurence and I have joint accounts now, so handing over cash was more discreet.' She raised her eyes to Eve's. 'Laurence doesn't know about the loan. It was my savings; mine to do with as I liked. And I'm managing.'

Perhaps that was true. The workshop in Blyworth must cost a fair amount, but Laurence might be paying for that. The move to Suffolk was for his sabbatical; it was down to him that Poppy was away from her usual workspace.

Logically, Eve didn't see Poppy's motive for murder. She'd never get her money back now. All the same, the situation left her uneasy. She'd kept the loan secret from Laurence but it was bound to come out. Another example of lies told. Information left out. And the look in Poppy's eyes as she'd spoken told Eve there was more going on under the surface. She might have forgiven the loss of her money, but Eve guessed there was something else that had affected her and Emory's relationship.

'You might want to tell the police about the loan if you haven't already.' Poppy's agonised expression answered that question. 'They'll see for themselves once they trawl through Emory's financial records.' They already knew his bank balance, according to Robin. They might be reviewing his past transactions right now.

'I know.' Her voice was little above a whisper.

Eve could understand her reluctance. Palmer was sure to decide she'd murdered Emory out of hurt and anger once he knew about the cash. But withholding the information would look worse, all the more so after she'd lied about speaking to Laurence on Sunday night. It seemed to Eve that Poppy found it easier to fib or gloss over the truth than to face reality.

'Did you, Laurence and Emory socialise all together?' Eve asked on impulse. She wanted to confirm the impression she'd had: that officially, Emory and Laurence were only nodding acquaintances.

Poppy's look in response was sharp. 'No. Emory and Laurence hardly knew each other.'

After some general questions about Poppy's early memories of her godfather, Eve paid the lovely Lars for their teas. Thank goodness Viv was occupied out the back and they could sneak away without being quizzed. She'd be in the doghouse later though, for not updating her friend instantly.

Eve drove Poppy back to the hall, then left for home, her head milling with thoughts.

Finding out about the loan to Emory was a victory of sorts, but it was outweighed by all the mysteries she hadn't solved. Because she was certain Poppy had lied to her, just as she had to the police. She knew more than she was saying about Emory and Laurence's interactions. And she was holding back information about her visit to Magpie Lodge. Another snippet of Poppy's conversation with Emory had come back to her. Eve had caught the words *something I wanted to tell you*, and Poppy's tone had been intense. It was something that mattered, Eve was sure. But then Laurence had arrived and her chance to confide was gone. Eve guessed Sunday had been the first opportunity she'd had to sneak off and meet Emory alone again. What had she told him? Was it something about Laurence? How hard he was to live with, maybe – and that their marriage wasn't working? It was the kind of issue you might bring up with an uncle figure and Poppy was short of shoulders to cry on. Motherless and isolated from her friends down in London. And her dad's connection with Laurence might make it hard to confide in him. Laurence said they often agreed – it implied there was a meeting of minds. Talking to Emory instead made sense. But why had he allowed her to leave in tears? What had made her walk out before she'd composed herself? There must have been something else: something bigger, more fundamental.

Eve wasn't even sure she bought Poppy's reasons for her nervousness about the séance. Yes, Laurence was foul and likely to create a scene, but was that really enough? Eve didn't think so. Emory had been a robust person; not the sort to be floored by her husband's insults. Eve could understand her wanting to avoid the unpleasantness herself, but that didn't seem sufficient cause for the trembling.

As she parked by the village green and exited the car, her mind turned back to Poppy's uncontrolled sobbing during the interview. Of course she was devastated by Emory's death, but her tears had been gentle at first. It was when she'd talked about him being a link to her mum that she'd gone to pieces.

She turned into Haunted Lane, her mind still wrestling with the puzzle. What was it about the link that Emory provided that had made her disintegrate like that? And what would explain the dynamic between Emory and Laurence? Laurence had been angry on the village green, jabbing at Emory's chest. He had a roomful of people as an alibi, but Eve felt sure the answer was important.

Back at Elizabeth's Cottage, Eve's bubbling questions about Poppy filled her with the urge to share. She called Robin and told him about the loan in confidence.

'I know it's significant, but passing the information to the police feels wrong unless it's crucial.'

'*They'll find out soon enough anyway,*' Robin said, which both reassured her and made her tense. '*It will fuel Palmer's suspicions.*'

'I know, though I don't think it's the loan that gives her a motive. Emory can't pay her back now he's dead, and the timing makes no sense. He lost her money months back, when the hotel had to be sold. Why wait to kill him if that's the reason?'

There was a pause. '*He wasn't on the spot back then. Maybe*

*something pushed her over the edge; the same thing which made
her cry on Sunday.'*

Eve sighed. His thoughts mirrored hers. 'I definitely think
there's a lot more to learn; how to uncover it is the question.'

'What do you think of her?'

'I flip-flop on that. She's a bundle of nerves and emotion.
The fact that she's at such a low ebb makes me feel sorry for her,
and I wish she had friends closer at hand. Laurence is so belittling but he's all she's got, currently. But her turmoil might have
made her do something desperate. I can't tell until I understand
the secrets she's keeping.' Eve tried to imagine Poppy grasping
Emory by the ankles, using all her strength to hoist them up,
forcing him under water. Then, keeping that up, watching a
man she was so close to struggle and drown. It was such a ruthless and sustained attack. She took a deep breath, gathering her
thoughts. 'Whoever killed Emory acted in a cold and calcu-
lating way. My guess is they had a crystal-clear end goal. I can
imagine they might have been full of anger, but not that they'd
snapped. If they acted in a moment of madness, they'd have had
time to pull back from the brink.' How long had it taken Emory
to stop fighting for his life? The thought chilled Eve to the core.
'But without knowing what Poppy and Emory really talked
about at Magpie Lodge, I can't tell if that rules her in or out.'

*'And bear in mind that even if Poppy came to her senses
before it was too late, she might still have carried on. If she finds
it hard to face reality, how do you think she'd feel if she'd come
that close to killing Emory? Would she have let go of him and
expected him to forgive her? Or might she have been too scared?
She could have decided to finish the job out of self-preservation,
even if she was horrified at what she was doing.'*

Eve felt goosebumps rise on her arms. His words had hit
home.

14

After the call with Robin, Eve checked her appearance in the mirror by the front door. Her boots were still clean and there was no need to change out of the green tweed dress she'd put on to visit the hall that morning. It was smart as well as warm. Eve always dressed carefully when seeing bereaved friends and relatives. It showed respect.

She was due to interview Brenda Goody at Sycamore Cottage before lunch. The CSIs had finished their work and there was a chance she'd get to meet Kelvin Brady too. She really hoped so. She was impatient for that afternoon as well. She had an appointment to visit the Fultons, who both had clear motives for the killing. Maybe she'd find evidence of their guilt.

Gus helped with the getting-ready process by scampering about her feet and pressing his nose to the mirror, a giddy look in his eye.

'I'm afraid I need to head out alone,' she told him. 'But we'll go for another stroll at lunchtime, yes we will!'

She left the cottage wrapped up warm. As she walked, she focused on Brenda and her lodger. Brenda's alibi was clear – she'd been in the Cross Keys all evening – but Kelvin had slipped out. It might be irrelevant to the case, but his story of meeting a man called John Smith, yet not having his number, sounded concocted. He hadn't had time to kill Emory according to Brenda, but could she be sure? Either way, Eve bet he was hiding something. She wanted to know how much contact he'd had with Emory and if they'd got on. As for Brenda, she'd be invaluable when it came to the obituary, as well as for insights into Emory and Roger's relationship as they'd grown up. If things had been strained that far back, it would add weight to Roger's motive for murder.

Eve was approaching Sycamore Cottage now. The house stood on the Old Toll Road, the main route out of Saxford St Peter, which also led towards Fairview Hall and Magpie Lodge. Eve had walked past it on Emory's ghost tour, without knowing who it belonged to. It was shielded from the road by a dense dark-green yew hedge, so Eve could only get an idea of its char- acter as she reached the gate to the driveway.

It was a pretty place, painted a creamy yellow and thatched, with windows in the eaves, just like Elizabeth's Cottage. The front door was turquoise blue. It must have cost a fair amount, but that didn't surprise Eve now she'd researched Brenda, ready for the interview. After her childminding days she'd married and set up a successful travel agency with her husband. He'd died five years earlier, and Brenda had sold the business a couple of years previously ('ready for a well-earned rest', according to Moira). It was sad that she and her husband hadn't had the chance to enjoy their retirement together. Their marriage had been a happy one, by all accounts.

Eve was curious about Brenda's decision to take a lodger. Moira said she thought the money from the travel business hadn't gone as far as she'd anticipated. (She'd tutted a little.) But Eve wasn't so sure. It sounded as though the agency had been thriving when Brenda sold it, three years after her husband's death. That suggested she was an excellent businesswoman; she must have a good head for figures. Eve guessed she'd have worked out exactly what she needed to live on for her retirement. But if she was right, why had Brenda decided to share her home?

Eve walked up Sycamore Cottage's gravel drive. The place was well kept, but on this ice-cold grey day, aspects of the garden looked bedraggled. The soil in the flower beds was edged with frost – it must be rock-hard – and the leafless shrubs looked defeated. It was the time of year when decay was everywhere. There was a beautiful birdbath with decorative iron scrollwork, but what struck Eve was the shallow layer of ice it contained. She thought of the garden birds, fluffed up against the cold, unable to drink.

The details accentuated Eve's sombre feelings as she knocked at the door. The thought of Emory opening up the cosy cottage, ready to get warm and enjoy his bath, filled her head. How had he coped in Magpie Lodge with just a wood burner? She remembered Angie's description of plaster crumbling off the walls. Yet he'd insisted on staying there, even when Roger offered to rent him somewhere in Blyworth. Bloody-mindedness perhaps – a refusal to allow his brother and sister-in-law to assuage their guilt at not giving him house room.

She was dragged out of her thoughts as the door of Sycamore Cottage was pulled inwards. Eve guessed the woman who opened up was in her early seventies. She was generously curvaceous, with beautiful brown eyes. Eve could see the laughter lines around them, but today they were red-rimmed. She had a nasty bruise on her leg, too.

Her eyes followed Eve's. 'An icy puddle on the front path.' She shook her head. 'Just a small patch but I slipped on it when I ran out of the house after finding...' She stopped. 'After finding Emory in the bath.'

Eve held out her hand and introduced herself. 'I'm sorry,'

she said, as Brenda led her inside. 'More visitors must be the last thing you need.'

Brenda waved away her comment. 'It's nice to pay tribute to Emory.' She took a tissue from her pocket and dabbed her eyes. 'I was very fond of him.' Her voice juddered and she took a deep breath.

'I only met him a week before he died,' Eve said, as Brenda led her through to a comfortable sitting room with a couch and armchairs upholstered in a cheerful chintz. 'But I warmed to him. And then he gave me some of his ghost walk takings towards the charities I support.'

Eve was feeling increasingly guilty that she'd accepted the donation. He must have still owed Poppy a lot. It was like she'd said; he wasn't remotely clear-sighted.

'He was a dear.' Brenda took Eve's coat and hat and motioned her to a seat.

Eve glanced up to see a man in the doorway. He was a little younger than Brenda perhaps, tall and broad, his hair streaked with grey. He was handsome in a rugged way, with appraising eyes and a slightly flirty smile. Not someone Eve would trust.

'Ah, here's Kelvin,' Brenda said. She smiled and a little colour came to her cheeks. Not embarrassment, but pleasure, Eve decided.

She seized her moment and sprang up from the sofa to shake the man's hand. 'It's good to meet you. I'd love to ask you about Emory too, if you don't mind. I imagine you must have got to know him recently and the more input I have the better.'

That wasn't strictly true for the obituary – it all depended on the quality of the information – but it was certainly accurate as far as the murder investigation went.

'Of course.' Kelvin gave her a full-beam smile. 'I'd be happy to talk to you.'

But to his left, she glimpsed Brenda's anxious expression.

Eve moved back towards her place on the couch. 'I suppose

Emory was in and out quite regularly since his return to Saxford?' She kept her eyes on Kelvin. It felt uncomfortably rude, but she had her reasons for focusing on him first.

'That's right. I'd heard all about him from Brenda, of course. How she used to look after him and his brother when they were nippers.'

Brenda was hovering in the doorway, still clutching Eve's hat and coat, bound for the hall. She was a conscientious hostess. Any minute...

'Would you like some tea?' she said at last. It was what Eve had hoped for; she was keen to talk with Kelvin in private. He might be more unguarded that way.

'That would be wonderful. It's so cold outside. Thank you.'

Brenda smiled, but her face was pinched and she looked over her shoulder as she left the room.

'So Brenda talked to you about minding Emory and Roger before she knew Emory was coming back to Saxford?' It implied she and Kelvin had become friends and that Emory had still been part of her life.

The man nodded, leaning towards her and smiling. 'That's right. I always got the impression she was fonder of Emory than Roger. He brought out her motherly instincts. She's good-hearted, is Brenda.'

'And what did you think of Emory?'

He cocked his head, the smile still there. 'Very pleasant.' His brow furrowed. 'Though he was still happy to let Brenda mother him. She couldn't resist his vulnerability. Don't tell her I said so, but he had her eating out of his hand. Not that I minded. Just so long as he didn't take advantage, like. Brenda hasn't had an easy time since her old man died. Emotionally, I mean. It's been hard. I look out for her.'

Eve nodded. 'That's nice.' She wondered, though. The idea of Emory manipulating Brenda jarred. He hadn't struck her as an operator. He'd lost Poppy Rice's money, but he was making efforts to pay her back, and the charity donation seemed like a genuine impulse too. She felt he'd been chaotic, not deliberately dishonest or hurtful. That didn't stop Kelvin being protective, of course. Emory's actions could still have caused upset; he'd been thoughtless.

Brenda reappeared at that moment with the tea. 'Here we are.' The cups were tinkling on the tray as she came into the room. Eve sensed she'd been rushing.

'Don't mind us if you've finished talking,' Brenda said to Kelvin as she poured their teas. 'I know you're always busy.'

Eve wondered what he got up to. He could be retired.

Kelvin picked up his cup and gave Brenda a charming smile. 'Right you are.' He turned to Eve. 'Nice to meet you. I expect we'll bump into each other in the village.'

She smiled and nodded, while taking her cup from Brenda.

'He seems nice,' she said, as soon as he'd left the room. The door was almost closed but she kept her voice low.

'Yes, he is!' Brenda beamed. 'I'm so lucky to have found such a wonderful lodger.'

Once again Eve wondered why she needed one. The house was warm, in good repair, and full of nice furniture. Maybe it was company she was after.

'He's been so handy about the place,' Brenda went on. 'Putting up shelves, mowing the lawn in summer and walking me home from the Cross Keys when I feel like an evening out.' Her words seemed to confirm Eve's hunch.

'I gather you were there for Jo's birthday when Emory was killed.'

Brenda's shoulders rose and fell, her mouth instantly slack. 'That's right. To think that while I was out, having such a lovely evening...' She let the sentence hang. 'Kelvin's taking me back there tonight, to try to wipe the memory and take my mind off things. It won't work, but I do appreciate it. He really looks after me.'

He certainly seemed to be giving her a lot of pleasure. It made Eve anxious; she was already anticipating her disappointment if he wasn't as nice as he seemed.

'That's lovely. It must have been horrific, coming back here to find Emory.' Eve didn't want to press on an open wound, but she was keen to hear her account of returning home on Sunday. There might be clues – things that only she might notice.

Brenda's hands twisted in her lap and tears came to her eyes. 'I can't see how I'll ever want to lie in the bath again. I can't even go upstairs without crying.'

Eve put a hand on her arm for a moment. 'I'm so sorry.'

'Poor Emory. It was heart-breaking to see him just lying there. That feeling of disbelief, and then the horror of it all being too late, and how different it could have been if I'd never gone out.'

'You mustn't blame yourself. No one could have predicted anything so awful.'

She nodded. 'I know that in my heart of hearts, but I keep thinking what might have been. It was so odd to look at my own familiar bathroom and know such violence had taken place. Yet everything else was so peaceful. So normal, if you know what I mean. The fluffy towels I bought in Blyworth on the heated rail, the bath caddy across the tub. There were even some bubbles still. I could smell the bubble bath.' She took an unsteady breath and wiped her eyes with the back of her hand. 'The bath is one of my luxuries. It's huge and he'd filled it deep. The wooden floor was all dark where the water must have splashed over the sides.'

Brenda started to cry again as Eve's mind filled with the image of Emory thrashing around as his killer held his legs, the deep water making their job easier.

Brenda gulped. 'I could see he was dead straight away of course, but something inside me refused to accept it. I rushed to the bath and struggled to pull him up, out of the water. But he was so heavy. A dead weight. I ended up slipping and dropping him again and he went back under. I felt like I'd put him through a final indignity.' She closed her eyes and tears seeped out from under her lids.

'It must have been harrowing.' Eve gave her hostess a moment before continuing. 'If you feel up to it,' she said at last, 'I'd like to ask you about Emory when he was little. It's wonderful to find someone outside the family who's known him since childhood.'

Brenda blew her nose and smiled fondly, though her eyes still glistened. 'He was always the naughty one, that's for sure: mischievous as a pre-schooler, and that continued. I used to mind him and Roger after school. If they had homework you could guarantee Roger would be the one at the kitchen table, getting it done. I can still picture him – this was in my old house – bent over his exercise books. To be fair, Roger was two years older, but Emory never changed as he grew up. He'd disappear the moment my back was turned.' She shook her head and laughed quietly. 'But he was never idle. Ten to one, he'd be off doing something he found more interesting. I'd find him in the garden watching the bees, or hiding in a corner somewhere, drawing or writing a story.' Her eyes met Eve's. 'It was ghosts he wrote about back then, too. I asked him if he'd seen one once and he told me about a grey figure who walked in the woods on his family's old estate. At the time, I thought he was just repeating stories about the poor maid who was murdered there. But later, when he started to investigate hauntings around the country, I guessed he really had seen something. Why choose that career otherwise?'

Or maybe Emory had noticed how captivated Brenda had been by those early stories and enjoyed her reaction. He might have hoped to entertain other people in the same way, even if he'd never truly believed in ghosts himself. She could imagine him doing that. At heart, she sensed he'd wanted to make people happy, whether it was by telling them enthralling stories or passing on 'messages from the other side' that left them feeling better. She guessed that had been his aim at the séance with Poppy Rice, yet it hadn't worked. She'd been anxious and fearful. Eve still needed to unearth the real reason behind that.

'I'm afraid Roger loved it when Emory misbehaved,' Brenda went on. 'It made him look angelic by comparison and he lapped up his parents' approval.'

She stopped suddenly and Eve guessed her thoughts. 'Don't worry, I won't quote you on that if you'd rather not, but your other information is perfect. *Icon*'s readers will be so interested to hear all of this. And can you tell me, did you keep in touch with Emory while he lived in London?'

She smiled. 'Oh yes. Well, as much as we could. He'd send me postcards every month or so, with little snippets of news. Pictures of places he'd visited when he was researching his books. That carried on until he came back here.'

That was significant. He hadn't forgotten about Brenda, either in his heyday, when he'd been busy partying, or later when life was a struggle.

'That's sweet. I hope it doesn't seem intrusive asking, but I wondered about the Dower House. I suppose it was bequeathed to Roger as the eldest son?' Eve wondered if the bequest had soured the brothers' relationship.

'That's right,' Brenda said, sighing. 'Old Mr and Mrs Fulton were traditional sorts. But they left Emory a sizeable amount in their will to compensate for it. I'm afraid he burned through it. He's never been good with money.'

That resolved that question. Emory might still have been resentful. The Dower House was part of his family heritage. But Eve doubted that had come between him and Roger. He'd been treated fairly, and he hadn't struck Eve as the sentimental sort. He'd lived for the moment. But something had distanced them. Roger hadn't been prepared to cross Selina and insist

Emory stayed with them at the Dower House. He hadn't even put his foot down over the bathroom. It might just be the brothers' personalities. They were like chalk and cheese, and petty disagreements could build up over the years.

'And what about more recently? How did you find Emory?'

Brenda put her hands to her face. 'Cheerful. We spoke on the Friday before he died. I wanted to wish him luck for the ghost tour. I would have gone, but honestly, it was a long walk and so cold. If only I'd known... I'd have walked it gladly if I'd realised it was my last chance to see him.'

Eve put a hand on her arm. 'I'm so sorry.'

The woman nodded.

'I must leave you in peace, but before I go, I'm keen to ask more people about Emory's work. Did he ever tell your fortune, or perform a séance for you?'

'Oh goodness me no!' She'd answered very quickly. 'Sorry,' she added, almost immediately. 'It's just that, well, I don't really believe in all that stuff.'

But she'd believed in the ghosts Emory saw, once he started writing books about them. She hadn't been too shy to admit it. Gut instinct told Eve she was lying just as Poppy had. Not only about her beliefs, but about consulting Emory. Why would she do that?

Eve felt she'd outstayed her welcome. She made haste now, getting up from the couch and turning towards the door. 'Thanks so much for talking to me. It's been wonderful to hear more about Emory. He sounds like a very special person.'

Brenda nodded and walked with her to the front door, handing over her coat and hat. 'He was. I'm glad I was able to help.'

Eve's mind was full of questions as she walked back down Brenda Goody's path, but chief amongst them now was why Kelvin the lodger had listened in to her entire conversation with Brenda. Or at least, she assumed so.

As she'd risen from the couch, turning quickly, she'd seen his shadow falling across the hallway carpet. It was lucky for her that the sun had finally found a gap in the clouds or she might never have realised. The shadow had been visible through the narrow gap that Kelvin had left open himself.

And the moment Eve had started to thank Brenda, the shadow had made itself scarce.

15

Back at Elizabeth's Cottage, Eve sat at the kitchen table with a bowl of spiced parsnip soup and a hunk of warmed crusty bread, the butter melting as she applied it. She'd taken Gus on a brisk walk up towards Blind Eye Wood before lunch and it had left her hungry.

'What's Kelvin Brady's game?'

Gus pottered out from under the table, his questioning brown eyes on hers. He was a marvellous sounding board, albeit non-committal. 'Either he was scared what Brenda might say, or there are things he wanted to know about Emory.' Eve reviewed the interview. There'd been nothing that related to the lodger as far as she knew, but she was convinced Brenda was hiding something. She suspected Emory had offered his spiritualist services in some form and she'd accepted. Had her fortune told perhaps, or agreed to a séance. She'd dismissed the topic far too quickly.

But all thoughts of that question were banished when she checked her email. Robin had been in touch. The tech team had managed to access the search history on Emory's phone, and some photographs too. Greg had sneaked him copies.

The pictures were interesting. Amongst those taken recently were some in the woods – presumably the ones bordering Magpie Lodge, though the digital location stamp wasn't accurate enough to confirm it. There was one of Coco too, pulling an exaggerated pose just outside the Dower House. She was wearing a black beanie and thick black coat over something that looked like a spacesuit. The outfit was finished off with some heavy black boots with thick soles. She looked the height of edgy chic. Eve could see Roger in the background, through one of the windows, though he wasn't engaging with them, let alone joining in the fun. A lot of the others were of Brenda's house. There were several of the room Eve had sat in that morning: a couple with Brenda, and another with a woman Eve didn't recognise.

She referred back to the list in Robin's email and found she was Brenda's niece.

A final photo showed the same room, but with no people in shot. *Odd.*

There were similarly random pictures of other rooms Eve didn't recognise, but they were all at Sycamore Cottage, according to the email. Some had been taken during Emory's latest stay in Saxford, some on a previous trip two years earlier. In between there were other photos that meant less to Eve, though she guessed one might be the 'haunted' manor Emory had bought: a large forbidding-looking house with dark windows.

She frowned and sipped her coffee. The collection warranted more thought, but she was impatient for a complete overview of the latest information and moved on to his search history.

It was just as interesting. The day before his death, he'd been looking up long-haul travel destinations: adventurous options like West Africa, southern India and Laos.

She swallowed another mouthful of the heartening soup. 'I

know he was impractical,' she said to Gus, 'and I can imagine he might have wanted to escape, but this is taking things to extremes. How could he have afforded the flights?' She'd been convinced he was genuinely trying to pay Poppy back. Had that all been for show, giving her a pittance while he secretly saved? She couldn't believe it. Leaving his character aside, he hadn't had enough income to start salting cash away.

There was more too. He'd been looking up universities after he'd returned home from the ghost walk. As with the travel, he'd homed in on the less conventional options. Oxford, Cambridge and Bathurst, where Coco was headed, didn't feature. He'd looked at places known for their radical ideas in cities with active music scenes and plenty of options for clubbing. Again, she could kind of get it. He'd come to a full stop, with nowhere to live, his inheritance spent, in debt to his friends. He might have decided he'd like to start again – expand his education in the hope of a new career, perhaps. But it would have involved a large loan to cover the fees and he'd been Eve's age. It would have been quite an investment at his stage in life. She could understand him doing it if he'd been comfortably off, but that wasn't the case.

Robin had ended his email with the words 'Odd, huh?'

He was right there.

Maybe the ghost walk had left Emory feeling desperate to change his life and the searches reflected his dreams, rather than what was possible. But he'd been thorough. Was there any chance he'd been expecting to come into money – a lot of money – in the near future? Enough to pay Poppy back and indulge his fantasies? If so, where the heck from? Her mind flitted to Selina Fulton. He could have planned to blackmail her over her affair. Eve found it hard to believe – it seemed to go against Emory's character – but maybe she'd misread him. Or perhaps he disapproved of her behaviour so thoroughly he'd decided she was fair game.

It would add to Selina's motive, and she had the opportunity. Eve had created a timeline for the day of Emory's death now, and she looked at it once again.

Afternoon (precise time unspecified): Poppy Rice seen leaving Magpie Lodge in tears.

7.00 p.m.: Brenda Goody and Kelvin Brady leave Sycamore Cottage for the Cross Keys.

7.30 p.m.: Private view at Rice and Fulton begins. Ada Rice present from start to finish at 10 p.m. Laurence Rice present for second half.

7.30 p.m.: Brenda Goody and Kelvin Brady have dinner at the pub.

8.00 p.m.: (approx.) Emory arrives at Sycamore Cottage (according to a neighbour).

8.15 p.m.: (approx.) Someone heard slamming door at Sycamore Cottage. (If it was the killer, this could have been them pretending to leave.)

8.45 p.m.: Laurence Rice arrives at the private view at Rice and Fulton – stays until the end (10 p.m.).

Mid-evening (timing uncertain – could have been later): Kelvin Brady leaves the Cross Keys for five minutes. (If he and Brenda are being honest/remembering correctly. Brenda had been drinking and Kelvin can't provide the number of the friend he spotted through the window, 'John Smith'.)

9.10 p.m.: Coco sees her parents at the Dower House on her return from a cigarette walk.

9.13 p.m.: Coco disappears into her 'rooms' with an ex-boyfriend. (He and their internet history bear this out.)

9.30 p.m.: Laurence Rice calls Poppy on Fairview Hall's landline. The call connects for under a minute. Poppy ultimately admits it went to the hall's answerphone.

9.35 p.m.: Emory murdered. (Call to the horoscope line was cut when his phone fell into the bathwater.)

10.00 p.m.: Private view at Rice and Fulton ends. Ada and Laurence Rice leave.

11.00 p.m.: Coco emerges from her 'rooms' with the ex. Selina and Roger present. (But no alibi for either of them between 9.13 and 11.00 p.m.)

After 11.00 p.m.: Brenda Goody and Kelvin Brady leave the Cross Keys (after Jo's birthday fireworks).

As for Emory's photos and search history, Eve intended to revisit them after interviewing the Fultons. If he'd had genuine plans to travel or study she doubted he'd told his brother and sister-in-law, but Coco might know something.

16

As Eve approached the Dower House, crunching her way up its gravel drive, past topiary covered in hoar frost and a pond thick with ice, she thought through the interviews ahead of her.

She needed to get a lot out of her conversations with the Fultons, beyond any knowledge they might have of Emory's plans for the future. If she could get Roger and Selina to talk unguardedly, she might be able to judge whether their feelings were strong enough for them to have killed Emory. And it would be interesting to know if either Coco or Roger had any idea Selina was having an affair, though that might be harder to uncover. If her secret was still under wraps, she had all the more reason to kill over it.

Eve's aims were still circling in her head when she caught sight of Coco. She was smoking a cigarette, lolling against the end wall of the red-brick house. Opposite her was a garage Eve thought might have once been stables. It looked as old as the house and would accommodate several vehicles.

Coco glanced lazily in Eve's direction as she approached. 'Mum and Dad said you were coming. I don't think they want me talking to you.' Her smoky breath created clouds in the frigid air.

'Why not?' Eve was level with her now.

She shrugged. 'They didn't like my friendship with Emory. The way we seemed to be on the same wavelength. They don't trust me an inch.'

Eve could understand that entirely, though she could also imagine why a child would kick back against parents like Roger and Selina. Coco had the air of someone who'd do almost anything to irk them, just for a laugh. She bet they'd been flabbergasted when she'd decided to study after all. Maybe their sudden fervent approval amused her. Eve could imagine her enjoying university life too. She was the sort who'd break all the rules and get herself talked about. Eve took a deep breath and kept her expression even, despite her inner thoughts.

As their eyes met, Coco's look was insolent. Maybe Eve had been categorised as another boring adult, but Coco was an adult herself now. Twenty-eight, Ada Rice had said. She ought to be past that stage. She had a pop-art style sticking plaster on her arm with the words 'Don't ask' on it. She was probably dying for people to enquire, so Eve didn't.

'Shall I talk to you first?' Coco said. 'Before Mum and Dad interfere?'

Eve would have liked to say no on principle. She'd be pandering to Coco's ego and Roger and Selina would think she was late. In reality, though, they'd forgive her if she said Coco had intercepted her. And besides, she really wanted to hear what the woman had to say. It might be her only chance; she didn't want to miss it.

She was preoccupied with Emory's relationship with Coco – surprised he'd given her the time of day, in fact. But he might have figured she could use a friend – an alternative to her oppressive parents. And if their closeness irritated Roger and

Selina, Eve could imagine him pursuing it for that reason, just to tease them.

'All right,' she said at last. As Coco turned, ready to lead her down the drive, she caught Selina watching them from the Dower House. She was very still.

'So you and Emory got on?' Eve said, as they walked through the woods of the old estate.

Coco shot her a sidelong glance. 'He was better than any other member of my family. We had a laugh. I'll miss him. He livened things up no end.' Then her look turned sour. 'He could still be bossy, though.'

Eve smiled. 'Really? What about?'

'Just the standard stuff. Wanting me to do well, make something of my life.'

'Did he encourage you to apply to university?'

She raised an eyebrow, looking down at Eve from under her black beanie. 'It was my idea. I know I'm capable, it's just my parents who don't.'

'Speaking of studying, I heard on the grapevine that Emory was considering enrolling on a degree course himself. And that he'd been talking about travelling.' It was an exaggeration, but she couldn't admit she'd got leaked information from the police.

Coco frowned. 'How very surprising. He was flat broke. But of course,' she smiled, 'Mum and Dad were itching to get rid of him.' If she realised the impression her words created she clearly didn't care. 'Maybe they decided to bribe him, so he'd go away. They seemed quite desperate.'

That was a possibility Eve hadn't considered. But she still doubted Emory would have left without paying Poppy back first. He'd been a renegade, but he'd had a moral code. She couldn't imagine the Fultons would have covered his debts as well as his future costs. Unless they'd offered him cash on the spur of the moment, then fallen back on a cheaper way to rid themselves of his presence... She could imagine that.

'They both felt just as strongly?' Eve could see why Selina would – she had a lot to fear from Emory – but she hadn't discovered such an urgent reason for Roger to want his brother gone.

'Absolutely.'

'Do they always present a united front?' Eve noticed Coco tended to mention them in the same breath. Mum and Dad this, Mum and Dad that...

The young woman rolled her eyes. 'They do. They're always on my case.'

'It's kind of nice to see a couple singing from the same hymn sheet, I suppose.' Eve didn't expect Coco to agree, but she might produce a snide reply if she knew their marriage was built on lies.

'Not from my perspective. It's like having a pair of well-disciplined prison guards following me around.'

It wasn't conclusive, but Eve guessed she was in the dark about Selina's affair. She doubted Coco would have missed the opportunity to snipe if she knew their partnership was flawed.

As she had the thought, a young man in a long grey coat came loping around the corner towards them.

'Oh good grief, it's Jonny. My ex, only we got it together again the night Emory died.' She turned to Eve and rolled her eyes. 'By the time we'd finished I realised it had been a mistake to rekindle things. He's having trouble taking "get lost" for an answer.'

Jonny was carrying a large bouquet of flowers. Coco moved towards him with a heavy tread, her arms folded.

'Jonny, I don't want you here, fussing over me like an aged aunt. For heaven's sake, take the flowers home and give them to your mother.'

It was excruciating to watch. The poor man turned puce, his eye catching Eve's. But though she felt for him, it had been a useful exchange to witness. Boyfriends, ex or otherwise, didn't make convincing alibis, but Eve couldn't see him providing Coco with a false one given the way she was treating him. His neck was still a deep red as he walked into the distance.

Coco had no discernible motive anyway, and her search history suggested she and Jonny had been browsing the web when Emory was killed, but Eve found her deeply unpleasant. It was good to dot the 'i's and cross the 't's.

She was on the point of asking Coco more about Emory when she realised they had company from the opposite direction. Coco's dad.

'Roger Fulton,' he said, putting out a gloved hand to shake hers. 'Delighted to see you again, Eve, albeit under such sad circumstances. We met at the fundraiser.'

She nodded and smiled. They'd exchanged the usual pleasantries as she'd entered the Dower House, but that was it. She'd been one in a long line of visitors.

'Selina said she saw Coco marching you off the moment you arrived,' Roger said, all bluff bonhomie. 'Of course, I can understand her wanting to show you the estate, but you must be freezing, Eve. Come back to the Dower House. Selina's got the kettle on.'

Genuine concern for her core temperature, or secret worry about what Coco might say? Eve couldn't help thinking it was the latter. Roger Fulton had been running. He fought to control it, but he was out of breath. And he'd been right to be concerned. Coco hadn't minced her words about her parents' desire to rid themselves of Emory. But maybe there was more she could have given away too. Was Roger guilty, and worried that his daughter might have found out?

17

As Roger walked Eve back towards the Dower House, he managed to catch his breath.

'I was devastated to hear what had happened to Emory, Eve,' he said, turning to face her and carefully meeting her eye as she walked. It was just as Angie had said, his sincerity felt false: too posed.

'I'm so sorry for your loss, Roger,' she replied, gazing back at him. She bet he'd been on a management training course and had memorised the slides on communication.

'Thank you.' He shook his head in a way that convinced Eve he was acting. 'I can't believe he was relying on Brenda for bathing facilities rather than using ours. I'd offered, of course.'

Eve knew he was lying now. He hadn't been ignorant of the fact. Angie said it had come up in the row between Roger and the chair of the Blyworth and Villages Charitable Trust. 'Maybe it felt too awkward to accept. He was already relying on your generosity.'

'That could be it, Eve.'

She suppressed a shudder. He clearly hadn't realised she was being sarcastic. Roger might have offered to find Emory an alternative to Magpie Lodge, but it wasn't the same as welcoming him to the Dower House. From what Coco said, he'd happily have paid through the nose to keep Emory at arm's length. Eve still didn't quite understand why he'd felt so strongly. She wondered how she could get him to forget his pose. She'd glean far more that way.

'I went to Brenda Goody's house this morning,' she said at last. 'She mentioned Emory sent her postcards the entire time he was in London. I thought that was touching.'

His eyes widened. She'd surprised him at least. 'I didn't know that.'

If she carried on going, she might make him forget himself. 'She talked about the two of you, of course, and how she minded you after school. How good and studious you were, and how Emory used to sneak off and draw pictures or make up stories.'

She carried on in the same vein, focusing on the brothers' shared childhood. She wanted to dig into the past. If she could trigger some fond memories, it might work. It took a while, but as they turned up the drive of the Dower House, Roger bit his lip. 'I keep imagining him in that great bath of Brenda's. Dead amongst all her comfortable belongings.' He closed his eyes for a moment.

His words brought back Brenda's description of finding Emory's body in vivid detail. She tried to breathe evenly.

'It's as though I've got a horrific photograph in my head,' Roger added.

At last she'd got him sounding genuine and the horror in his voice chilled her. He could be remembering reality, not just sharing imagined images. But of course, he and his brother had known the house well. If he was visualising the scene, he'd be able to conjure up the details.

'I'm so sorry,' she said again.

A moment later, he was leading her through the front door of the Dower House, into the hallway and through to the drawing room where the villagers had gathered for the fundraiser.

Selina appeared, looking as smart as ever in a calf-length fitted dress and jacket. 'Would you like a cup of tea?'

Once again, Eve was glad to accept a hot drink. As she settled herself on a couch and took out her notebook, Selina placed a loaded tray on an occasional table.

'Thanks so much for seeing me,' Eve said. 'This must be a terrible time for you both.' Her eyes were on Selina, her mind on the two arguments she'd heard her have with Emory, at the Dower House and behind the church. She must have felt threatened. And once again, Eve wondered why they'd had that second conversation. It seemed very possible that Emory had been warning her he was about to reveal her secret unless she told Roger first.

Selina was focusing on pouring the tea, a look of apparent concentration on her face, but she hadn't let it brew for long enough. It was so weak that Roger put a hand on hers to stop her.

'It needs a bit longer.'

Selina put the pot down and shook her head. 'I'm sorry.' She glanced quickly at Eve. 'You're right. It's been a massive shock. I can hardly function.'

The news was horrifying, of course, but she'd had over twenty-four hours to process it now. Eve guessed it wasn't just shock that was affecting her. She was stressed to the point of snapping. You could see it in her taut movements as well as her lack of concentration. She might be guilty, or imagine that Roger was.

'I'm due to drop in at the shop tomorrow.' Selina's words came quickly. She was filling the silence – not uncommon with nervous interviewees. 'But I won't be much good to Ada, who will no doubt comment on it. She's twice mentioned how useful our assistant Rachel is, since Emory died. More useful than me, is clearly what she means. She's not one to tolerate human frailty. And her son seems much the same. A Bathurst professor! That makes so much sense. I'm obviously delighted that Coco's finally decided to attend university, but I hope the place doesn't turn her into one of their standard superior—'

'Darling!' Roger reached over to take the cosy off the teapot again. 'Perhaps we can pour now.'

Eve had heard the chair of the charitable trust had been to Bathurst too. Roger was probably keen to keep his wife's insults to a minimum in front of a stranger.

His tone had been gentle though, and the way he'd put a hand on hers to stop her from pouring the tea was tender. There were no signs of tension in his actions. Eve had a feeling he didn't know about Selina's affair any more than Coco did. It strengthened her motive. Killing Emory would likely have kept her secret.

'So, how can we help, Eve?' Roger asked, as Selina organised their drinks. His guard was back up.

'After hearing Brenda Goody's memories this morning, I'd love yours of Emory as he was growing up. A brother's perspective is special.'

Roger nodded, a look of studied sincerity on his face. 'He was inquisitive.' He smiled briefly. 'It tended to get him into trouble. As Brenda said, he couldn't bear to sit still. When it came to learning, our teachers gave him up as a lost cause.' He shook his head, with a deliberately fond look in his eye. 'While I was fascinated by my subjects, he was captivated by the stories people told him, not what he read in books. People liked him, but he hadn't got that staying power that's so necessary. He let friends down time and again because he didn't focus. He'd adopt people, topics or causes when they amused him, then drop them again later. And he always thought he knew best.' It was fascinating to watch Roger. The line of his mouth had gradually thinned as he spoke, but when Eve put down her teacup, reminding him of her presence, the fond look was back. He turned to meet her eyes. 'But really, Eve, most of his behaviour was down to a lively and original mind.'

'I see, Roger.' She must stop mimicking him. She'd have to go through what he said with a fine-toothed comb. It didn't quite hang together. Of course Emory had been unreliable – he'd died owing Poppy money – but he hadn't dropped the people he cared about. Brenda Goody's postcards proved it. It was interesting that Roger had been unaware of that habit. Perhaps he was no longer close to Brenda himself.

'What about your memories of the time you and Emory spent with Brenda Goody after school?' It would be interesting to contrast his views with the childminder's.

Just for a second, she caught another flash of emotion in his eyes. They'd had *some* good times back then, she imagined, even if the wedge between them was already growing.

'I remember us picking blackberries in her garden once,' he said, but when he spoke again his tone turned tetchy. 'She indulged Emory, I'm afraid. My father got quite angry about it. It wasn't doing him any good, you see. But I don't imagine anyone else would have wanted to step into her shoes and take over. He was such a handful. Of course, we owe her a debt of gratitude more recently for welcoming Emory into her home.' *Yeah, right.* He'd definitely said that for form's sake. 'But I still wish he'd come to us.'

Selina nodded, just as Eve remembered she'd complained that Emory was too dirty to use their facilities, according to Angie.

'Brenda hadn't mentioned the arrangement to you?'

'Our paths don't cross much these days. It's funny' – he shook his head – 'we spent so much time with her as children, with the run of her house. Now, I bump into her in the village periodically, but that's about it. I suppose she would have thought it was indelicate to bring it up there.'

'That makes sense. What was Emory like as a teenager?'

'As wild as they come.' It was Selina who'd spoken.

'You were living in Saxford then too?'

'Wessingham,' Selina replied. 'But we were all of a similar age and we attended the same school, just beyond Blyworth.' She put her hand in her husband's and entwined her fingers with his. 'You were worried about him even back then, weren't you, Roger?'

The man nodded. 'He'd disappear and we'd find he'd skipped class and hitched to London or something of the sort.'

'Was he already interested in the supernatural?'

Roger shrugged. 'In a superficial way. He always had a vivid imagination. I remember him telling ghost stories for the school once, at a winter fundraiser. He drew quite a crowd and they were all captivated. I suspect that's when he found out that the supernatural sells.' He sighed. 'It's a crying shame he didn't apply himself academically or put in the effort to get organised.'

The storytelling would work well in Eve's obituary and she was getting a clear idea of the early dynamic between Roger and Emory too. There'd been resentment between them for a long time. Roger was clearly jealous of the way Brenda had indulged his brother, and possibly of his ability to charm people. The lawyer was successful and maybe he'd get the knighthood he was after, but he had to rely on hard work and sucking up to people, not natural charisma. Over the years, jealousy and irritation would have built up and then he was faced with his brother once again. Emory's careless talk and jibes at Selina had threatened Roger's reputation, but even that, coupled with long-term resentment, didn't strike Eve as a hugely persuasive motive. Yet Roger's tone when he spoke of his brother was bitter, and when he'd talked about visualising Emory in the bath, something had set her hair on end.

'I was interested in his recent history too,' she went on. 'Were either of you aware he was considering studying for a degree, or possibly going travelling?' Was Coco right? Had they offered to pay to get him out of their hair? Or could he have tried to blackmail Selina for the money?

But they both looked blank. No looks of recognition or of guilt. 'Where did you hear that?' Roger asked.

'That's the trouble, I can't remember now. Someone in the village.' Eve hoped her acting skills were better than his. It looked as though Coco had been wrong about her parents giving Emory money. If he was expecting a large influx of cash, Eve guessed it was from another source.

'I'm curious about Magpie Lodge, too,' she went on. '*Icon* often print photographs of places associated with my subjects. Would there be any chance of seeing inside? The place looks so atmospheric.'

'Ah.' Roger put his cup down. 'I... ah, I'm afraid not.' He glanced sideways at his wife. 'I think we'd find it too upsetting to have the press marching about in there.'

'Of course. I'm sorry.' There was no point in pushing it. She'd guessed they'd say no, but she'd love to get a look herself. She knew the forensics team would have crawled all over the place, but there was always the chance it would tell her something. It was where Emory had had his dramatic last meeting with Poppy and the site of the recent break-in. She still couldn't imagine what the intruder had been after. It was frustrating.

At that moment there was a knock at the front door. 'Excuse me.' Selina got up, straightening the skirt of her dress before nipping out of the room.

'Perhaps you could tell me—' Roger began, but he was interrupted by Selina calling his name. 'I'm sorry; I'll just be a moment.'

Suddenly, Eve found herself alone in the Fulton's sedate drawing room. As her eyes ran over the space, she remembered the peacock-blue book Emory had taken from the bookcase. The scene came back to her. Selina had seen, crossed the room in three short strides and snatched it from his hands before ramming it back into place.

Listening out for her hosts returning, Eve crossed the room to the same bookcase. She'd be curious to know what the book had been.

But after scanning the shelves she was left thwarted. It was no longer there.

18

Back at home, Eve emailed Robin an update before preparing for an evening with Viv at the Cross Keys. She'd sent Eve a text early that morning, demanding a debrief, and it was easiest to give in gracefully. Besides, it was secretly fun to bounce ideas off Viv, and there were few nicer places to be on a bitterly cold January evening. Eve swapped her formal tweed dress for rust-red jeans and a soft black jumper and reapplied her make-up.

Five minutes later, she and Gus walked into the pub's cosy glow. The heat from the huge log fire matched the warm atmosphere: everywhere there was light and cheer, fighting against the dark outside and the horror of recent events. Tealights twinkled, and flames reflected in glasses. The whole place smelled of woodsmoke and fine food, which made her stomach rumble.

'I've reserved you table nine,' Toby Falconer said, raising an eyebrow and grinning as she approached the bar. He knew Eve's habits. It was a quiet table, away from the hubbub, where Eve and Viv could exchange news privately.

Gus had already dashed over to Toby's schnauzer, Hetty. They were performing their comical, disruptive greeting. Jo

Falconer, Toby's sister-in-law and the pub's fierce cook, had no patience with their bouncing but she was currently behind the scenes. Eve couldn't help being relieved, though she was pretty used to Jo now. Her bark was worse than her bite. Mostly.

'Thank you!' Eve said, in response to Toby's comment about the table. As she asked for a Rioja, Viv appeared and uttered a breathless greeting, her cheeks flushed. 'I've been waiting all day for this,' she said to Toby. 'I need Eve to tell me everything!'

They finished ordering then set up camp at their table.

'Toby looks happy, doesn't he?' Viv said. 'It's his love life, I reckon.'

He was carrying on a long-distance relationship with an actress. It seemed to be working – against the odds – which gave Eve a warm glow. It was nice to have something positive to focus on.

Eve was glad they could see so much of the pub from where they sat. Across the room, in a secluded corner, Brenda Goody was sitting with Kelvin the lodger. Eve hadn't spotted her as they'd come in. Their eyes met momentarily and Brenda raised her hand in greeting. She still looked stricken.

'Poor woman,' Viv said, picking up her glass of Shiraz. 'She looks done in, doesn't she?'

As they watched, a villager approached Brenda's table and leaned in for a quick word, putting a hand on her shoulder. Eve bet there'd be a constant stream of people doing the same. She imagined Brenda had plenty of friends: she'd been so kind and welcoming that morning. But also, of course, the villagers would be curious and scared too. Eve had already noticed that the pub was busy for a Tuesday. People flocked to the Cross Keys and Monty's when anything dramatic happened. They wanted news and reassurance.

'I can understand her coming out,' Viv said, still looking at Brenda. 'I did something similar after Oliver died. It was better to get all the stilted conversations over with in one go.'

Eve nodded. It had been hugely tough for Viv too; her husband had died so young. All the same, Brenda didn't look equal to the ordeal. 'I gather it was Kelvin's idea to visit the pub. She mentioned it earlier. He wanted to take her mind off Emory, but she said it wouldn't work.'

'Nice of him to try, I guess.' Viv lowered her voice. 'Have you heard anything more about his whereabouts on the night of the murder?'

Eve picked up her Rioja, took a sip and explained his movements, passing the information off as gossip. Of course, she and Viv had been in the Cross Keys that night too, but the place had been packed, and neither of them had met Kelvin by then.

When Eve got to the bit about him meeting a man called John Smith who couldn't be traced, Viv sat back in her chair.

'Blimey. That sounds a bit fishy.'

Eve nodded. 'Brenda says he was only gone five minutes. Not enough time to run up the Old Toll Road to Sycamore Cottage, drown poor Emory and make it back again. So he's in the clear as far as I know and I haven't found a motive for him. All the same, the timing's not certain – the booze was flowing freely that evening. And it's odd that his excuse for exiting the pub is so flaky. Plus, he secretly listened in to my interview with Brenda.'

Viv's eyebrows shot up, but she was prevented from saying more by the arrival of Jo Falconer with their food. They'd both chosen game pie with winter greens and roast potatoes.

'Smells delish!' Viv said, over the top of Eve's own enthusiastic thanks. It was quite true, but surely Jo must realise people fell over themselves with compliments because she was so scary?

The cook beamed but didn't look surprised.

'What's the gossip?' Viv said to her. 'Have you heard anything about the murder?'

The cook's look turned grim. 'Appalling business. Lots of

press in, ready to make money out of someone else's misery. Wolfing down their food without letting it touch the sides.' She threw back her head. 'I ask you!'

'Dreadful.' The lack of reverence towards her cooking was clearly what rankled most.

Jo nodded in Brenda and Kelvin's direction. 'I saw Emory in here late last week, sitting in a corner with that Kelvin Brady. Might have been lunchtime, Friday. I don't know what was going on, but it wasn't pretty. I got as far as asking Matt to keep an eye on them in case we needed to boot them out, but in the end they took their quarrel outside.' Matt was Toby's brother, and Jo's husband.

As Jo sashayed back towards the kitchens, Viv gave Eve a superior smile. 'I hope you can see how helpful I am as your Watson! Would you have got that interesting little nugget if I hadn't pressed Jo for information?'

Eve cocked her head. 'All right, all right. There's no need to get above yourself.'

Viv stuck out her tongue. Behind her, more customers were entering the Cross Keys. An icy draught whistled through the room before the last one pushed the door closed. Leading the newcomers was Ada Rice. Poppy and Laurence followed just behind. Once they were safely settled, Eve filled Viv in on the latest news about Poppy. In between sentences, she took mouthfuls of game pie. The meat and gravy were sensational: rich and flavoursome. 'I feel conflicted,' she said at last. 'Poppy doesn't have an alibi and she's certainly lied. I still don't really know why she was so opposed to the séance either. She claims she was protective of Emory's feelings but my hunch is there's more to it than that. If one of the secrets she's keeping is damaging, and her mother knew about it, she could have worried it would come out during the séance. She keeps saying she doesn't believe in spiritualism but I'm pretty sure she's lying.'

'But Emory sounded fond of her. I mean, he wouldn't have aired her dirty linen in front of Laurence?'

'Not intentionally, I'm sure, but she might have imagined he'd go into a trance and come straight out with whatever it was. It all depends on what she believes. I know it seems ridiculous.'

Viv tutted and folded her arms. 'You might have closed your mind to everything outside your experience, Ms Smartypants, but not everyone's that narrow-minded. There are more things in heaven and earth, and all that.'

For a second, Eve thought of the footfalls she sometimes heard, out in Haunted Lane, but rationally, she was still sure she'd dreamed them. Nothing else made sense. 'So if you were Poppy and had something to hide – some secret your mother knew about – you'd have been worried too?'

'For sure, if I thought he might blurt it out.'

'So it's possible that accounts for her anxiety over the séance, then.'

Viv nodded. 'I'd say she's generally anxious. I've got her down as vulnerable and troubled. There's something about her eyes.'

'I noticed the same thing.' She'd been clinging on to Laurence's arm and gazing up at him again as they took their seats in the Cross Keys. Eve hadn't seen Laurence's expression but she remembered the way he'd shrugged her off at the hall. Selina Fulton's comments about Laurence's father-in-law's influence over his career came back to her. Perhaps that was all that was keeping him in the marriage. It sounded as though Laurence and Poppy's dad got on well at present. That might change if Laurence filed for divorce. Eve's stomach tensed as she thought of the dismissive way he'd treated her. He'd be doing her harm incrementally with each cruel word.

'So,' Viv said, breaking into her thoughts. 'Do you think Poppy's the sort to kill?'

Eve visualised Emory thrashing around like crazy as the

murderer held his legs. 'It depends on her motive. When someone you trust like a father lets you down, it's all the more painful. What if she'd discovered Emory had plans to travel, and imagined he might leave without paying her back? That could have tipped her over the edge – at least to the point where she was too scared to stop what she was doing.' Robin had had a point. 'And I've a feeling I don't know the half of it yet. I need to find out more.'

Viv nodded as she put her fork down. 'What else have you found out since yesterday?'

Eve sipped her wine and filled Viv in on her chats with Ada Rice and Angie in Blyworth, as well as her visit to Brenda and Kelvin and the Fultons.

As she spoke, she noticed Poppy Rice spill salt on the table. A second later she pinched some of it up with her fingers and threw it over her left shoulder. It wasn't the same as believing in séances – it might just be a childhood habit – but it looked as though Poppy was several degrees more superstitious than Eve was.

Viv was still digesting Eve's latest news, her brow furrowed. 'Okay, I think I've got it. So although Kelvin's suspicious – and he rowed with Emory – everyone's fairly sure he hadn't the time to commit murder. And Lawrence was in a roomful of people too. So apart from Poppy, you're left with the alibi-less Roger and Selina Fulton.'

Eve nodded. 'Selina's motive is compelling. I don't buy Roger's to the same extent, but he's a pompous man who lives off his reputation, and it sounds as though his and Emory's relationship started to deteriorate back when they were kids. There's been plenty of time for tensions to escalate.

'And he and Selina probably thought they were stuck with him. I could imagine them trying threats but then resorting to violence if they were desperate enough. That would fit for Selina, given the hold he had over her. Either that or Emory might have dabbled in blackmail.' She paused, feeling uncomfortable with the thought. It was like trying on a pair of shoes that didn't fit properly, but there was that hint that he might have been expecting a windfall.

'So Selina is still top of the list, with Roger and Poppy as possibilities.'

Eve nodded. 'But there's one important point we mustn't overlook. We know someone was heard slamming the door of Sycamore Cottage around fifteen minutes after Emory arrived.'

'I remember.' Viv nodded. 'And we reckoned it could have been the killer, pretending to leave, then hiding, ready to strike when he was in the bath.'

'That's right. The neighbour certainly thought the slammer was on their way out. But whether they were coming or going, if they waited around to kill Emory, Roger and Selina are out of it. They were both at the Dower House when Coco came in from her walk at ten past nine. And if it wasn't the killer, that means Emory had a second visitor on Sunday night.'

19

After her visit to the Cross Keys, Eve sat at home by the fire with Gus, going through her notes from the interview with Roger and Selina Fulton. As she'd talked about them with Viv, she'd developed a fidgety feeling, which danced on the edge of her mind, refusing to be pinned down. She was sure she'd picked up on some oddity without realising it. Now she was desperate to work out what it was.

She made plans for the following day too. She would contact Poppy again. Find out if she knew that Emory had been researching university courses and travel options. If she'd suspected he planned to cut and run, Eve hoped she'd be able to tell from Poppy's reaction.

After focusing on the suspects, Eve's mind drifted back to the one clue in the case that might relate to any of them: the break-in at Magpie Lodge. It might be unconnected to Emory's death, but it was a big coincidence if so; perhaps the intruder had been his killer. She'd aired the same thought in her email to Robin earlier. It seemed important.

She wished Roger Fulton had let her see inside. She remembered the look on Emory's face when he'd discovered the forced window. Something told her the incident hadn't been a total surprise. Not that he'd anticipated it, but that it made some kind of sense.

Robin hadn't mentioned the police removing anything valuable from the lodge; that probably meant the intruder had taken what they'd come for, but it wasn't certain. What if it was something well hidden, and they'd missed it?

As time wore on, Eve couldn't shift thoughts of Magpie Lodge from her head. She glanced out of the window at the frost-encrusted privet hedge bordering her tiny front garden. It was well below freezing outside, but not enough to put her off. In fact, it might help. It was getting late and on a night like this she doubted the Rices or the Fultons would be strolling through the woods. She could walk over to Magpie Lodge before bed and peer through the window at least. She guessed the police would have finished with it, and it was well away from the hall and the Dower House.

She pulled on an extra black jumper and a moment later she'd added her coat, boots and hat.

For once, Gus didn't look too enthusiastic for a walk. He'd been lying on the rug but opened one eye and began to get up. The rough and tumble with Hetty must have worn him out.

'Don't worry, Gus,' she said, bending to give him a pat, 'this should probably be a solo mission in any case. I'll be back before you know it.'

He relaxed again, though he watched her through half-closed eyes as she made for the door. She hoped he wasn't going to wait up, worrying.

Twenty minutes later, Eve took the side road towards Thorington. It would lead her to the main entrance of the old estate, and Magpie Lodge. The route Emory had used on the ghost tour was a shortcut, but it would mean walking past the hall. She felt nervous now and glanced regularly over her shoulder, but there was no one walking behind her, just a van in the distance on the road.

A moment later, still monitoring her surroundings, she slipped through the trees. It meant she could avoid approaching via the main track. Better safe than sorry.

The lodge was ahead now, eerie and dark with its corrugated metal cladding, and holes left for the windows. She kept close to the trunk of a huge oak and stood absolutely still, listening...

Nothing. No footsteps, no sound of frozen leaf matter crunching underfoot. The birds were silent too. Shafts of moonlight reached the ground, stretching out long fingers where the trees were leafless.

Eve moved closer to the lodge. She'd wondered if there might be police tape across the door and windows but all signs of their presence was gone. Of course, they'd had two days to gather evidence and the place was small. She guessed it hadn't taken long.

She paused again to listen, then approached one of the windows cautiously. She was reaching for her phone to use as a torch when the hand came down on her shoulder.

She didn't scream. All the air went out of her, so she could hardly breathe.

An instant after she felt the hand, she saw the face.

Robin. His eyebrow raised. 'Planning something?' He looked torn between anxiety and amusement.

'Heck, Robin.' She spoke in a murmur. 'You almost gave me a heart attack. What are you doing here?'

He was smiling now. 'You mentioned your desire to see inside Magpie Lodge twice in your email.'

Had she? That wasn't like her. It didn't say much for her writing style, given her profession. 'It's been on my mind.'

'So I gathered.' He kept his voice as soft as hers. 'I decided to give you a ring this evening. I tried your landline first and when you didn't answer, your mobile.'

She'd had her phone on silent since she'd entered the woods. 'It got your antennae quivering?'

'Correct. I knew you wouldn't have silenced it if you were still in the pub with Viv. I decided I'd nip over in case you were giving in to temptation.'

Eve kicked herself. She hadn't recognised Robin's van in the distance, behind its bright headlights.

She shook her head. 'I was only going to peek through the window. But look...' She showed him the frame behind the cladding. The wood was still splintered from the break-in, the catch barely holding the window in place.

'That's careless.' Robin was frowning. 'I can only assume the CSIs had all they needed and weren't too worried about security going forward. Palmer probably told the Fultons to get it sorted, but if the place is as dilapidated as you say, maybe they don't see the urgency.'

'Perhaps not.'

Robin raised an eyebrow. 'I'm glad I turned up when I did. Are you telling me you wouldn't have been tempted if you'd noticed how easy it would be to get inside?'

Eve would have been nervous, but he was probably right. In a whisper, she explained her reasons for wanting to snoop. 'You do see, don't you? There's just a chance something's been missed. And if the police have finished, would it be problematic, morally, to have a look? I mean, the Fultons clearly don't care about the place, and it's not as though I'm wrecking a crime scene. There's a lot at stake.'

He put his head on one side. 'True...' At last, he sighed. 'Go on then. You go in and I'll keep watch. If anyone comes, I'll head them off and I'll be loud about it so you hear. I'll tell them I thought I saw an intruder in the woods or something. That'll give you enough time to get out.'

'Thank you.' Eve took a deep breath and wondered what the heck she was doing. She got to work on the damaged window frame: jiggling it, applying pressure. At last, it moved just enough to allow her to slip the catch up. Her way was clear.

Climbing in wasn't easy. She wished she'd worn a shorter coat but she hadn't anticipated such a hands-on approach. In the end, she took off her outer layer and threw it into Emory's old living room, keeping her gloves on. Moments later she was through. She dragged the coat back on immediately.

Despite her adrenaline rush and the sense of urgency, she paused to stand and stare. By the light of her phone torch, she could see the extraordinary state of Emory's old living quarters.

20

Magpie Lodge was one big room inside. Eve remembered the mention of an outdoor WC somewhere. What would it have been like to use it in this weather?

The place was bitterly cold, with little protection from the winter. Eve wouldn't have dared to switch on a light, but when she looked, she found to her astonishment that there was no switch, and no fitting overhead. No plug sockets either. The place was without electricity. What had Emory done for light? Sweeping her phone torch round the room she saw an old oil lamp on a shelf. He hadn't even been able to charge his mobile. Maybe the Dower House had an outdoor socket he'd been able to use, or he'd got a solar charger. She'd expected the accommodation to be basic, but this was something else.

To her right, one wall rose up into the roof area. Odd bits of plaster were still attached but it was mainly bare brick – it looked like it might collapse if the wind blew too hard. She could see part of the structure of the place too: warped timber, smothered with dead ivy. Embedded in the roof-high wall was a chimney with a wood-burning stove, and a recess next to it, which was empty.

To her other side, there was a sleeping platform at attic height and below it a Belfast sink, and taps, a two-ring gas cooker, a couple of cupboards and a table with two wooden chairs. Eve could see why the CSIs hadn't taken long.

Within moments, she was climbing up to the sleeping platform, gripping the ladder's sides. It felt horribly rickety. Using both hands was essential, so her phone was back in her pocket and she ascended in near darkness. She'd noted the position of the beams beforehand and guessed there might have been two floors once. Perhaps the upper one had collapsed. She tried not to think of it as she climbed higher up the ladder. Emory had been a lot bigger than she was. If it took his weight she ought to be okay.

The plaster over the bed was cracked. She couldn't imagine how Emory had slept at night. She'd have had nightmares about it falling on her head. Suddenly, his genial smile filled her mind. He might have been out to get his own back on Selina but he hadn't let his circumstances get him down. Maybe he knew things could have been different if he'd behaved differently. But despite his relaxed attitude, Eve was sure he must have been keen to get out.

The mattress he'd slept on was set on a low base. To its right, the ceiling was even worse. The tiles were visible, and where the lodge's wall met the eaves there was an old bird's nest. There was one cupboard up there. Eve checked it, though she knew she'd be repeating the work of the CSIs. It was empty except for a pile of Emory's clothes. She recognised the jumper he'd been wearing at the fundraiser. It still smelled of woodsmoke, and sadness washed over her. After that, she shone her torch at the base of the bed, but it was solid and flush against the floor. There was nothing under the mattress or mixed up with the bedding. Eve put it all back carefully, straining for any noise from Robin as she did so, her heart hammering.

Down on the ground floor, Eve checked the recess next to the chimney, but it was empty apart from a battered old enamel kettle. She went to peer inside the wood burner next, then felt round its back too. She looked inside the kitchen cupboards and the gas cooker, felt behind the sink and then peered at the floor-boards. There was probably nothing to find, but it felt as though she'd taken a big risk, coming in. She wasn't going to leave without being thorough.

If she had something valuable to hide, where would she put it?

In an instant, Eve was back at the wall with the fireplace and the recess. What about the bare bricks? How many of them were actually loose? The wall was deep enough for the chimney and the recess; there might be space for other hidey-holes behind the bricks. She ran her torch over the wobbly structure, biting her lip as the minutes ticked by. Every second of delay increased the risk of discovery.

She moved the sleeping-platform ladder to balance it against the brick wall instead. She was glad Robin couldn't see her. He'd be sure to tell her to stop, but she wouldn't climb high, just enough to check the point where the chimney breast narrowed. She was three rungs up when she saw it. A brown cardboard box resting on top of one of the warped timbers that formed the lodge's structure. A tangle of dead ivy would hide it from view for those at ground level.

Holding her breath, Eve reached for the box, leaning her weight heavily against the wall to ensure she remained stable.

Within seconds, she'd carried it down the ladder. Her heart beat faster as she took off the lid.

There were two things inside: a strange but beautiful box, decorated with a grid pattern and curious markings, faint with age, and the peacock-blue book which had once been in the Dower House.

. . .

An hour later, Robin and Eve were thawing out in front of the fire in the living room at Elizabeth's Cottage. Gus had woken briefly on their return, but was asleep again now, snoring lightly. He clearly thought little of Eve's antisocially timed adventures. Robin was always cautious about visiting Eve at home, but it was late, and he'd parked his van by his house in Dark Lane before doubling back to meet her. It was unlikely he'd been seen.

They each had glasses of brandy and mugs of hot chocolate. 'Let's have another look,' he said.

Eve turned her phone to show him the photos she'd taken of Emory's treasures at Magpie Lodge. She'd left the originals in situ for the police to find; the evidence was too important to keep to herself. Robin had agreed to tip off Greg Boles. They knew he'd be discreet and invent a good excuse for going back to the lodge so he could 'discover' them.

Robin's eyes met hers. 'What do you think about the box? A game of some kind?'

Eve shrugged. 'Maybe. Or something for telling fortunes, perhaps? It reminds me of that ancient Egyptian game, senet. I think I read somewhere that people believed that connected the living with the underworld. It would fit with Emory's interests.'

But it wasn't senet, and they hadn't managed to identify it online since they'd got back. They'd each searched, entering a basic description into Google: 'game' 'box' 'grid' 'four by eight' 'markings'. All they'd got was a load of maths games for school children. An image search hadn't done any better. Whatever it was, it must be rare.

She scrolled on to the next photograph she'd taken, which was of a drawer in the box, containing counters. 'It looks old, doesn't it?'

Robin nodded. 'And if it's really ancient it could be worth a fortune.'

'You're thinking Emory could have stolen it, and the proceeds might be enough for the travel and university degree?'

Robin reached out to touch her hand. 'I'm sorry. I know you liked him, but it sounds as though he was a mixed bag.'

Eve sipped her brandy. 'I'm sure he was, but I honestly couldn't see him pinching something to pay his way. He was busy paying Poppy off in instalments – all very conventional – and if he was that money-grubbing, why give me a percentage of his takings?'

'Not everyone's as rational as you are.'

Eve still couldn't believe it. 'I can't imagine where he'd have stolen it from, anyway. If it's a museum piece he'd have been dealing with tight security.'

'Maybe it belonged to someone who hadn't realised its value. Someone wealthy perhaps – it might have lessened his feelings of guilt. And although he seemed to be doing right by Poppy when he died, he clearly didn't worry about borrowing from her in the first place.'

He was right. Emory had had a duty of care to his goddaughter. Eve couldn't deny he'd failed miserably. 'I suppose it's possible,' she said at last, a sinking feeling pulling at her chest. He'd sure as heck been flawed. Her hunch that his moral code would have steered him away from theft wasn't really evidence-based. It *might* depend on who he was stealing from. She sipped her hot chocolate. She'd only just stopped shivering.

'What about the book?'

Eve scrolled on to show him the relevant photos. 'It was a volume of spooky-sounding fairy stories. The old-fashioned sort that are quite frightening. The inscription's interesting.' The hairs on the back of her neck had lifted when she'd read it:

For Roger and Selina

I guess the best man won, but hang on a second, I am the best man! I'm afraid your child's going to have an awful uncle. Emory x

Robin's eyes met hers. 'Wow. So it looks like Emory was in a relationship with Selina before Roger was?'

'I'd guess so. And that Roger knew that. I assume Emory must have been best man at their wedding. I wonder if Selina was already pregnant when she married.'

'Sounds plausible. You're sure that's the book Emory was looking at at the Dower House?'

Eve nodded. 'Certain. It was gone when I had the chance to check.' She thought it through. 'I can't see Selina giving it to him. She snatched it away when he picked it up. I'd guess he pinched it.'

'I wonder why he'd do that. A keepsake? Or regretting the inscription? But he can't have wanted to keep his relationship with Selina secret from Roger. It was addressed to both of them; he must have seen it at the time.'

Eve nodded. 'Yes, I agree. But taking it after all these years must mean something.'

They sat in silence for a while.

'I can't help wondering about his cryptic comment,' Eve said at last. 'That bit about "but hang on a second, I *am* the best man..." Was that just a pun, or did he feel he'd won in some way after all? And what about "I'm afraid your child's going to have an awful uncle"?'

'Robin, what if he didn't mean he, Emory, would be an awful uncle? What if he was talking about Roger, and Emory was Coco's father?'

21

Eve took Gus for a walk along the estuary path the following morning. Out across the stretch of brackish water, she spotted a group of Slavonian grebes, with their golden ear tufts. Gus paused and nosed into the reeds in response to their trilling calls, but they were well out of his reach.

'Grebe hunting is strictly forbidden anyway.'

He gave her a disdainful look.

As they turned to walk home, reeds to their right, a ditch and fields to their left, Eve reviewed the situation. She was glad the police would find the hidden possessions. The book was relevant and perhaps they could uncover the history of the ancient-looking box too. Eve still hoped Emory had had it legitimately, but doubt gnawed at her insides.

Was that what his intruder had been after? It looked valuable, as Robin said, but the theory left her puzzled. Who would have known he'd got it? If he'd stolen it and its rightful owner had guessed, they would have gone to the police, not broken in. Unless they'd come by it dishonestly themselves, of course.

Or maybe a third party had guessed he'd pinched it and

decided to help themselves. The whole village knew Emory was out that evening.

Back at home, she paced the living room. It was frustrating. She couldn't think how to find out more. The question of Coco's parentage was an easier line of enquiry. Who might know about Emory and Selina's past, and when their relationship had ended? Moira was no good – if she'd been aware, the whole village would be too. But a moment later the answer came to her. Brenda. She'd been Emory's champion and he'd trusted her. Eve arranged to meet the woman at Monty's for a cup of tea. As she got ready to leave, pulling on a green cardigan over her rust-coloured dress with its swishy skirt, she pondered the implications. If Emory believed he was Coco's father, he might have wanted to let her know. His current visit might have convinced him the time was right; he'd started to bond with her. And he knew Selina was having an affair – it would be hard for her to beg him not to risk her family's stability. And if Emory told Coco, Roger would likely find out next, assuming he didn't know already. It would strengthen Selina's motive for murder. She might have killed to protect her daughter as well as her own position. If she and Roger divorced and Roger discovered Coco was Emory's, would he still leave her the Dower House in his will?

And of course, Roger might have found out already – and recently. That would make his motive much stronger. Selina had been quick to call Emory wild when Eve interviewed the pair the previous day. Eve remembered the way she'd turned to Roger just afterwards and held his hand. Had the comment and the affectionate move been an attempt to make sure he didn't suspect? Or to show him that whatever she'd done in the past, she realised her mistake now?

Twenty minutes later, Eve sat in Monty's, appreciating the bunting strung across the bay windows which cheered up the spartan view of leafless trees outside. The ground was still frozen hard, the puddles like skating rinks. She couldn't remember such an unrelenting winter.

Brenda sat opposite Eve, still pale and hollow-eyed, silent as Viv set down a cake stand sporting her chocolate intense selection.

Brenda had looked lost when Eve asked what she'd like, so Viv had suggested it. She considered it fortifying. She turned to Brenda now, tucking a strand of hair behind one ear. 'How are you bearing up?'

The woman nodded. 'I'm all right. The police have been in and out but I don't think they're making much progress. They've asked poor Kelvin a lot of questions.' She looked around anxiously and lowered her voice. 'I hear they've interviewed Poppy Rice more than once too.'

Eve bet they were ignoring the Fultons. Palmer never liked well-connected suspects – not when pursuing them might affect his career.

After Viv had left them, Eve took a deep breath and began. 'Brenda, I wonder if you can help me. This isn't to do with Emory's obituary – I won't quote anything you say. It's just that I'm starting to piece together information that might help find his killer. It's the police's business, of course, but I'd like to help if I can. And it's a matter of self-preservation too. I know I might come face to face with the murderer when I conduct my interviews. I'd rather be one step ahead.'

'I can understand that. And it would be a huge relief if you managed to work out who did it. Kelvin was with me almost constantly, but I'd swear the police still suspect him.' She shook her head. 'It's worrying. He had no motive at all.'

Eve thought of the row Jo said he'd had with Emory, but she kept quiet. If he'd only left the pub for five minutes, he couldn't have done it.

'I know how close you and Emory were.' Taking a deep breath, she went for it. 'I suspect Coco might be Emory's child and if I'm right, I'm guessing you know it's a possibility.' She kept her voice very low and the ebb and flow of teashop chatter continued around her.

Brenda's eyes met hers, her emotions clear to see: from shock, to something like relief, then sorrow. They filled with tears and she shook her head. 'I predicted there'd be heartache long before it happened. Emory thought he and Selina were two of a kind. Both wild and rebellious. Their affair lasted almost a year – officially – but who's to say when it finally petered out? Emory never told me outright that Coco was his, but I'm sure that's what he thought. You could see it in the way he acted. Their closeness. The presents he sent her, even when he was hard up. I'm sure that's why he insisted on staying at Magpie Lodge rather than letting Roger farm him out to Blyworth.

'As for Selina, she always had an eye to the main chance.' Her voice had dropped to a whisper. 'She knew which way her bread was buttered. Roger and Emory looked quite alike in those days and Roger had a certain suave charm. And he was the steady one, who'd have the money to support her. She wanted her own business. In the early days it was quirky second-hand stuff, not the overpriced nonsense they have now. Roger invested and they've been successful. Selina's a canny businesswoman.' She gave a hollow laugh. 'She could have opted for bank loans but I reckon Roger was less paperwork and he came with a lovely old house attached.'

Ouch. But it fitted with Eve's impression of Selina.

'Emory had money too, of course. Like I said, his parents compensated him for not getting the house, but he frittered the funds away in no time. Invested most of it in a scheme that went down the pan, and he spent a lot on partying. For a while it looked as though he'd make up for all that with his book earnings, but,' she sighed, 'the proceeds went the same way.'

'Do you think Roger knows Selina was still sleeping with Emory after they got together?'

Brenda finished a layered chocolate heart cake and frowned. 'I don't know. We're not close and he's a proud man. He'd never admit it if he did.'

'But it would have had a profound effect, if he'd found out?'

'I'm sure it would. He was always jealous of Emory, despite everything. Emory had such charm.' Brenda's eyes met Eve's. 'I've been worried about it. What he might have done, if... Well, you know. I should have told the police, but it's so hard. If they were both sleeping with Selina then I presume Emory couldn't be certain he was Coco's dad. And if Coco doesn't know, me speaking up will throw everything into turmoil.'

'I understand, but they might ask you. I guessed and they might too.' Especially once they saw the blue book.

Brenda nodded and sighed. 'I just don't want to make things worse for Coco. I've heard all the talk. She's been off the rails for years and I know how pleased everyone is that she's finally going to university. And Bathurst too – Roger must be bursting with pride.'

'Does he ever talk to you about Coco?'

She shook her head. 'He's very gracious of course, remembers to send me Christmas cards. Always signs off with "fondest, Roger". But Emory was the fondest. Roger treats me like an old retainer.' She gave Eve a sad look. 'Emory treated me as a friend.'

22

Back at home, Eve scanned her list of queries and decided to call Poppy Rice. She was still wondering about the box she'd found at Magpie Lodge, and in particular what Emory had intended to do with it. If there was any chance he'd stolen it, she wanted to believe he'd planned to sell it so he could pay Poppy back. If so, there was a chance she might confirm it. Eve doubted Emory would have admitted to thieving, but he might have hinted that his circumstances were about to improve. She dialled the woman's mobile number.

'*That's all right,*' Poppy said, when Eve explained she had more questions. '*I'm over at my workshop, but I can't concentrate anyway.*'

'Thank you. It's not strictly in relation to the obituary.'

Eve heard Poppy draw in a long breath. '*I heard you sometimes help the police with their enquiries. And that you've helped suspects prove their innocence before. Ask me anything you'd like.*'

She sounded tired and anxious, but keen to talk. That ought to mean she was innocent but Eve didn't feel she could trust her instincts where Poppy was concerned.

'I just wondered,' she hesitated, 'had Emory given you the impression he might be able to pay you back in full sometime soon?'

Eve could hear the frown in the woman's voice. '*No. Why do you ask?*' She didn't sound annoyed, only puzzled. For once, Eve was pretty sure she'd got an honest reaction.

'Someone mentioned he might be expecting an influx of cash. They might have been wrong.' Eve decided a white lie was excusable, under the circumstances.

'*That's strange. He hadn't said anything to me, and I think he would have.*' But then she stopped abruptly. '*Or maybe not.*' She paused as though the thoughts in her head were coalescing. '*It might depend on how he hoped to acquire the funds.*'

She sounded bitter, and Eve's heart sank. Was Robin right? Maybe Poppy knew Emory wasn't a hundred per cent honest. It wasn't how she'd thought his story would go; certainly not how she wanted it to pan out. 'How do you mean?'

There was a moment's silence. '*If it was uncertain, perhaps he didn't want to raise my expectations.*' But Eve was sure Poppy had sanitised her reply for her benefit.

'I'd also heard Emory had been asking about long-haul travel destinations. Places in West Africa, southern India and other bits of Asia. And that he'd been finding out about different universities.'

'*That really is odd.*' Poppy's response was immediate. '*I mean, I can imagine him wanting to travel, but I don't see how he'd have got the money. And the universities? No. He was very anti-establishment.*'

'I gather it was places known for their radical ideas, not the more traditional options.'

'*It still doesn't make sense. He didn't believe in formal learning. And why do a degree now? I'd say someone's got that wrong.*'

Eve thanked her and rang off. 'She was pretty unequivocal,' she said to Gus. 'And the degree thing always seemed unlikely.

As Poppy said, why now? Yet we know he was researching that very topic.' She stood up and stretched, causing Gus to leap backwards. 'Did I give you a fright?' Sensing he was in some way owed, Gus rolled onto his back for a tummy tickle.

As Eve obliged, she thought through the implications of the call. What Poppy said made sense. And thinking about it, if Emory had been keen on studying, he'd have looked at the courses, not just the pages on university life. So...? So, he must have been looking for another reason. She paused in her tickling as a possible answer came to her, and Gus shot her an accusatory look. 'Logic says he was looking with someone else in mind. But who does he know who's at that stage in life?' She started tickling again, rather erratically. 'I can only think of Coco.' She followed the idea through. Poppy said Emory was very anti-establishment. What if he'd hated the idea of his own daughter studying somewhere like Bathurst? He could see the sort of person it produced. He might have decided Poppy's husband was a prime example. She gave Gus a final pat and went to her laptop where a quick search showed Laurence had studied there too. Bathurst through and through. Emory might have felt compelled to suggest alternatives: edgy universities or, better still, more travel. It sounded as though the 'university of life' would have been his preference.

Suddenly, the argument she'd overheard between Selina and Emory took on new meaning. Yes, he'd known about her affair; he'd told Selina she had no right to take the moral high ground. But Eve had a hunch the rest had been about Coco.

It's family, Emory had said. *Blood's thicker than water. I've every right to say what I think.* Eve had assumed he'd been referring to Roger, but it was clear they weren't close. Now it seemed more likely he'd been speaking as a father, albeit an absentee, unacknowledged one. And then there'd been Selina's reaction.

Don't you dare! she'd retorted. *You'll upset everything. The damage you'll cause.* And then she'd ridiculed the idea of

Emory giving advice. *It's not as though you've made a success of your life*, she'd said. *Not like Roger and I have.*

Eve's idea, that he'd wanted Coco to consider different options, fitted. And Selina must have got wind of it. Maybe Roger had too. At the age of twenty-eight, Coco was finally living up to her parents' expectations but Emory was set to throw things off course.

And when Selina tried to reason with him at the church, he wasn't having any of it.

Eve imagined Roger going to visit him that night at Sycamore Cottage, furious at his interference. This was something that could have pushed his anger to boiling point: Emory had been carelessly trashing Roger's reputation and to cap it all he was steering Coco away from university again – something that could affect her entire future. And maybe Roger had started to suspect she wasn't his.

'I'm beginning to think his motive is as strong as Selina's,' she said to Gus. 'And he could have sneaked over to kill Emory while Selina watched TV and Coco performed bedroom gymnastics with her ex. But if so, there's still Emory's mystery visitor to account for, earlier in the evening. Either Roger went over to Sycamore Cottage twice, returning home between times to chat with Selina and Coco – which sounds wildly unlikely – or Emory had a previous caller who left him alive.'

23

Eve was still preoccupied with her theories when a knock on the door sent Gus into a frenzy of barking.

Opening up, she found Molly Walker outside. Molly was a cleaner at a local stately home and a friend of Moira's. Eve often bumped into her in the village store.

'Hello! Come on in.' Not that she'd find it easy. Gus was mobbing her on the doormat.

Molly bent to make a fuss of him, then stood up and ran her hands through her wiry hair. 'You're sure I'm not interrupting?' She bit her lip. 'I didn't want to call at lunchtime but I thought it would be easier to talk when Dylan's not around.'

Dylan was her boisterous five-year-old son, who attended the local primary school. Eve had seen him in action. He'd once climbed onto her kitchen counter and attempted to deconstruct the toaster. Eve was glad Molly had come alone.

'It's fine. Would you like a sandwich while you're here?'

Molly shook her head. 'Thanks, but I couldn't. I won't keep you long.'

'A coffee then.' Eve moved to the kettle and motioned Molly

to take a seat at the kitchen table. 'Is something wrong?' She was plucking at her coat sleeve.

'I bumped into a friend who said you'd had tea with Brenda Goody in Monty's this morning.'

That was Saxford for you. You couldn't sneeze without someone reporting it. 'That's right.'

'She's a family friend. She and my mother were close.' Eve pieced it together. Molly must be in her late thirties. Her late mother might have been around Brenda's age. 'I still see a lot of her,' Molly went on. 'She minds Dylan sometimes and she looked after me, back in the day. This was before she moved to Sycamore Cottage with her husband.'

'We've talked twice now. I like her.'

Molly nodded. 'She's lovely. That's why I'm here, to be honest. I guessed you were asking her about Emory. Are you looking into his murder too?'

Molly knew she'd been involved in police investigations in the past. Eve nodded and Molly's frown deepened.

'That's what I thought. Well, it's about Kelvin. You met him? What did you think?'

Eve poured their coffees and sat down opposite the woman. 'It's a good question. I can see how fond Brenda is of him.'

Molly put her head in her hands. 'It's the first time I've seen her happy since she was widowed. She and her husband had such a full life. They travelled the world, researching destinations for their business. They loved each other so dearly, and then all of a sudden he was gone. It was an awful blow.' She looked up again, her eyes full of worry. 'Then six months ago, along comes this charming, confident man who bumps into her three times in one week. And before anyone knows what's what, he's moved in as her lodger.' She shook her head. 'Brenda says he was in Saxford looking for a place to stay. The way she tells it, he couldn't find anywhere decent and it was logical to offer him a room. I know she doesn't need the money. My bet is he's paying peanuts or nothing at all. She's always been generous and not all that worldly. She's fallen for Kelvin, that's quite clear. She told me they've kissed. She was so excited. She says he's being a gentleman and not pushing her to go further than she wants. She feels odd, getting close to someone for the first time since her husband died.'

'But you think he's up to no good?'

Molly sipped her coffee. 'Didn't you get a feeling about him?'

Eve stuck to the facts. 'He listened in to my conversation with Brenda, and Jo at the pub mentioned she'd heard him rowing with Emory. It made me wonder.' To say nothing of the suspicious-sounding account he'd given the police. John Smith indeed...

'I think I know the reasons for both those things.'

Eve's heart beat faster as she leaned forward, cupping her coffee in her hands. 'I'd love to hear, if you don't mind telling me.'

Molly nodded. 'The day before Emory died, I went round to Brenda's for tea and she seemed troubled. When I asked what was wrong, she said she'd visited Emory that morning and agreed to let him do her cards. He told fortunes in all sorts of ways and she was curious; she thought it would be fun. You know how it is when you're in a new relationship. You want someone to tell you there's a happy-ever-after ahead. But instead, Emory said someone was playing her false and that he was anxious for her; she needed to watch out. Brenda claimed she couldn't imagine who the fortune referred to. I was gentle, but I suggested Kelvin.' Molly stared down into her cup. 'She was upset. Not angry exactly, but protesting. I felt uncomfortable, so I got up to leave and as I did, I heard a door creak.'

'Kelvin was listening in then, too?'

Molly was plucking at her sleeve again. 'I'm not sure. Brenda said he was out, but I wonder if he'd sneaked back in.

Especially now you've mentioned his and Emory's row in the pub. Maybe he thought Emory was trying to muddy his name. He probably wanted to know where he stood.'

'Maybe.' Eve wondered what Kelvin had to hide.

'And there's more. Brenda's behaving as though Kelvin has a cast-iron alibi for Emory's murder, but I don't think that's right.'

Eve went still. 'What makes you say that?'

'When Kelvin left the pub, she, Moira and I got chatting. She finished her drink and we got through another round during that time. I'd say he was gone a lot longer than five minutes.'

'You've told the police?'

Molly nodded. 'But I don't think they took much notice. I couldn't be certain, whereas Brenda claimed she was. It's not that she'd deliberately protect him. She adored Emory. He was like the son she never had. But I think she might be blinkered enough to believe Kelvin's above suspicion.'

Eve let the facts sink in as Molly got up to leave. She felt goosebumps crawl over her arms. She could imagine the fortune referring to Kelvin too. What had Emory suspected about him? He couldn't have had proof, or she assumed he'd have spoken more plainly. As it was, maybe he'd stuck to hints, but he'd been confident enough to confront Kelvin in the pub. Perhaps that had led to his murder.

But despite Eve's preoccupation with the lodger, she found her mind straying back to Roger as she watched Molly retreat down the road from her sitting room window. She had that weird sensation again – the same one she'd had the previous day. Something during their chat had jarred, and deep down, she knew it related to Emory's brother.

If only she could work out what it was.

24

As she ate pâté on toast for lunch, Eve added researching Kelvin Brady to her list of actions. It sounded as though he'd appeared in Saxford abruptly and made a dead set at Brenda from the start. He might have spotted her and been attracted, but the truth could be more sinister. Her insides pulled taut as she imagined him doing research of his own: finding out about Brenda's nice house and her comfortable circumstances, perhaps.

'I really hope I'm wrong, Gus,' she said as she helped him on with his tartan coat a short while later. She was wrapped up warm too, with two jumpers under hers, in lieu of fur.

She couldn't sit around, waiting for inspiration to strike. She had some vague notion that retracing her steps towards the Dower House might help. She still couldn't identify what had jarred during her interview with Roger Fulton, and why her chat with Molly Walker had sparked the feeling once again. There was a link somewhere. She needed to catch the elusive thought now, before it left her.

At the top of Haunted Lane, she turned right, feeling the pull of Fairview Hall and its estate. As she walked over the bridge that crossed the Sax, she stared out over the marshes and estuary. Her mind was normally soothed by the view, but today it was filled with too many questions.

Had Roger suspected Emory might be Coco's biological dad? And, if Eve's theories were correct, how angry had he been at Emory's attempts to put her off Bathurst? Very, she imagined. Reputation was everything to him, and Eve was sure that would extend to Coco. If she disgraced herself, his contacts in Blyworth would all be talking about it. How close had Emory come to blowing their precarious family set-up out of the water? He'd had all the means necessary, and Selina had hurt him twice over – rejecting him in favour of Roger and then treating him as an enemy, despite their former closeness. She could see how he might have been tempted.

And then there was Kelvin. What was he hiding from Brenda and how had Emory found out?

And finally, what had really gone on between Emory, Poppy and Laurence? Laurence couldn't be the killer, but if she could find out why he'd broken up Poppy's meeting with her godfather it might explain a lot. Whatever Poppy had been going to say to Emory at Monty's had probably come out at Magpie Lodge instead. That interaction had left her sobbing in public view, and just hours later, Emory was dead.

She was lost in thought, pausing as Gus sniffed at some frozen leaf matter on the edge of the Fairview woods, when she heard sirens.

An ambulance, racing up from the direction of Darsham. It manoeuvred at speed down the track which passed Magpie Lodge. Eve had no idea what was going on but in an instant, adrenaline had taken over. Her heart was thudding like a badly balanced wind-up toy, her mouth dry.

A police car screeched as it braked round the corner and Eve darted back amongst the trees. The last thing she wanted was Palmer seeing her there. He'd probably accuse her of being involved. She wasn't going home though. Not yet. She wanted to know what was up.

After a moment's hesitation, Eve walked through the trees, keeping away from the main paths and tracks.

Two more vehicles followed the first one. One a patrol car, one unmarked. She thought she recognised Palmer's froglike posture in the passenger seat. She tracked their lights in the semi-darkness of the woods.

They'd turned towards the Dower House.

Eve put her finger to her lips as she caught Gus's eye. He seemed to share her tension and stayed close to her feet, keeping quiet as they crept nearer.

She was close enough to the Dower House to see the apron of gravel parking and garden now. From somewhere inside, she heard crying that made her palms go clammy. Gus let out a low whine and she bent to fuss him, but it was for mutual comfort, not to keep him quiet. She doubted they'd be heard. The sound from the Dower House was hoarse, yet high, almost like the whinny of a horse but harsher. More urgent. Scared. The paramedics were emerging with someone on a stretcher. Eve could see the patient struggling, reaching to their neck with one hand, the other flailing with outstretched fingers.

Selina Fulton came running out. She was leaning over the stretcher as someone – one of the police team? – tried to steer her out of the way so the medics could do their job.

A moment later, Roger appeared too. He stood in the doorway, blocking the police behind him; they had to manhandle him out of the way. He had a hand up in his hair. Eve guessed he was in a state of shock.

The keening must be coming from Coco, the frantic figure on the stretcher.

25

The moment Eve got back to Elizabeth's Cottage she called Robin to update him. She guessed it would be a while before Greg got in touch with more information. He'd be busy dealing with the fallout.

Half an hour later, Eve slipped out to buy milk from Moira's store and got the first snippets of news. Rumours were rife and varied.

'Apparently someone tried to poison Coco,' Moira said, leaning forward eagerly over the counter. 'Does that fit with what you know, Eve? Only you've always got your finger on the pulse, as they say, and people are asking.'

'I'm afraid I don't know.' Eve could hardly admit she'd spied on the family as Coco was carried away. In her mind's eye the image of her was still vivid, one hand at her throat, the other arm flailing. The hoarse keening noise she made had chilled Eve to the bone.

After she'd settled up with Moira, Viv dashed to meet her on the green.

Eve gave her an accusatory look. She was always running

out on her customers in situations like these. Tammy was on duty too, but it was against Eve's rules.

'Don't be strict,' Viv said. 'Everyone in the teashop's full of this business with Coco. Someone saw an ambulance. They know I'm after news and they want it just as much as I do. Do you know if she's all right?'

Viv was a different prospect to Moira; Eve admitted what she'd seen and why she'd been there. 'But no one else must know I watched the whole thing,' she finished.

'Blimey,' Viv said. 'Perhaps it's drugs? A bad trip?'

'What kind of adolescence did you have?'

Viv gave her a wide-eyed look. 'I watch documentaries, thank you very much. I hope she's all right. Maybe Emory's death sent her off the rails.' She smiled ingratiatingly. 'You will let me know when you've found out more, won't you?'

'As if I'd get the choice!'

Viv laughed and trotted back to the teashop.

It was over an hour later when Eve and Gus made their way to Robin's cottage. They used the hidden route as usual, through Blind Eye Wood and his back garden. The villagers would be full of questions if they knew Eve visited Robin regularly. As ever, she thought how nice it would be to see him openly – meet up for a quiet drink at the Cross Keys, saunter carelessly up the coast with Gus at their feet. But the minute their relationship got out, people like Moira would ask her about his past. She'd have to lie and do it convincingly, or risk putting him in danger. Secrecy was the only realistic option.

Five minutes later, Robin was updating her, his expression grim. 'The keening you heard wasn't caused by a bad trip, but it did result from terror. You said she sounded hoarse?'

Eve nodded.

'That makes sense. Her parents say someone was halfway through strangling her when they arrived home and scared them off.'

They were in his cosy sitting room: a small snug space that ran front to back in his fisherman's cottage, adjacent to his kitchen. The effect of the soft couch and the glowing table lamps was cocooning. It gave Robin's words even more power to shock; the news was like a cold clammy hand, reaching into a place you thought was safe.

'That's horrific. Have the police made an arrest?'

He shook his head slowly. 'Coco says the attacker came at her from behind; she's got no idea who it was. They ran for it when her parents arrived home, and she was too out of it to look round and identify them. She says she can't remember anything after a certain point. Just the terror. She thinks she fell to the floor.'

'Heck. And Roger and Selina didn't see them either?'

'Apparently not. Coco was up in her bedroom. There's more than one staircase at the Dower House and they were too shocked to start searching. All they heard was a door slamming. They were busy tending to Coco and calling an ambulance.'

'Understandable. How did the attacker get in?'

'They forced the French windows downstairs. They weren't all that secure. It wouldn't have made much noise.

'The CSIs are looking for evidence of course, but unless they find something in Coco's rooms it might not help much. Half the village has been in and out of the Dower House expressing condolences since Sunday, according to Greg. If the person who attacked Coco paid a legitimate visit recently, proof they were on site will count for nothing.'

'I can imagine. I went there myself.' Images of Coco, cocky and dismissive, walking through the woods, filled her head. 'Will she be okay?'

'Greg says the medics are keeping her in overnight – she's very bruised with a sore throat – but it's more for her mental state than physical.' He met Eve's eyes and leaned in to give her a hug. Gus – aware of the atmosphere but not the cause –

looked up anxiously so that in moments they were both focused on him. He was good at keeping Eve grounded.

She took a sip of the coffee Robin had made her. 'So where were Roger and Selina?'

'They'd gone into town. Selina popped into Rice and Fulton. She hasn't been back properly since Emory's death. She said she was worried Ada might feel put out.'

'I could see her trying to take over in Selina's absence too. There's a bit of rivalry between them. What about Roger?'

'He's asked junior partners in his law firm to see his clients this week. Greg says he thinks it's for show – that it wouldn't be seemly to carry on as normal.'

'That figures.'

'But he paid a visit to the offices of the Blyworth and Villages Charitable Trust. He claims he needed to pick up some papers for a meeting. But no one's sure why he felt obliged, under the circumstances. It's not until the week after next.'

'You think he made it up? That he might have come home sooner and attacked Coco himself?'

Robin's gaze was steady. 'I wouldn't rule it out. We've only got their word for it that they went into town together at all. Roger could have forced the French windows to make it look like an outside job. No one saw him at the charity's offices. It's a large building and there's no CCTV so it doesn't prove anything, one way or the other. I know it's hard to imagine a father attacking their child, but it does happen. And these are unusual circumstances. He might have attempted to kill her out of desperation if she knew he was guilty.'

'But if that's the case, Selina must have lied to cover for him. She'd never have done that when he'd attacked her child.'

'She might feel the consequences would be even worse if she told the police. People think in warped ways. Maybe she fears for Coco's future if it comes out that her father's a killer. She might figure that he lost control and it won't happen again.

And she'd have a selfish motive too. If Roger went down for murder, it would leave her life in tatters.'

Eve shook her head. Surely Selina wouldn't prioritise her own well-being over her daughter's? But part of Robin's argument sounded possible. 'What about Coco? If she has proof that Roger killed Emory, she's been keeping quiet. I'm not sure she'd have done that to protect him.'

'I know she's a rebel, but I expect he read her bedtime stories when she was little and played with her in the park. She might love him underneath it all.'

Eve hesitated. 'True... Coco got on so well with Emory, but I do see that reporting Roger would have been a huge move.' She shuddered. 'I can think of another possibility though, and it fits better with her character as far as I'm concerned. Coco might know or have guessed the killer's identity and she's wild. I'd say she enjoys power.' Eve remembered the way she'd treated her on-off boyfriend, bringing him running when she wanted, then sending him off again. 'I could imagine her blackmailing the killer rather than reporting them to the police, whether it was one of her parents, or another suspect.

'If it was Roger who attacked her, I wonder if she's genuinely unaware of the fact.' Surely she wouldn't stay quiet under those circumstances. 'What about Selina?' she asked at last.

'Even she could be guilty. She was definitely in Blyworth to start with; she popped in to her and Ada's shop. But after that she claims she walked around waiting for Roger. He might be lying for her, for similar reasons.'

Eve shook her head. 'I can't imagine her going for Coco like that. Her own daughter? She just wouldn't.'

'You mean *you* wouldn't.' He took her hand.

'But I saw her, Robin. She was desperate to get to Coco when the paramedics took her away. One of the officers had to pull her off. It was Roger who stood in the doorway.' She remembered how he'd blocked the way, just staring, stock-still.

'The police are checking CCTV in Blyworth anyway. There might be footage to back her story. But Roger's likely to remain a question mark. They'd parked in a side street close to the charity's headquarters. It's where the town gives way to one of the residential areas; there are no cameras there.

'The other possibility is that it's all an elaborate fake. Coco might know one of her parents is guilty and have gone along with the scheme to make them look innocent. In which case one of them went through the motions of strangling her and she was never meant to die. But if so, they went perilously close to getting it wrong. The medical evidence is unequivocal.'

Eve shook her head. 'And I heard her, Robin. I'd swear her terror was genuine. It still sends shivers through me thinking of it.'

'I'll pass your thoughts on to Greg. It never seemed likely anyway. I'd say the attacker meant business. Apart from her parents, who else would you suggest for the perpetrator?'

Eve took a sip of her coffee and reviewed what she knew. 'The original suspects still stand – unless they have alibis this time?'

'None that I've heard of yet. The police will check.'

'Coco knew Emory well; there's every chance she has information – knowingly or unknowingly – that might lead to his killer. So that's Poppy Rice, and you can add Kelvin Brady to the list. Molly Walker thinks he might have had time to kill Emory after all.' She explained what the woman had said. 'Always assuming her attacker and Emory's killer are one and the same. I suppose it's not impossible someone had a separate motive to harm her.'

'Anyone spring to mind?'

For a second Eve thought of her ex, Jonny, but though she'd treated him appallingly, she didn't buy it. He was too timid.

'Not really. It seems more likely someone thinks she knows too much.'

Robin nodded. 'Makes sense.'

It left them with a new puzzle. What could Coco have seen or heard that meant she was a threat to the killer?

26

As promised, Eve updated Viv over a cup of tea at Monty's. The teashop was already shut and Viv was clearing up after the hordes, cloth in hand. Eve stepped in to help as she relayed the news she'd got from Robin.

'I'd heard about the attempted strangulation. Monty's has been buzzing with rumours,' Viv said. 'Murmurs of Coco everywhere I turned. I could see reporters heading into the Cross Keys too. That must have made Jo's day. And of course, the whole ghost story link is kicking off again.'

'Excuse me?'

'The two murdered maids Emory told us about. The second one, Mildred, was found strangled in the woods. People are saying Coco's near miss is another warning to the Fultons.'

'They think it's supernatural?'

'Some of them.' Viv gave her an exasperated look. 'Come on, you can see why! It's quite a coincidence, the way Emory's murder and the attack on Coco mirror the story. And everyone's still talking about how Roger Fulton's great-grandfather was probably guilty.'

'Don't tell me you believe we've got a killer ghost on our hands.'

Viv cocked her head and gave Eve a withering look. 'Certainly not. I believe in ghosts. You can't grow up in Elizabeth's Cottage and not.' Her parents had lived there before Eve. 'I'm willing to admit the footfalls on Haunted Lane are real, even if you're not.' She ignored Eve's open mouth. 'But I can't imagine insubstantial ghostly hands dragging Emory under water, or half throttling Coco. That would be ridiculous. Moira's quite excited about it though.'

Eve could imagine.

As they walked out of the teashop and Viv locked up, they spotted a figure tiptoeing through the icy dark of early evening. Her long red hair gleamed in the lamplight.

Poppy Rice.

Eve had been convinced she was making for a car – a smart little Alfa Romeo – but at that moment she glanced up and spotted them.

'Hello. I just nipped into Saxford to pick up a couple of things from your village shop. Isn't it lovely? I've been making good use of it since we arrived.'

Beyond her, Eve could see Moira was just closing. She turned the sign on the door and glanced in their direction.

'It's great.' Eve smiled, but Poppy's words seemed stilted and overly perky. Why was she so awkward? Had she come into the village for gossip? Was she anxious to find out what the police thought about the attack on Coco? Moira was the right person to pick, if so.

'It's nice to be out and get some fresh air,' Poppy added. 'I think I might take a turn around the village before I head back.'

'Good idea.' Eve tried to ignore Viv's meaningful glances until Poppy was out of earshot. 'You are so unsubtle,' she said, when it was safe to do so.

'Is it me though, or was she being weird?'

'It's not you. I'd swear she was about to drive off until she saw us. And she's the first person I've met this afternoon who hasn't mentioned Coco.'

'Good point.'

Eve took a deep breath, damping down her frustration. 'Why is she lying again? I'm not sure I've had a straightforward response from her yet. Mind if I wait at your house for a bit, to see if she comes back?' Viv lived right next door to the teashop.

Her friend rubbed her hands. Eve guessed it was ten per cent cold and ninety per cent glee. 'Be my guest. So long as I can keep watch too.'

They stood in Viv's sitting room with the lights off and peered out at the village green, one each side of the window. Eve could feel the cold of the night seeping in around the frame. Viv's cats were unimpressed. She'd fed them rapidly on her way in, but they were too mystified by their owner's behaviour to concentrate on eating. Two of them were circling Eve's legs. Fluffy and Scruffy, she thought, though there were several more and it was hard to tell in the dark.

'She's coming back already,' Viv hissed.

She was right. Poppy was approaching the Alfa Romeo again, her hair swishing as she turned to glance over her shoulder.

'She's watchful.'

'Definitely.'

She approached the car unnaturally, almost as though she was about to overshoot it again, then unlocked the doors and slipped in quickly at the last minute.

'I'd like to follow her,' Eve said.

'Seriously?' There was a note of awe in Viv's voice.

Eve was already moving towards the door. 'You were the one who said she's behaving oddly. And she's one of the suspects.' Eve's Clubman was parked by the village green as usual. It would be easy enough to go after her.

'I know. Can I come?'

'Do I have a choice?'

Viv laughed and followed Eve out of the house.

'We'll have to be quick.' Eve had unlocked her car and Viv leaped into the passenger seat.

Poppy's car was already out of sight, but she'd exited the village on the Old Toll Road and there were no immediate turn-offs. A moment later, they could see her tail lights ahead.

'She's going at quite a lick,' Viv said. 'I suppose she might be late for supper. I wouldn't fancy upsetting Ada Rice.'

But it was only ten past six according to the car's dashboard. 'I don't think it's that.'

Eve was proved right when Poppy overshot the turning to Fairview Hall and drove on in the direction of Blyworth.

They followed her at a distance. Eve was anxious when they reached town, and Viv was leaning forward, as though the extra inches would give her a better idea of where Poppy was going. They mustn't lose her. Eve's eyes focused on the tail lights again. Poppy was taking the through route. Once she was beyond the town centre she made a turn for a residential area. Eve had been there before. It was a down-at-heel part of Blyworth, with its own set of local stores.

It was outside these that Poppy pulled up. Eve drove past, so as not to attract attention, but she only overshot by a short way. In moments, she and Viv had got out and were edging back along the pavement, peering round a hedge as Poppy walked towards the row of stores. Three were still open: an off licence, a fish and chip shop and a bookmaker.

Poppy went inside the bookmaker's.

'She's sneaked out to put on a bet?' Viv was incredulous. 'I'd never have thought someone like her would pop into the book-ie's regularly. She looks so prissy somehow. And why not go online?'

Eve considered that for a moment, a theory forming, albeit

one based on thin evidence. 'If you go online you have to use a bank card to pay. Here, she can hand over cash. She mentioned she and Laurence have joint accounts these days; if she uses cash, in person, she could keep her gambling secret. Maybe it's more than the occasional flutter? She looked pretty shifty when she left Saxford.' Eve knew she was making a leap. Maybe the excitement of tailing Poppy had got the better of her. But if Poppy was at ease with her mission, why avoid setting off as Eve and Viv watched?

The possibility that she had a habit took her mind back to their first talk at Fairview Hall. 'Doing her betting in person presents a different threat. No wonder she didn't want to speak to the press about Emory. She asked me if I'd need a photo of her before she agreed to an interview. At the time I assumed she was avoiding the limelight generally – especially as a suspect. Now, I wonder if it was fear at being recognised by staff here. If they realised one of their customers was a well-to-do connection of a murdered celebrity they'd be sure to gossip. If she has a gambling habit, word might easily have got back to Ada and Laurence.'

'That makes sense. But why go to Saxford before coming here?'

'I suppose she needed an excuse to leave the hall. Or at least, she did in her own mind. She strikes me as the nervous sort. She probably told Laurence and co that she was going to Moira's and then to get some fresh air, just like she told us. But she didn't want to risk someone who might chat to the family seeing her drive off shortly after six. She was being very careful.'

She must have worked herself up into a frenzy of anxiety. Eve could imagine her fears spiralling out of control. And there was something intense about her. Eve thought of the way she clung on to Laurence, as though she was desperate to keep their relationship going.

'If she has a problem, her mother might have known,' Eve

said. 'It could explain why she was nervous about the séance. It's like I thought before: maybe she imagined Emory in a trance, coming out with something that would give her away.' Assuming her guess was right, there was a new mystery to solve. 'If she bets in cash, where does that cash come from? She was getting the odd repayment from Emory, but I imagine they were few and far between, but lots of withdrawals from the joint account would alert Laurence, so that's not likely.' She frowned. 'Fairview Hall must be full of valuables. What if she's been pinching small items here and there and selling them? Her marriage might be over if Laurence finds out the truth.' It would give him an excellent excuse to divorce her without fallout at work. Poppy's dad could hardly blame him under those circumstances.

Viv leaned forward eagerly. 'And she might have thought Emory was in a position to give her away after the séance: that he'd found out more from her mum than he was letting on. That sounds like a motive for murder.'

'It's possible.' But as their suppositions swirled, the facts settled in Eve's mind, and Emory and Poppy's conversation in Monty's came back to her. 'But actually, I don't think that's what happened. Poppy was sad, that day she and Emory came in for tea. At one point, she said something like: *I know, I should have told you. And you're right of course, I've been meaning to, but it's not easy.* And then a second later she added, *You don't understand. Please, Emory, don't push me on this. I can't. Not now.*'

'You think they were talking about her gambling? That he already knew?'

'And was suggesting she confided in someone to get help.' Eve nodded. 'It would fit. But it doesn't explain Poppy's upset the day Emory died, or Laurence's grievance against him. There are layers of secrets; if I'm right, we've only unveiled one. But we might have uncovered nothing at all – one trip to a bookmaker's, albeit in strange circumstances, does not a habit make. I'll need to talk to Poppy again to check.'

She'd have to plan her approach; it would be an awkward conversation.

Twenty minutes later, Eve and Viv were back in Saxford. Parking on Haunted Lane was forbidden, and Eve's original space had gone, but she found an alternative close to the turn-off to Ferry Lane.

'That tiny house on the corner's where Brenda Goody lived before she got married,' Viv said, pointing. 'It was her parents' home but I gather they were out a lot. Her mum was a nurse and her dad a haulier. I suppose Brenda must have had the run of the place when she was minding Roger and Emory. Just as well. It still must have been hell with so little space.' Viv had three boys, though they were all young adults now. 'Brenda inherited the house when her parents died.'

It was a tidy-looking whitewashed cottage with a red-tiled roof. A similar size to Robin's. Viv was right. Looking after two boisterous children there must have been a challenge, though the garden was long and they were close to the beach.

The thought played in her head as Eve locked the car. And then suddenly, its import hit home. At last she knew why Roger's words had jarred. And why her chat with Molly Walker had accentuated that feeling.

Eve needed to talk to Roger Fulton again. It was too late that night, especially after what had happened to Coco, but the matter was urgent.

And before that, she must call Brenda Goody to check her facts.

27

The following morning, Eve was ready to carry out her plan. Her call to Brenda had confirmed her hunch and another visit to Roger Fulton was called for.

A sense of purpose fought with nerves at the thought, and her heart hammered uncomfortably. Robin's arguments came back to her. He could be the killer. What if Selina was out and Coco still in hospital? She didn't want to be alone with him.

'It's no use looking at me like that,' she said to Gus, who'd got up eagerly when she rose from her seat. 'You're plenty brave enough but I won't risk taking you.'

Instead, she called Robin, who was trained, and never took to barking or rolling over to have his tummy tickled at awkward moments. By the time she approached the Dower House, a bouquet of flowers from Moira's in hand, he'd texted to say he was in position. He couldn't make his involvement public – not with the secrets he was keeping from the police – but she felt secure, knowing he'd be hidden just outside the house. He would listen for raised voices, ready to wade in if there was trouble.

Robin was assuming Roger would see her in the drawing

room where the fundraiser had taken place. He'd advised her not to go upstairs, or to any rooms with no exterior window.

A trickle of fear snaked its way down her back. What if Roger tried to get her isolated and she couldn't think of a reason to avoid it? If he was guilty, she'd be in danger the moment he guessed she was frightened of him.

She took a deep breath and knocked on the door of the Dower House. They must have had other well-wishers visiting but there were no cars parked outside. Maybe they'd all come the day before.

It was Roger himself who opened up, which did nothing for Eve's nerves. 'I was so sorry to hear about Coco,' she said, proffering the flowers. 'I wondered if you'd mind giving her these?'

'That's kind of you, Eve.' He replied without a pause, his tone smooth. 'Selina's just fetching her from the hospital now. I'll see that Coco gets them.'

The temptation to thank him, turn tail and walk away was strong. But in some ways, it was a good opportunity. Roger might be more unguarded without them there. If she wanted the truth, this was her chance, and Robin was close at hand.

'I wondered if I could possibly have a word with you too. I hate to disturb you at such a difficult time, but I have a couple of extra questions about Emory.'

Roger's look changed subtly. The polite pasted-on smile was still there, but there was a wariness in his eyes.

'It won't take a moment.'

He stood back suddenly. 'Of course.' Perhaps he'd rather they spoke in private too. Her stomach tensed.

It was a relief when he showed her to the drawing room, as she and Robin had hoped. He motioned her to a seat. 'Coffee?'

But Eve didn't want to waste time. Selina and Coco might be back any minute. 'I'm fine, thanks.'

'So, Eve, your extra questions?' He raised an eyebrow.

She tried to steady her breathing. It was best just to go for it.

'I know you were in Brenda Goody's cottage, the night Emory died.'

Roger went absolutely still and Eve held her breath. Should she have gone to the police with her theory? Handed the job over to them? But Palmer would never have followed it up. Despite her words, the accusation was an educated guess. The DI would have scoffed at her reasoning. Told her to mind her own business. Yet she could see from Roger's face that she was right.

In a fraction of a second, he'd pulled himself together. 'How can you possibly know that?'

'You don't deny it then?'

'That's not what I meant, I—'

'When I came to interview you, you talked about your horror at the way Emory had died.' She took her notebook from her bag; she already had it at the right page. 'You told me: "I keep imagining him in that great bath of Brenda's." The image you created was accurate. Brenda told me herself that her bath is huge. *Now*. Now that she's living on the Old Toll Road in that lovely house she and her husband bought. But you said yourself you're out of touch with her. The bathroom you knew, back in Brenda's old house on Ferry Lane, was tiny, as was the tub.' Brenda had confirmed it, and that Roger had never been inside Sycamore Cottage – or not with permission, anyway. 'You were picturing her current bathroom. One you should never have seen.'

She'd almost clicked when Molly mentioned Brenda looking after the brothers at her parents' house. When Viv showed her the place in person, the penny had finally dropped. Until then she'd failed to string the facts together; she'd been imagining the brothers running in and out of Sycamore Cottage. Brenda said Roger treated her like an old retainer, sending an annual Christmas card for propriety's sake. It hadn't seemed likely that he'd visited her after the childminding stopped.

Roger was sitting on the edge of the couch. Eve was primed too. Ready to yell, jump up and run if he showed any signs of attacking her. He stayed seated, but there was a tic going in his cheek.

At last, his shoulders went down. 'All right. I was there. But for heaven's sake, I didn't kill him! He wasn't even in the bath when I arrived.' He put his head in his hands for a moment, clutching at his hair. When he spoke again his voice was barely controlled. 'I went to find him at the lodge. I was furious. He'd been trying to talk Coco out of taking up her place at Bathurst. I mean, as if he hadn't caused enough trouble!' His eyes met Eve's. 'I love my daughter – love her dearly – but she's like Emory in some ways. She'd try the patience of a saint. She's had a record number of gap years, as you probably know, and finally she was about to come good. And then I find – via Selina – that Emory was trying to torpedo my plans for her. Selina had tried to talk him out of interfering but he wasn't having any of it, so she came to me.'

'And you went to Emory.'

'Yes, but to yell at him, not to drown him! I went to the lodge first, but he was out.' He looked down at his lap. 'In truth, I knew he was using Brenda's bathroom. Selina didn't make him feel welcome at our place.' Eve could imagine her not wanting him around – an ex-lover who knew about her current affair. 'Sure enough, when I went off in the direction of Brenda's I could see Emory in the distance under a streetlamp. I arrived at Sycamore Cottage just after he did. He hadn't even locked the door. We got into a slanging match. Emory wouldn't give an inch. He kept telling me I didn't understand.' Roger's fists were balled-up tight. 'He walked away while I was talking to him. He said he was going to have his bath and I could do what I liked. I followed him up the stairs and gave him a great shove against the bathroom wall.' He stood up suddenly, shaking, and Eve flinched in spite of herself. 'Most people would understand that! He wound everyone up. He sullied my name with my clients without even thinking about it. It was all a joke to him but he was ruining my chances. He was painfully thoughtless. You must see that. But when he calmly turned on the taps and started to undress I knew there was nothing I could do. I was incandescent with rage, if you must know. Emory told me to show myself out and I did just that.'

Giving the door an almighty slam behind him. It fitted with the neighbour's report. They hadn't mentioned the shouting but they'd likely missed it. The houses were detached with decent-sized gardens. It was the external door slamming that would carry. It explained why the front door had remained unlocked. There was no latch.

'I was back here way before Emory was killed,' Roger said, sagging down onto the couch as though he was exhausted. 'I think Coco knew I was upset when she saw me.'

'She was the first person you talked to?'

'I bumped into her outside our gates. She was on her way out for a walk.' He made it sound healthy, but Eve remembered it had been a cigarette stroll. 'She asked where I'd been. I was probably red in the face.'

'Did you tell her what had happened?'

He shook his head. 'I didn't want anyone to know. I feel terrible that our last words were angry ones.'

Hmm. The threat of the police and his high-profile friends finding out was likely off-putting too.

'I changed the subject. Asked her about going to university. I wanted to check the state of play. I wasn't sure if Emory had already got to her, you see – made her question her choices. She looked at me as though I was mad – but that's kids for you – and said she couldn't wait to go.'

But Coco wasn't a kid. Perhaps it didn't help that Roger was still treating her like one.

'By the time she came back, I'd calmed down. Selina was

around too. We stayed here all evening. It seemed pointless explaining my visit to the police when I wasn't involved, Eve.'

'I understand, Roger.' She fixed him with her gaze. 'But it might help them piece things together.'

'Detective Inspector Palmer's a top man, of course. I've every respect for him.'

That had to be a lie. 'I was thinking Greg Boles might be the person to talk to. He's very discreet. He wouldn't make a fuss unless he had to. And since I've worked it out, others probably will too.' Eve would ask Robin to pass Greg the information if Roger didn't do it himself. It was too important to ignore.

'That's a point.' She could see his mind working. The lesser of the two evils. She'd expected him to be angry at her interference, but in fact he looked relieved.

At that moment, Eve heard a car draw up outside.

Roger glanced out of the window. 'That's Selina and Coco back.'

Eve rose. 'I'd better give you some space.'

'Thank you.'

He saw her to the door. As she left she caught a brief glimpse of Coco in the passenger seat of her mother's car, her face white, her eyes huge. A very different woman from the one she'd talked with in the woods. Eve didn't believe anyone could act fear so well, especially not someone as self-assured as Coco.

28

Eve met Robin in the woods on the Fairview Hall estate.

'It went smoothly then?'

He pulled her into his arms and she nodded. 'It was weird, I thought he'd be angry. Defensive. But it was as though he was relieved to get the story out. I suppose it's been hanging over him since Sunday. He's been waiting for the axe to fall – he must have guessed someone could have seen or heard him.'

'So, what are your thoughts?' He let her go and strode next to her, hands in pockets, black beanie pulled down on his head to keep out the cold.

Eve relayed their conversation. 'My hunch is he's innocent. He's got a very obvious fake, public-facing voice, but when he told me the tale he forgot to use it. He only went back into smarmy mode when he was trying to justify not telling the police. I think that's when his filter switched back on. And his story fits with the slamming door the neighbour heard. When he was nearing home he bumped into Coco and she calmed his nerves about her plans for university. It probably meant the fight had gone out of him by the time Emory was killed.'

'Could be. He still had a very good motive though, if he'd

found out about Selina two-timing him when they were engaged, and Coco's possible parentage.'

'True, but the way he talked convinced me he doesn't know. He said: "I love my daughter – love her dearly – but she's like Emory in some ways. She'd try the patience of a saint." I'm sure I'd have seen it in his eyes or detected bitterness in his voice if he'd known. If anything, he sounded proprietorial. Irritated but still proud. Every inch the Victorian dad.'

'Interesting.'

She nodded. 'And that being the case, I'm guessing Coco has no inkling she might be Emory's either. I'll bet she'd have had it out with them all if she knew.

'I'm sure Emory felt acutely invested in her future. I believe he thought he was acting for the best, not just making mischief. But he was a drifter. I'd say he cared, but perhaps he was glad to avoid the responsibility after all. In fact, I've been wondering if that's why he pinched the book he gave to Selina and Roger when they got married.'

Robin raised an eyebrow. 'To preserve the status quo?'

Eve nodded. 'I suspect he was angry when he wrote his cryptic message and half hoped Roger would guess its meaning. But that was over twenty-eight years ago. Feelings change. Maybe seeing it again made him think hard about what he wanted, and in the end that wasn't for Roger or Coco to guess the truth. That could have been for selfish reasons or for Coco's sake. It's clear he minded about her future. He might not have wanted to throw her life into turmoil.'

'You could be right.'

'I think Roger might talk to Greg of his own accord.'

'But if not, would you like me to suggest he interviews him again, discreetly?'

'That would be great. Thank you.'

Robin nodded. 'So where does this leave your investigation?'

'With Selina and Roger relegated to rank outsiders. I can't help it. Selina was beside herself when Coco was carried away by the medics.' She held up a gloved hand. 'But I know. I won't discount them completely unless I find concrete proof.'

He grinned and kissed her.

'I'd like to talk to Poppy now I have an inkling what her secret is, just to make sure I'm right and that Emory knew about her gambling problem, if that's what it is. I might get a clue as to what caused the rift the day he died too, and why he and Laurence were on such bad terms.' She met Robin's eye. 'Don't worry – I'll choose a public venue.'

'Top marks.'

'So patronising.'

He laughed.

'And Kelvin Brady's still a worry. Do the police know if he has an alibi for Coco yet?'

'He hasn't. He claims he was home at Sycamore Cottage but Brenda was visiting a friend so she can't vouch for him. He got shirty, apparently. As far as he's concerned, his alibi for Emory's murder ought to be enough to strike him from the suspect list.'

'But if Molly Walker's right he had time to kill him, and Jo Falconer confirms they argued two days before the murder. But I still don't know what their quarrel was about. When Emory told Brenda's fortune, he just said someone was "playing her false". Molly Walker immediately thought of Kelvin, and I agree.' She sighed. 'It sounds as though Emory had strong suspicions of some kind of wrongdoing, but no proof. He might have tried talking to her about Kelvin directly, of course, but he probably had to pull back just like Molly did, or risk their friendship. I imagine the fortune was another way of trying to seed doubt in her mind, to protect her. Perhaps he was looking for hard evidence to convince her when he was killed. What about Poppy? Does she have an alibi for the attack?'

Robin shook his head. 'She'd been at her workshop in Blyworth apparently, but she says she couldn't concentrate so she drove back to the hall and went off for a walk.'

The news left Eve with two main suspects, and lots of questions.

Back at Elizabeth's Cottage, Eve's mind was crowded with queries and she made herself pull back. She needed to be methodical. Pinpoint each area of doubt and work at it until the mist cleared. For Poppy, that meant checking if her gambling was a habit, whether Emory had known about it, and pulling out all the stops to understand the rift between them, the day he died. She texted the jeweller, asking her to call, and Poppy did so while she was making a coffee and telling Gus about Roger Fulton's confession.

When Eve explained she wanted to meet again, Poppy sounded nervous, and suggested a sandwich bar in Blyworth that lunchtime. She was certainly on edge, and her nerves convinced Eve the meet-up would be worthwhile. If she believed in an afterlife, as Eve suspected, it ought to make her less likely to commit such unspeakable acts, but once again her clinginess towards Laurence filled Eve's head. If he was her be-all and end-all, and she thought Emory threatened their future, it wasn't impossible. People were contradictory; that was one thing obituary writing had taught her.

With the meet-up arranged, Eve took Gus for a walk, then settled down to start her research into Kelvin Brady. She'd wanted to do it sooner, but the drama over Coco, then following Poppy to the bookmakers and challenging Roger Fulton had delayed her.

Kelvin was a hard man to track down. He had no LinkedIn profile – the wrong generation perhaps – and no Facebook either. But after endless scrolling down pages of links she found a review on Trustpilot, which tied him to a firm of electricians in Ipswich. The comment said how skilled and friendly he was.

'I might call his firm, Gus,' she said, bending to give him a pat. 'I've got to start somewhere.' She'd already formed a plan.

She dialled and a woman picked up. '*Cosgrove Electricians. How may I help?*'

'I'm having some trouble with my circuit breaker. It keeps tripping out and I wondered if someone could help.'

'*I'm sure that can be arranged. Have you used us before?*'

'I haven't, but Kelvin Brady's been recommended to me.'

'*Ah.*' There was a distinct pause. '*I'm afraid Mr Brady's no longer with us. He left six months ago now.*' Around the time Brenda had taken him in as a lodger. There was something about the receptionist's clipped tone that made Eve wonder. Had they let him go? And if so, why? The review on Trustpilot was complimentary.

'I'm sorry to hear that. Do you know if he's operating independently now?'

'*I'm afraid I couldn't say.*' She spoke firmly, as though she was pleased to have cut off all ties. '*To be one hundred per cent frank, I'm afraid we're not prepared to recommend him any longer.*' She proceeded to offer Eve a slot with another electrician. Guiltily, Eve pretended there was a knock at the door and said she'd call back.

She added: *Left previous job under a cloud?* to her notes on Kelvin. But he'd charmed his clients, by the sound of it, and known his stuff too. The firm might just have lost patience because he'd gone independent and pinched some of their customers.

She went back to the jumble of photos that Emory had taken of Brenda's house. She wondered if they'd got anything to do with Kelvin. If she was right, and Emory's fortune-telling session had been to warn Brenda about her lodger, something must have made him worry. It would explain his heated row with Kelvin at the Cross Keys too.

'The photos seem so random,' she said to Gus, who'd just got up and was making for his water bowl. 'That's got to mean something. I'm sure they're less haphazard than they appear.'

She frowned, frustrated. It was no good trying to work it out now. She only had twenty minutes to drive to Blyworth to meet Poppy Rice.

29

Eve sat opposite Poppy in the small sandwich bar she'd suggested. It was warm, the windows misted, and nearly every table was taken. The air was filled with the smell of freshly baked bread, cheeses and cured meats.

Eve had bought them both lunch, but Poppy hadn't touched her baguette and Eve wasn't hungry either. You could feel the tension in the air. Everyone else in the café was chatting animatedly. Eve and Poppy sipped their coffees.

Eve made up her mind and put down her cup. As with Roger, it was better to wade straight in. She watched Poppy closely as she spoke. 'I'm sorry, I have to confess this isn't strictly about the obituary. You already know I overheard you talking to Emory, the day you came into Monty's. Part of your conversation's just fallen into place. Do you remember, you said something like, "You're right of course, I've been meaning to, but it's not easy." You looked upset, and then a moment later you told him he didn't understand, and asked him not to push you. "I can't," you said. "Not now."'

She flushed. 'I don't remember.'

'Poppy, I know what you were talking about.' A bluff often

worked; it felt dishonest, but it was in a good cause. Eve didn't break eye contact.

Poppy's blue eyes met hers as she dashed her coffee down, knocking the cup against the edge of the saucer. 'How on earth? Wait, I saw you last night. What happened? Did you follow me?'

Her voice was loud and several customers looked around. Their glances in Eve's direction were suspicious and unfriendly, but Eve felt a rush of satisfaction. Poppy had done the job for her; made the link between the previous conversation and her gambling without Eve asking any leading questions. She'd been right, she was sure now; Poppy's gambling had become a problem, and Emory had known.

Eve rushed to explain. 'You were acting oddly. Please understand that I'm interviewing all Emory's closest friends and contacts.' She lowered her voice. 'I know one of them's probably his killer. I don't want to interfere or cause trouble. I'm certainly not out to reveal any secrets you have. But I can't just sit back and ignore things that make me nervous. It's self-preservation. You would do the same in my shoes.'

There was a long pause, but at last Poppy straightened her coffee cup. 'It was a huge liberty that you took. You must have watched me.'

'I was concerned in case it was relevant to Emory's death.' She spoke very quietly. The gawpers at the neighbouring tables had finally gone back to their food. She didn't want to set them off again. 'If you're in trouble, I'm honestly sorry.' She really was. 'But I wanted to ask you about it. I could see how anxious you were not to have Emory round to do the séance. You looked scared when Laurence suggested it on the ghost walk. And then afterwards, when I came to ask you how it had gone, you were tense. I wondered if you thought your mother's spirit might have given away your secret to Emory.'

'And that I'd killed him to keep him quiet?' Her voice rose again but when heads turned she toned it down.

'It wouldn't be a bad motive, if the future of your marriage depends on it.' Eve held her gaze. 'It was something I had to rule out. And then I remembered your conversation with Emory in Monty's. I guessed he already knew, so the séance didn't change things. Emory could have given you away at any time.'

Tears came to the woman's eyes. 'He wouldn't have though – not deliberately, to hurt me. I knew that.'

Eve was sure she was right. He'd been thoughtless but kind, and he knew what it was like to struggle and push your way through tough times. She nodded. 'I believe you. I liked him.'

'I did too. I did, I did.' Her words were odd. She sounded as though she was trying to convince herself, and there were tears in her eyes.

Eve turned her mind back to the séance. 'So, were you worried Emory might give you away to Laurence by accident? By coming out with something your mother said in the heat of the moment, perhaps?'

But Poppy shook her head. 'Emory didn't lose control like that.'

Eve leaned forward. 'He'd done a session for you before?'

She hesitated, her eyes down. 'I sat in on one once as a child.' She was still fighting tears.

That raised more questions than it answered. 'Then why were you so anxious about the séance? Laurence said you were physically shaking.'

Poppy hesitated. 'I know I told you I don't believe in spiritualism, but it's hard not to get taken up in the moment. And in the past I've wanted to believe. Did believe, in fact. And I was ashamed. I promised my mum when she was ill that I'd get help with my addiction. I swore to her I'd beat it. I managed it for a while. For a year and a half after her death the promise kept me clean. But then it all started to fall apart again. I couldn't bear the idea of making contact with her, and her disappointment and worry.' She looked up at Eve, and the hollow grief in her eyes was hard to watch.

Whatever else was true or false, Eve was sure Poppy had loved her mother. Now she was lonely and grieving, battling her addiction. Eve's heart went out to her.

'That's why I was shaking.' Poppy took a juddering breath. 'It wasn't fear, it was sorrow. Laurence didn't notice I was fighting tears. And I'm certain now that Emory never managed to reach her and that was worse. The message he passed on was just to make me feel better.'

Eve found herself believing this version of events. It fitted and the raw emotion in her voice was convincing.

'Emory asked to have a private word with Laurence after we'd finished,' Poppy went on. 'That made me anxious at the time. I knew he wanted me to get help; to see someone about my problem. Although he wouldn't have given away my secret maliciously, I wondered if he might resort to telling Laurence in the hope that he'd help me. Laurence wouldn't understand a bit, but Emory wouldn't have got that.' She shook her head. She'd picked up her paper napkin and was twisting it in her hands. 'With the odd exception, he thought everyone was as well-meaning as he was, deep down. It made him act stupidly sometimes.' She tore the corner off the napkin, a sudden angry movement. 'Laurence sounded furious when Emory spoke to him. I could hear his tone but not their words, and my stomach was in knots; I was imagining it was his reaction to my gambling. And then Emory's voice rose too. I sat there feeling sick.'

'Emory told him?'

She shook her head. 'When I asked Laurence what they'd talked about, he said Emory just said he thought something was troubling me. Laurence saw it as interfering. He said he'd told him he was quite sure he'd know if there was a problem. And then he asked me if there was.' She gave a small, sad smile. 'Of course, I told him Emory had it all wrong. He seemed to buy that.'

How could he not notice when she was so obviously suffering? He might be a brilliant academic but he clearly sucked at life. And it was mean to get angry with someone who only had Poppy's best interests at heart. Unless that wasn't the real reason for his and Emory's cross words. Eve's mind went to their row on the village green again. Their quarrel at the hall could secretly have been a continuation of that argument.

'Have you tried going to anyone for help? Does your dad know what a difficult time you're having?' Eve was still wondering how she got the money to carry on. She couldn't be winning every time. No one ever did.

Poppy looked down, her hair falling over her face. 'Dad never picked up on my problem. He cares, but he was never around as much as Mum.'

It sounded as though Emory was the only living person who'd shared her secret. She was so alone. Eve's insides ached for her.

'I haven't managed to get help yet.' Poppy's shoulders rose and fell. 'I'm broke and out of control. I pinched one of Ada's knick-knacks recently to sell in a moment of desperation, when I needed to repay a loan. Can you imagine what she'd say if she found out?' She clutched at her red hair. 'To think that I lent Emory my savings to stop myself from gambling. With no spare cash, I thought I'd be able to beat the habit, and help Emory into the bargain. And ultimately, get an income from his thriving business, even. How wrong can you get? Thank goodness Laurence is paying the rent on my workshop.'

Poppy had her head in her hands and her voice was quiet when she spoke again. 'I didn't kill Emory to protect myself. And whoever murdered him must have attacked Coco too.' She glanced up, tears building again. 'You can't think I'd do that!' She took a deep breath. 'Besides, the evening of the séance would have convinced Emory that telling Laurence wouldn't help. Just mentioning I might be troubled made him angry. I heard him, don't forget.' She gulped. 'Laurence sounded spiteful, full of loathing. He can deal with physical illnesses all right, but you can forget other afflictions.' She blew her nose on the torn paper napkin.

Eve believed her – that she wouldn't kill for that reason. But she still didn't know what had happened the day Emory died. 'What did you talk about at Magpie Lodge, Poppy?'

For a second, Eve thought Poppy was going to blow up at her, but after a moment she shook her head. 'We discussed my gambling problem and my mum. That's why I was so upset.'

But Eve's radar was going off again. Poppy was back to lying, she was sure of it. It was something in her eyes, and in any case, her claim made no sense. Emory wouldn't have let her go off in tears after that. If she'd dashed out in her misery he'd have followed her. The witness would have seen them together, as Emory tried to comfort her. Eve was sure the scene had resulted from an argument, not a heart-to-heart. Each time she thought she was getting somewhere, Poppy threw her off course with more invented excuses. It was so frustrating.

In the end, she and Poppy decided to wrap their baguettes and take them away. Eve asked if there was anything she could do to help, but Poppy said she'd handle it 'when the time was right'. Eve wished she could believe her. From what she'd read, conquering addiction was one of the hardest things in the world, even if you had help. She'd want to check in on Poppy again to keep digging for the truth, but she'd like to offer support too, if she'd accept it.

As Eve walked back to her car she thought about what she'd learned. In theory, Emory had been an ongoing threat to Poppy, but he was no fan of Laurence's – she was sure he'd never have shared Poppy's private business with him. And she was convinced Poppy believed that too.

All well and good, but Eve couldn't forget her final lie about her talk with Emory at the lodge, nor the strange words and the look in her eye as she'd said them. *I liked him*, Eve had said of Emory. *I did too*, Poppy had replied. *I did, I did.*

She had once, Eve guessed, but something had set off an inner battle: one which had rocked her opinion of Emory after years of loving him like a father.

Eve couldn't ignore that profound shift. And Poppy had been scared enough to lie to the police. It was enough to keep her on the suspect list.

Eve couldn't rest until she understood Emory's final day.

30

As the tension of her meeting with Poppy fell away, Eve found she was ravenous. She ate her baguette in her car, parked on a side street in Blyworth.

Back in Saxford, she and Gus took a brisk walk down the estuary path, the wind finding its way between Eve's coat collar and scarf and biting at her chin and cheeks. As they walked home, they bumped into Daphne, Eve's neighbour on Haunted Lane, who paused to ask after them.

Eve gave her their latest updates, and within minutes, she'd been ushered into the living room of Hope Cottage, the home Daphne shared with her partner, Sylvia. It was seventeenth-century like Eve's, and slumped down on one side, as though it had finally found a comfortable resting position. All around were signs of her neighbours' professions. Daphne's glorious ceramics with their crackle glazes and intense colours – blues, greens and purples – sat on shelves in a studio area at the back of the open-plan room. Meanwhile, Sylvia's photographs were framed on the walls and sat in albums on shelves too.

It was Daphne's connections that had caused her to invite

Eve in. It turned out Poppy Rice's grandmother had been local and a ceramicist, just like Daphne.

'A fearsome rival,' Daphne said, smiling warmly as she handed Eve a cup of coffee. 'We used to exhibit at the same exhibitions across East Anglia. Poor Kitty, she was a wonderful character.' She shook her head. 'She died a couple of years ago now, at a ripe old age, but she had to deal with such tragedy. She had twin girls, but one, Lavender, died when she was only thirty in a skiing accident. And then the second – Poppy's mother, Helena – succumbed to cancer in her mid-fifties. Awful.'

The mention of twins sent Eve's mind straight to her own. The idea of losing either of them – and the pain they'd endure if one lost the other – didn't bear thinking about.

Sylvia joined them. She sat erect in an emerald-green chair, upholstered in velvet. Eve was on their peacock-blue couch. 'Kitty certainly had a tough lot.'

'Let me get us something to eat.' Daphne disappeared into the couples' tiny kitchen, cosy like a ship's galley, while Sylvia bent to make a fuss of Gus, her long grey plait falling forward.

Gus was a big fan of their neighbours, but although he rolled over as usual to let Sylvia tickle his tummy, he kept a keen eye on Orlando, the couple's marmalade cat. There was a long-standing animosity between them. Eve always felt Orlando had the upper hand. He was peering down his whiskers at Gus now, eyes half closed, expression superior.

Sylvia caught the direction of Eve's gaze, glanced at Orlando and laughed. 'Don't take any notice of him,' she said to Gus. 'You're only pandering to his ego.'

At that moment Daphne arrived back with a plateful of sloe-gin spice cakes; she must have picked them up at Monty's.

'I hope you're not sick of them,' Sylvia said.

Daphne raised her eyes to heaven. 'That's tactless. Who could be sick of anything Viv and Eve produce?'

Sylvia simply grinned and took one. 'I must say, they're the only thing keeping me going in this relentless cold.'

'We've been having them warm from the oven with a glass of brandy before bed,' Daphne said, blushing slightly.

'Sounds like heaven.' Eve made a mental note to try it herself and felt a tiny stab of envy. Their arrangement sounded so companionable. Robin's complicated past was much harder for him than for her, but just occasionally she found herself ruing it for selfish reasons. She'd love to be with someone she could relax with; to share happy evenings together or with friends, to walk up the beach openly – do all the things that other people did.

'So.' Sylvia gave Gus a final pat and sat up straight again. 'You want to know about Poppy Rice. And this is to do with the murder enquiry?'

Eve nodded. 'There was some upset between her and Emory the day he died.' She didn't want to mention the loan. She'd trust her neighbours with her life – they even knew about her and Robin, though not Robin's history. But the loan wasn't her secret to tell. 'The thing is, I saw her with Emory just days before he died and she seemed fond of him. And it was clear she had something to confide, too. She never got the chance to share it because Laurence interrupted them, but it was enough to make me think she trusted him.' She sighed and sipped her coffee. 'And yet it seems like something fundamental happened between them on that final day. I can't overlook it.'

Sylvia nodded. 'She's always struck me as rather vulnerable. I put it down to upbringing. Helena adored Poppy – they were very close – and after the sorrow of losing her twin, I believe she wanted to protect her from everything. A mistake.'

Daphne cocked her head. 'Though very understandable.'

Sylvia gave a wry smile. 'No doubt, but foolish. From what I've seen of Poppy, she hasn't learned self-preservation. She says yes when she should say no. Personally, I would have refused to come and live with Ada Rice for six months for a start. Saying "yes" to Laurence led to that.'

'We can't know the exact background,' Daphne said.

'I know, but from what I've seen of him I'm not a fan. He's very much like Ada, and that's not intended as a compliment.' She fixed her look on Daphne. 'You feel the same, admit it.'

Her partner sighed. 'I suppose he is a little standoffish. But I feel I shouldn't judge, without knowing him better.'

Sylvia turned to Eve. 'But I'm quite happy to. Some of my opinions are based on village gossip, it's true. But we knew from Kitty that Helena didn't approve of Laurence. He's as respectable as they come, of course, but apparently she told Poppy she didn't think he'd make her happy. And looking at her, I'd say she was right. She looks pinched and miserable. And far too clingy; as though she's leaning on him more than she ought.'

Eve had come to the same conclusion, of course. She took a mouthful of her sloe-gin spice cake. The rich liquor-soaked fruit helped her think. 'Poppy mentioned her mother when I interviewed her at Monty's. I gather she died three years ago?'

'It must be quite that now.' Daphne sighed. 'A year before Kitty. Such a tragedy when the children go first.'

'Do you know when Poppy married Laurence?'

Sylvia frowned. 'Around eighteen months ago. I wonder if she'd have gone through with it if her mother had still been alive. Kitty always gave the impression that Poppy listened to what Helena said; I think she might have seen sense. As it was, he got her at a low ebb. She was still grieving.'

Daphne shook her head. 'I think you might be right. After Helena's death, Poppy came to stay with Kitty for a bit and people in the village rallied round but none of them knew her well. She seemed very much alone.' It would have been a few months before Eve came to live in Saxford. 'Emory came to see her, though. I remember that. So many people in the village seemed to disapprove of him. There was always gossip about his "wild times" down in London. But he cared about the people he loved. Helena saw his true worth and asked him to be godfather to Poppy. The way he dashed up to Suffolk to comfort her showed she got that right.'

But they didn't know about the loan she'd given him. Of course, he might not have asked for it. Maybe the suggestion had come from Poppy; she said she'd wanted to invest her savings. But if so, Eve felt he should have turned it down. He'd taken too much of a risk. 'Do you know how Helena met Emory?' Eve was curious. The mix of rich, over-protective Helena and big-hearted but unreliable Emory seemed an odd one.

'I'm not sure,' Sylvia said, 'but I believe their paths crossed both here and in London. Their shared Suffolk background was a talking point. He was kind to Helena after her twin died.' She ate some of her cake. 'And of course, if you believe in such nonsense, he held out the possibility of contact with loved ones "beyond the grave".'

'I can understand people believing,' Daphne said, 'or at least, wanting to believe. I think I would.' Her eyes were on Sylvia, and they glistened slightly, making Eve feel emotional. 'It would be a tiny slice of comfort at the most dreadful time.'

'If it turns out I'm wrong, I promise to come back and haunt you,' Sylvia said, with a bark of a laugh.

'Oh you!'

'Do you think Helena believed?' Eve asked.

'I think she did,' Sylvia said, with a note of resignation in her voice. 'She brought Emory up to Suffolk to see her mother when Lavender died.' She turned her intelligent eyes on Eve. 'Nothing much was said about it, but why else would he visit her? Do you think Emory truly believed he could contact the dead?'

'I'm honestly not sure. I certainly think he faked some of the fortunes he told to pass on warnings, that kind of thing. And I suspect it was the same with some of his séances. He wanted to give comfort.'

'Either way, it sounds as though he had good intentions,' Daphne said. 'That was always my instinct too.'

'Did Emory know Laurence well?' Eve asked. Poppy had said not, but Eve wanted to get their take. She reached for her coffee as Gus shifted slightly at her feet. Orlando had left the room and he was relaxing.

Daphne frowned and looked at Sylvia. 'I don't think so?'

Sylvia nodded her agreement. 'I imagine that's probably right. Emory had left Suffolk by the time Laurence was born so there's been limited time for their paths to cross. As I say, Emory was around when Poppy came to visit after her mother's death, but Laurence didn't join her at that stage. I seem to remember they were down at the same time a couple of years ago though, but Laurence was busy socialising with his mother.' She raised an eyebrow. 'Why do you ask? Do you think he might have been involved in Emory's death?'

Eve shook her head. 'He was in a roomful of people at Rice and Fulton when Emory died and although I saw the pair of them quarrelling, he has no obvious motive. Besides, I can't really imagine him getting his hands dirty.'

'What a shame,' Sylvia said, taking another cake.

Back at Elizabeth's Cottage, Eve reviewed what Sylvia and Daphne had told her. She still had no idea what had caused the rift between Poppy and Emory, nor why Laurence had argued with Emory on the village green.

Eve shook her head as she dished up Gus's supper. 'I can only think that Emory or Poppy were on the point of sharing something that Laurence wanted kept private.'

But it must have been an odd balance of power, she reflected. Emory and Poppy could have told Laurence to go to hell, and got on with their private chat, yet they hadn't; not in Monty's anyway. Poppy might have wanted to avoid a public row, but it didn't explain Emory's reticence. It might imply that Laurence had some kind of hold over him.

The talk with her neighbours made her focus on Poppy's belief in spiritualism again. She'd admitted that she used to believe, and that less than a week earlier she'd still thought Emory might reach her mother. It had been enough to fill her with shame and anxiety. That all figured. Her grandmother and mother had believed in Emory's powers too.

Yet Poppy had claimed Emory had never tried to contact her mother before the séance at the hall, despite their obvious closeness. That couldn't have been down to shame. She said she'd managed to stop gambling for a couple of years – until six months after her marriage to Laurence, in fact.

So why hadn't she asked Emory to make contact, when it sounded as though he'd performed the same service for her grandmother?

31

That evening, Eve sat in the Cross Keys with Viv, warming herself by the fire. They were each part way through a venison-sausage casserole and well down glasses of Malbec. Eve had already updated Viv on the day's events, from her interviews with Roger Fulton and Poppy Rice to her talk with Sylvia and Daphne that afternoon.

'So you're still hot on the trail of Kelvin Brady, and the mystery over Poppy's final rift with Emory remains?'

Eve nodded. 'The other suspects seem less likely now, though I can't rule them out completely.' She kept her voice low. The attack on Coco was still having its effect. Half the village was in the pub, talking about it and Emory's murder.

'Moira says she dropped off flowers for Coco at the Dower House this afternoon,' Viv said, taking up her wine.

That figured. She'd be dying to know more. She must have got her customer-loathing husband Paul to mind the store. 'Did she see her?'

'Only her face at an upper-floor window. Moira says she looked terrified and darted away the moment their eyes met.' Viv lowered her voice slightly. The storekeeper was present, though not within earshot. 'To be fair, that could just be natural reaction to Moira's spying.'

Eve nodded. 'We've all been there.'

'But I've heard the same from another customer who dropped by,' Viv went on. 'Coco wouldn't come down. Apparently Selina says she went straight to her room when she got home and she hasn't come out since. She doesn't want to be alone in the house, either.'

'I guess that's understandable.' Eve would feel the same. She couldn't imagine the trauma, though she'd had some close calls herself, including in her own home. For a second, memories flashed through her head, but she pushed them away. Coco's state left her in a difficult position. Another interview would be ideal, but it sounded as though she needed some space and Eve would seem like a ghoul if she tried to talk her way in. On the upside, she'd already heard what Coco had told the police, thanks to Robin.

She was distracted from her thoughts by the appearance of Brenda Goody and Kelvin Brady, over near the bar.

'Brenda looks awful,' Viv said. 'Poor thing.'

Eve wished she had someone other than Kelvin to cheer her up. How would she cope if it turned out he was a killer? And was she safe? His row with Emory played on her mind, along with the guarded way his old employers had spoken about him. If he'd been sacked, then why? He'd been competent and friendly according to that review on Trustpilot. Maybe it was something that came to light later. What had Emory known?

Across the room, in a corner, Eve spotted Ada Rice was in too. Once again, she had Poppy and Laurence in tow. Perhaps she couldn't face cooking if she was still doing the lion's share of the work at Rice and Fulton. Eve doubted Laurence would offer to take on any of the domestic burden.

Brenda Goody was watching them, Eve noticed. Or at least,

staring in the opposite direction to Kelvin. She looked uncomfortable.

When she got up to go to the loo, Eve excused herself and decided to follow her. She wanted to know how she was doing, and to check she hadn't any worries about her lodger.

The ladies' was empty except for the two of them. Eve was out first and waited for Brenda to emerge from a cubicle, though she knew they might be disturbed any minute.

When the woman started washing her hands, Eve greeted her. 'How are you bearing up?'

Brenda's hands were twisting under the running tap. 'Not great, if I'm honest. It's still so hard to accept that Emory's dead and the attack on Coco is such a shock.' She chewed her lip and moved to the hand dryer.

'You seem anxious.' Eve stood closer to her. 'Is there something worrying you?'

Brenda shook her head. 'There is something on my mind, but it's no good, it doesn't fit. I was just thinking about Poppy, and how young women get involved in the most unsuitable relationships. It reminded me of something Emory said... He was worried—'

But at that moment Ada Rice came in and greeted them and Brenda clammed up. Within seconds she'd exited the loos. Eve followed her out.

'Ignore me. It makes no sense,' Brenda muttered, and before Eve could press her she'd re-joined Kelvin.

'Is she all right?' Viv asked, as Eve slid back into her seat at their table.

'I'm not sure. I thought she might be worried about Kelvin but it seems Poppy's the one on her mind. Something about her relationship with Laurence, and Emory being concerned.'

'I guess that makes sense. Emory must have seen what a rotten husband Laurence is; he would have been anxious. And you said yourself they'd argued more than once.'

Eve nodded. 'But I don't see how that sheds light on the killer's identity. I'm just wondering if Brenda knows more than we do. But whatever her idea was, she's decided it doesn't work for some reason.'

Eve couldn't figure it out, and gradually, as they finished their wine, her thoughts went back to Kelvin. He and Brenda had risen to leave and he was helping her on with her coat.

Eve overheard Brenda thanking him and wondered how she felt about returning to Sycamore Cottage. Maybe they were out because home was a painful place to be, with such harrowing recent memories.

It made her visualise Brenda's house with its cheerful and comfortable décor. She guessed it would never feel the same again.

And in that instant, with images of the house in her head, her thoughts drifted back to the odd photographs Emory had taken of its interior. Suddenly she had an idea.

'Oh my goodness; I think I might have worked out why Emory had all those weird photos of Brenda's house on his phone.' In her memory, they formed into pairs. Why hadn't she noticed it before? But they were all in different folders by date – not grouped that way.

Spot the difference. It had to be… 'Do you mind if we settle up with Toby now? I need to get back to work.'

32

The following morning, Eve stood outside a store called Peggy's Curiosity Shop in Little Mill Marsh, a down-at-heel village inland from Saxford. She'd found the store by googling; last time she'd visited the area, its unit had been boarded up. Eve couldn't help wondering if the new occupier had chosen the right premises. The store sat between a small supermarket with a 'Bargain Booze' poster in the window and a bookmaker's, which looked several degrees tattier than the one Poppy Rice had visited. It was the fourth store she'd called at that day, but also the least successful-looking. She'd been feeling discouraged, but something told her she'd found the right sort of place this time.

Once again, Eve pictured the photographs Emory had taken of Sycamore Cottage. Sometimes more than one of the same room. Some had been taken two years back on his previous visit, some during his most recent stay, after the arrival of Kelvin Brady. One was of an empty room, which had seemed bizarre. It made much more sense now she'd realised each photo was one of a pair: spot the difference, just like she'd thought the night before. Once again she cursed herself for not realising sooner, but it hadn't been that obvious. When Emory took the first pictures, he'd simply been recording a pleasant visit to his old child minder. They'd been framed to show her, not the objects in the background.

But it was the objects that were significant. Eve understood that now. Ones that were present in the photos two years ago, but missing in the most recent lot. They all looked special and exotic; mementos Brenda and her husband had collected on their travels, perhaps. Of course, Brenda might have sold them if she'd been short of cash, but there was every indication she was well off. So what had happened to them?

It was a puzzle, but the only theory Eve had come up with was that Kelvin had taken them and Emory was onto him. She frowned. If she was right, Brenda must have noticed the pieces going missing. How had Kelvin got round that, or was Eve simply wrong? But the theory explained the photos, and Emory's row with Kelvin the Friday before he died. Perhaps he'd challenged him, firmly believing he was up to no good. His next move would have been to try to prove it to Brenda. But she imagined he'd never got that far.

It was Eve's responsibility to take over where he'd left off.

When she pushed on the door, the young man behind the counter, who had dark hair tied back in a ponytail and bright dark eyes, leaped eagerly to attention. This place was less impersonal than the others she'd visited and she felt instantly guilty. Maybe she should buy something small. Her eyes ran over the shelves. They had a bowl full of antique marbles, which appealed. Eve had a selection back at Elizabeth's Cottage, stored in one of Daphne's crackle-glazed bowls. (Viv had been delighted when she'd spotted them, calling them one of Eve's 'weird and rare weaknesses'.)

Eve took four up to the counter, wondering what on earth she was doing. If she had to pay twenty pounds each time she wanted information she'd be broke.

The man smiled at her. 'An excellent choice. I love these myself.'

Transparent sales talk.

She hoped he'd be more honest when she asked her questions. 'I wonder if you can help me.' She peeled off a glove and took a printout of one of Emory's photographs from her bag. She'd blown up a section of it, enlarged to focus on Brenda's ornaments. 'I wondered if anyone's been in to offer you this item?' She pointed to a carved dark-wood figure. It was hard to pick out the details – the picture was a little pixilated – but it was clearly a woman in traditional Japanese dress.

The young man frowned and shook his head. 'It's a lovely piece, but it doesn't look familiar.' A note of anxiety crept into his voice. 'Are you police?'

'Oh no!' Eve tried for her most reassuring tone. 'A friend owned it and several other collectables, only I understand they were sold on. No one seems to know where they ended up, but I always rather liked them. I thought I'd try locally in case I can pick one up before it reaches its next buyer.'

'Right...' He was chewing his lip, his eyes wary.

She wasn't surprised he didn't believe her. She could have done with a better excuse for asking.

'What about this bronze bust?' Eve showed him her next photograph. 'Sorry, you can only see half of it. I never had a photo that included the whole thing.'

The young man's eyes changed as he bent to look this time, and he flinched slightly – a contraction in his frame. 'No. No, I haven't seen that either.' His smile was fixed now – painted on.

He leaned forward, took the remaining photos from Eve and shuffled through them swiftly. He wasn't even looking at them now. Too worried about giving himself away, Eve guessed. 'No, sorry.' He handed them back to her. 'I hope you manage to track them down elsewhere.'

She took a deep breath to combat her adrenaline. She bet

he'd given into temptation and taken the bronze without asking too many questions. The proceeds would probably pay several months' rent.

Eve felt utterly helpless. She was sure he was lying, but there was nothing she could do about it. It was possible Greg Boles could dig deeper if she asked Robin to pass on her suspicions, but would he take her seriously when the team were so busy? She had no proof and there was the obvious question: if her guesses were correct, why hadn't Brenda challenged Kelvin?

Maybe he'd told her he was taking the pieces to have them cleaned. Something like that might do it. It wasn't sustainable long-term, but he might be planning to do a flit at any moment. Maybe he'd have gone already if it hadn't been for Emory's death. Whether Kelvin had killed him or not, disappearing overnight in the aftermath, along with a load of valuables, was enough to trigger a full-scale manhunt. Eve guessed he was biding his time, but if she was right, he was working against the clock. Sooner or later, Brenda was bound to ask after her possessions.

A sinking feeling pulled at Eve's insides. She'd need to contact her about her suspicions. How on earth could she broach the topic?

She was about to leave when she noticed an odd flat circular object on a shelf. It had letters and numbers around the edge and she wondered...

'It's an antique ouija board,' the man said, following her gaze. There was a pack of tarot cards next to it in a decorative box. 'I've got a special interest in the occult.'

It was more believable than his marbles passion. She could see the spark of enthusiasm in his eyes. A thought occurred to her. She took out her phone and showed him the box she'd found at Magpie Lodge, with the strange markings and grid pattern on its lid. 'You don't know what this is, do you? I wondered if it was something for fortune-telling, though it might be a game. It had counters in the drawer you can see there.' She indicated with her forefinger.

The man was still twitchy, but after a moment he answered. 'Looks like a museum piece. You could be right about the fortune-telling; I'm not sure. If you'd like to bring it in?'

'It doesn't belong to me.'

His look shut down. He was probably back to thinking she was an investigator of some kind. 'I see. Well, I must get on.'

Eve took her marbles back to the car and thought about the implications of everything she'd heard.

Based on the storekeeper's body language, she was convinced her theory was correct: Kelvin had stolen from Brenda, and Emory had guessed the truth, though, like Eve, he'd had no evidence. She thought it through. His first move had likely been to raise the issue with Brenda; he could have asked after one of the missing treasures maybe. But if Brenda was in denial, she'd probably explained it away. Trotted out whatever excuse Kelvin had given her. How would Emory have reacted to that? Eve imagined the lack of concrete evidence would have held him back. He'd have been anxious for Brenda, but keen to maintain their friendship. If he upset her too badly, she might have refused to see him. So then perhaps he'd confronted Kelvin at the Cross Keys. Tried to get a confession most likely, but Kelvin had been aggressive and refused to admit to what he'd done. Ultimately, in the absence of proof, Emory had warned Brenda obliquely, via the fortune-telling session. Eve was sure his next move would have been to do what she'd done that morning, only he'd been busy, leading a ghost tour, performing a séance, confronting Selina and falling out with Poppy. He was killed before he could get any further.

If she was right, Kelvin had a massive motive. Up until now, it seemed he'd outrun whatever illicit activities he'd been caught up in, but Emory would have put a stop to that.

Eve tried a couple more antiques stores on her way home in the hope of finding concrete proof. It was possible Kelvin had sold Brenda's valuables on to more than one outlet to avoid arousing suspicion, but she got no further with her enquiries. The people she spoke to looked genuinely blank. Now she'd thought of it, she showed them her photos of Emory's mysterious box too. They each agreed the item looked 'special' and one of them muttered about a 'museum piece', just like the man at Peggy's Curiosity Shop.

On her way back into Saxford, Eve paused at Sycamore Cottage. Her plan was to claim she needed to follow up with Brenda on the obituary. She'd suggest tea at Monty's while they talked, to get her away from Kelvin for a short time. But the house looked shut-up, the windows dark, and when she knocked on the door there was no reply. She wrote a note asking Brenda to call and posted it through the letter box, but as she parked by the village green she still felt twitchy.

Before she got out of her car, she texted Robin to explain what had happened and suggested Greg might like to talk to Brenda again. It had to be worth a go. She was frightened for her.

33

Eve still felt anxious as she let herself back into Elizabeth's Cottage, but there was nothing more she could do about Brenda for the time being. She tried to focus on the box she'd found at Magpie Lodge instead, mulling over the words of the antiques traders she'd spoken to that morning. A museum piece... It suggested a new plan of action and she decided to text her son, Nick. He had lots of contacts at museums and galleries in London, thanks to his arts centre job. They tended to fetch up on the same fundraising courses.

Nick messaged back in seconds with contact details for a woman he'd met at the British Museum. He referred to her as

> the lovely Fi. But you'd better address her as Dr Prentice. She won't mind you emailing. She loves a challenge.

She texted back, with a winky emoticon.

> You seem on very good terms.

He replied with a blushy face.

Might be more to tell, one day soon.

Eve felt a warm spark of interest as she replied again with some hugs.

After that she composed a carefully worded email to Dr Prentice, saying she'd come across the box in a ruined house. (That couldn't be counted as dishonest. The lodge was a ruin.) She confirmed she'd informed the police and that it was in their hands now, but she was curious about the box's origins. She didn't want to say anything that might put her off Nick.

She called Robin next.

'*I've contacted Greg about Brenda,*' he said, before she could ask.

She breathed a sigh of relief and felt her shoulders relax a little. 'Thank you. I can't work out how Kelvin managed to take all those valuables without her protesting, but I'm pretty certain he did. If she discovers he's a thief, she might be in danger.'

'*Don't worry, he'll bring that up. He'll pass it off as a question sparked by a village gossip.*'

'That's me.'

'*A very useful one.*' She could hear the smile in his voice. '*He's grateful – they had no idea. So, what's next for you?*'

Eve explained about her research into Emory's box. 'Other than that, I'm going to focus on Poppy Rice. Apart from Kelvin, she's the only person still surrounded by unanswered questions.'

'*I wouldn't write Roger Fulton off. Even if he visited Emory earlier in the evening, he could have gone back to kill him later. He left the front door open. And I still think it's possible Selina lied to protect him.*'

'I take your point, but I think his anger would have worn off by then. If he was going to attack Emory, surely he'd have done it in the heat of their argument? Instead, he went home and talked to Coco who reassured him that she was still committed to going to Bathurst. I'm guessing that would have placated him.'

'*Unless something extra happened to send him over the edge. What if he'd found out about Selina two-timing him with Emory while they were engaged?*'

'True...' But Eve still didn't believe it. She was sure Roger had no idea Coco might be Emory's. He'd sounded fond but exasperated when he'd talked about her. There'd been no undercurrent.

'*So what's your plan with Poppy?*'

'Sylvia and Daphne have got me thinking. They had Emory and Laurence down as nodding acquaintances, nothing more, but my hunch is they're wrong. It doesn't fit with the argument I saw them have on the green. And Poppy said Laurence sounded furious when she heard them exchange words at the hall. You don't usually feel that kind of intensity with someone you barely know. On top of that, Poppy looked shifty when I asked if they ever socialised. She denied it, but I think she knows something about their connection, whatever it is.'

'*You think they might have met on a previous visit?*'

'It's possible. It sounds as though they overlapped in Saxford a couple of years back. If they ever met privately, I'm guessing it was most likely at Emory's lodgings.'

'*Do you know where he stayed?*'

'Not yet, but I'll ask around. Moira might know. I'll bet it wasn't at the Dower House, given his poor relationship with Roger and Selina. And I never got the impression he'd stayed at the lodge before.' Maybe he'd managed a cheap B & B; he'd been giving the odd talk back then. 'If I can find out, I might visit and see if anyone remembers seeing him and Laurence together. I've got no idea if it will help, but I'm certain there's more to uncover.'

After Robin had wished her good luck, she called Gus, ready to walk him to Blind Eye Wood. 'And we'll stop at Moira's on the way home,' she told him. He looked crestfallen. The hooks outside the village store weren't number one for canine entertainment. 'But only for a minute. Just a minute.'

It was still cold outside, but at long last a thaw was in progress. Before the ice there'd been days of rain and now the huge icy puddles, collected in ruts in Heath Lane, were starting to unfreeze. But the temperature was only just at melting point. The thickest bits would probably take days to thaw, especially if everything froze again overnight.

Moira beamed when Eve entered the store, bringing the prospect of news. Eve asked for a bottle of Shiraz and let her down gently.

'I'm afraid I haven't heard anything new.' Nothing she was willing to share, anyway. 'I'm actually after your knowledge, Moira.'

The storekeeper's smile, which had been fading, burst forth again. 'Well, of course I'll help if I can.' She rang the wine up on her old-fashioned cash register. 'If there's anything I can do to unlock the case...' They were alone, but she leaned forward and lowered her voice to a whisper. 'Don't worry. I won't say a word. You know me. I'm always discreet.'

Eve tried to keep a straight face and explained what she wanted to know.

Moira's brow furrowed. 'Yes, Emory did tell me. I asked him when he came in during that visit.'

It figured.

'Don't worry; the name will come to me in a moment. It was one of the pubs in Blyworth. I remember wondering if he was hard up at the time because the place has a bit of a reputation. One wouldn't choose to stay there. Something about a moon?'

'The Blue Moon?'

'That's it!' Moira beamed.

Eve had walked past the pub recently. It looked like a dive. 'When you say the place has a reputation?'

Moira gave Eve a conspiratorial look. 'It might just be gossip, but I've heard the landlord breaks the licensing rules. And that he isn't above taking a bribe!' Her eyes gleamed as Eve thanked her and turned to leave the store.

34

By the time Eve finally reached the Blue Moon in Blyworth she had Robin with her. She'd called him with an update after Moira's stories about the pub's landlord.

He had news too, but it wasn't reassuring. Like Eve, Greg had got no reply when he'd called at Sycamore Cottage and no more luck when he'd tried Brenda's mobile, though he'd left a message, asking her to call. A neighbour said she'd gone to Ipswich for the day with a friend and no one knew where Kelvin was. Greg had had to leave it at that.

Eve and Robin sat in Eve's car, looking at the Blue Moon's lacklustre exterior. Its pebble-dashed front had been painted navy blue but Eve guessed that had been several years ago now. The colour had faded and peeled off in places.

'You're sure you're happy to come in?'

Robin grinned. 'Wouldn't have it any other way. I doubt any Saxfordites will be around at this time of day.' It was only half past four and most of them stuck to the Cross Keys in any case, but it would be good not to bump into anyone associated with the case. 'We can keep an eye out, but I'd like to join you. I'm curious about the dodgy landlord.'

Eve relished the idea of a joint venture. She hadn't been nervous of going on her own, but openly entering a pub with him felt good. She shook her head inwardly. How many people would consider a brief outing to a run-down dive in Blyworth a treat? For a moment she allowed herself to fantasise about a parallel universe where the network of corrupt police officers he'd crossed had never existed. Though without them, of course, they'd never have met. Robin would still be back in London.

As she put her hand on the brass doorplate of the Blue Moon, nerves tickled her stomach. She sighed and entered the dingy pub. She bet the accommodation was grotty, but she could imagine Emory preferring it to staying with his brother. All those family tensions...

The carpet in the bar had a swirly blue pattern and the walls were blue too. What with that and the bar's dark wood the place was depressing. The wall lights were art deco in style, with orange shades. If they'd been in Eve's house she'd have taken them down and given them a good clean around a decade earlier.

The landlord was a large balding man with abundant grey whiskers, wearing an aging suit that somehow made him look more disreputable. Amusement lit his eyes as Eve and Robin walked towards the bar. He could tell they were out of place, Eve guessed, and was looking forward to having some fun at their expense.

There were a number of drinkers already present: a group of men who looked past retirement age in one corner, hunched round a newspaper, discussing something. Another mixed group looked up at a television on the wall which was showing a game show.

'We'll get the young ones in later with our special offer.' The landlord grinned and pointed at a notice advertising cocktails for £2.50. A suspiciously good deal around there. They probably went heavy with the mixers and very light on the spirits.

'I can imagine that pulls the teenagers in,' Robin said.

The landlord gave him an impassive look. 'I chuck out all under eighteens, of course. We're very strict here, aren't we, Jimbo?' He glanced at a man sitting further down the bar, who laughed.

'Absolutely. Kids round here know not to try it on.'

'What'll you have?' the landlord asked. 'Or are you here to make trouble?'

'Not at all.' Robin scanned the beer taps and asked for a half of some bitter Eve had never heard of.

'And a Coke please. Designated driver.'

'Plus whatever you're having,' Robin added.

The look in the landlord's eyes changed to something warmer. Eve imagined he'd reassessed the way their talk might pan out. Moira had said he was reputed to take bribes. Maybe he was anticipating one now, with the offer of a drink as a lead-in.

'Horrible weather we've been having,' he said. 'Wouldn't mind joining you. Something to keep out the cold.' He helped himself to a double whisky.

Eve proffered her credit card before Robin could beat her to it. The marbles she'd bought in Peggy's Curiosity Shop floated through her mind. Her expenses were mounting up but *Icon*'s fee was decent and the investigation was important. Each night Emory's friendly face filled her head. She wouldn't rest until she found out who'd robbed him of his future.

Eve took a photo from her bag. They'd agreed there was no point in beating about the bush.

'We wanted to ask about this man.' She showed him the picture of Laurence Rice. She'd found it on the Bathurst website – an informal shot from their social pages of him and

Poppy at a garden party. It looked more recent and representative than his official mugshot. 'We know you know him.'

She was bluffing, of course, but she sensed it was required. If the landlord detected weakness, he was definitely the sort to take advantage.

He raised an eyebrow. 'So what if I do? He hasn't been in for a while though. I only remember him because he was so stuck up. Wait a moment, is this about last Sunday? What are you? PIs?'

'Interested friends,' Robin said. 'I don't suppose we could talk in private?'

The man sighed heavily and turned to call over his shoulder. 'Lily!'

A young woman with blonde hair piled high on her head appeared from behind the scenes.

'Take over here for a minute, will you, love?'

'Sure.'

The man called Jimbo perked up. He was offering to buy Lily a drink as Eve and Robin followed the landlord to a back room.

'We're not interested in what happened on Sunday,' Eve said, though that was a lie. 'But why did you link this man' – she pointed to the photograph of Laurence – 'with Emory Fulton's murder? Did he visit while Emory was staying with you?'

The landlord sank onto a floral-patterned couch and motioned for them to sit too. 'How d'you know he lodged here? The police haven't asked about it. How's it even relevant? I like to keep things simple. Anything for a quiet life, that's me.'

'A mutual friend mentioned it.' Eve could understand him wanting to avoid police scrutiny. She imagined the place was full of underage drinkers come happy hour, and that might not be the only dodgy dealings at the pub. 'This won't do anything to threaten your peace and quiet. I just want to know if this man, Laurence Rice,' she showed his photo again, 'met Emory Fulton when he took a room here.'

The landlord frowned. 'It was a while back. You expect me to remember?' He looked expectantly at Robin.

'If you're not sure, don't worry,' Robin said. 'There are other people who'll know.'

The landlord slumped in his chair. 'I was hoping we might share at least one more drink.'

'If you tell us something useful, we'll probably want to celebrate.' Eve felt sour inside. He wasn't the kind of man who deserved favours, but in reality, there wasn't anyone else they could ask, despite Robin's bluff. And Eve *really* wanted to understand the connection between Laurence and Emory. It might not be relevant to the murder, but her gut told her it was important.

At last, the landlord sat forward and rubbed his hands. 'All right. I'll throw myself on your mercy.'

He took the photograph of Laurence and Poppy from Eve and jabbed his finger at each of them in turn. 'Both came in here, they did. Two years or so back when Emory Fulton came to stay. Not together, I don't mean. I had no idea they were an item. But I remember.' He peered at Poppy, with her dazzling smile and shiny red hair. 'She stuck in my mind because she's so beautiful.' He shook his head. 'And him because he was up himself. What are they? Married?'

Eve nodded.

'What a horrible notion. Right, well, anyway, she came in one afternoon and went to meet old Emory Fulton in his room. I remember him, of course. Wrote those ghost books. He was always on the telly at one point. The wife liked to watch. She's into that kind of stuff.

'Anyway, that woman came in and I remember how nervous she seemed. Nervous but excited. I wondered at first if she was Emory's girlfriend but he hugged her and it didn't look like that.

More like he was a favourite uncle or something. And she seemed relieved on her way out. A lot more relaxed, smiling.' He shook his head. 'Very pretty.

'But here's the odd thing. While she was upstairs with that Emory, this man here' – he pointed at the photo of Laurence – 'came into the bar. He was hiding himself in a corner behind a newspaper. I'd swear she never saw him as she left, but the moment the door closed behind her he was up at the bar, asking to speak to Emory Fulton too.'

'He asked for him by name?'

The landlord nodded. 'Yeah, but I don't reckon Emory was expecting him. I showed him up and when Emory answered the door he looked blank. But he let your guy in all right, once he'd given his name.'

Eve couldn't imagine what it all meant.

'And here's the pièce de résistance.' The landlord grinned. 'Something that has to be worth a whole bottle of whisky.' *Hmm.* 'A day later, the redhead came back. She looked nervous all over again. She was in with Emory for longer this time, and by the time she came out she was in tears, but they were happy tears. He hugged her again and he looked emotional too. I remember that.' He licked his lips. 'I was wishing I could give her a cuddle as well.'

They bought him another drink, while Eve fought the urge to squirm until they'd left the pub.

35

Early on Saturday morning, Eve walked towards Fairview Hall again, with Gus in tow. It was just above freezing and everything around her was dank and grey. Ice remained in most of the puddles she passed. Under her coat, her plum-coloured woollen trousers and Fair Isle sweater helped keep the icy draughts at bay.

Her destination seemed necessary. The image of Coco being carried away from the Dower House, flailing on the stretcher, still haunted her. Visiting the scene was like an exorcism. The notion brought Emory to mind.

But although she was preoccupied with the Fultons, thoughts of the Rices worked their way to the surface again. Poppy and Laurence had been on her mind all night. She'd spent most of it awake and when she had finally slept she'd dreamed of the hue and cry who'd hunted the boy Elizabeth had hidden. Their footfalls had seemed so real, but it wasn't surprising. Everything was in turmoil at the moment. Her mind was bound to be disturbed. She marshalled her thoughts again.

Poppy had adored her mother, Helena. They'd been very close, according to Sylvia.

And Helena had disapproved of Laurence, so much so that Sylvia doubted they'd have married if Helena had lived. Eve wondered if she'd thought it had been a marriage of convenience from Laurence's point of view. Wedding the daughter of Bathurst's vice chancellor could be seen as a shrewd move.

Eve imagined Helena's reservations had weighed heavily on Poppy's mind after her mother's death. Even if Laurence had swept her off her feet – he was exceptionally good-looking – she might still have had doubts. Accepting his proposal would have been going against her late mother's wishes.

Eve had paused when Gus did, in response to an exciting rustle amongst a patch of snowdrops. The flowers quivered and she held his leash tightly as her mind continued to run over the facts. In front of her, the scene faded as she searched for links. Suddenly she realised Gus was tugging her forward again, an impatient look in his eye.

'Sorry, buddy. My mind's so full.'

They walked on.

Eve was almost at the Dower House now. She'd chosen one of the main tracks through the wood. There was no one about and she'd got no intention of taking risks, even in daylight. She felt a lot more exposed than she had when she'd come to look at Magpie Lodge. The attack on Coco made a difference.

There were lights on downstairs at the Fultons' home. The upstairs rooms were in darkness, but Eve could see movement at one of the windows. A faint outline, the hint of Coco's long, platinum-blonde hair. As Eve walked on, she glanced over her shoulder, but Coco hadn't moved.

Eve wondered if she was keeping a lookout, thinking her attacker might come back for her. What did she know, that had made her a target? Once again, Eve wished she could set up another interview, but she couldn't think of a good excuse to worm her way in when Coco was living like a recluse.

As Eve switched course towards home, choosing a different

track for variety, Gus trotted ahead eagerly, off his leash, drawn to the sound of a robin flitting from branch to branch in a holly tree.

'Way out of your reach, Gus,' she said, but he ignored her.

Her mind returned to Laurence and Poppy.

Why had Poppy decided to marry Laurence? They didn't seem happy. It was almost as though Poppy could feel Laurence slipping away from her. And he seemed to be tolerating her at best. Maybe he *had* asked her to marry him for the wrong reasons.

And had Laurence had some hold over Emory, such that he'd break off his meet-up with Poppy without protest?

If so, it sounded as though Emory and Laurence had been keeping a secret from her.

Gradually, some terrible thoughts were coalescing.

Eve thought back to past conversations with Poppy. She'd admitted she'd believed in Emory's gift until recently – and claimed she'd sat in on one of his séances. She'd said it was when she was a child, but how likely was that? Would Helena have let her back then, when she might have been frightened? Now she thought about it, Eve couldn't imagine it for a minute. Her neighbours had said how protective Helena was.

So... so maybe Poppy had lied. Perhaps she had taken part in a séance with Emory as an adult, before the one at the hall. And who was she most likely to contact? Her mother, surely, despite her denials. She said she hadn't wanted to face her at the latest séance because of her gambling, but she'd managed to break the habit for two years after Helena's death before starting again.

Eve imagined Poppy, turning up to see Emory at the Blue Moon, excited but nervous. Had she asked him if he'd perform a séance so she could ask for Helena's blessing before marrying Laurence? Her mother had been dead for a year. Laurence had wooed her and Poppy had fallen in love, but in the background were Helena's words of caution. If Poppy believed in Emory's powers, wouldn't she have been tempted to try to get her approval? Suddenly, Eve was certain that's what had happened. Poppy had been keen to marry, but unsure of Laurence. Maybe she'd sensed he wasn't quite as passionate about her as he made out.

Laurence had picked up on Poppy's plan somehow. Maybe she'd admitted she was going to see her godfather and he'd guessed her intent. He probably hadn't known where Emory was staying, so he'd followed Poppy to the pub, then sneaked up to see Emory.

And when Poppy visited again, for the séance itself, Eve imagined, she'd come out so happy she was in tears. Then, six months later, she'd married Laurence.

It was after that that things had gone downhill. Eve imagined Poppy's gradual realisation that Laurence wasn't the charming companion that he'd seemed, followed by her descent into misery. She'd still have been grieving for her mother and her father had probably been too busy to provide support, even if she'd felt able to go to him. His chummy relationship with Laurence might have made it feel impossible. After six months of marriage, despairing Poppy had started to gamble again.

If Eve was right, Emory had been in a position to control the situation from his room at the Blue Moon. He'd had the casting vote on the marriage: the power to make or break Laurence's future. And Poppy's.

Then came the worst question of all. Why had he helped Laurence? He hadn't known him back then. A cold chill settled in Eve's core as she caught up with Gus.

There was only one conclusion she could come to: Laurence had paid Emory to tell Poppy that her mother approved.

Emory was still fond of Poppy, so he'd had a go at Laurence on the village green – maybe because he could see she was unhappy. And Laurence had got angry. If he'd really paid Emory, he'd probably been confident his secret was safe. Emory couldn't reveal what he'd done without admitting his own part in the deception.

Eve thought of Poppy leaving Magpie Lodge in tears the day he'd died. She was starting to think Emory had told her then. Maybe he couldn't live with the guilt. Perhaps he wanted her to know her mother hadn't really approved the marriage; that she ought to feel free to cut and run if she was miserable. He'd passed on that message obliquely during the séance at the hall – telling her her mother was thinking of her. She'd support her whatever she did.

Heck. It was one almighty betrayal.

She tried to imagine Laurence's feelings, back when he'd got proof of why Poppy had visited Emory at the Blue Moon. He'd have felt betrayed. Angry. Poppy hadn't loved him enough to accept him without her mother's blessing. And Emory – a man he regarded as a fraud – had the temerity to act as gatekeeper. Even though he'd done what Laurence wanted, Laurence probably still despised him. It would explain the tone of voice he'd used when they'd spoken privately at the hall.

Eve felt sick, but a moment later she was pulled out of her spiralling thoughts.

Gus had run well off the main track while her mind was elsewhere. Now he was standing rooted to the spot, close to a path that wound its way between a thicket of holly and hawthorn.

He was whining. There was something about the sound that reminded Eve of Coco's hoarse cries after someone had tried to strangle her.

Her palms went clammy, her breath short as she went to join him, bending to comfort him – or maybe herself – as she stared at what he'd seen.

A body, face down to one side of the path.

For a second, Eve's brain refused to process what she was seeing. It was as though a fog had descended. It was too awful to be true. But Eve recognised the hair and as she moved to one side, her legs shaking, the terrible truth rose up like a wave, making the blood rush in her head.

Brenda Goody lay on the ground in a thick padded coat, her arms and legs flung out at odd angles. Her hat had fallen off and was near her body. Her neck was bruised, her lips blue.

Eve sank to the ground next to her with a feeling of utter hopelessness. It was too late. There was nothing she could do.

36

Two and a half hours later, Viv opened Monty's door with a look of horror and ushered Eve straight through to the kitchen. Eve could feel people's eyes on her. They must know she'd found Brenda's body. She was late for her shift; the second time it had ever happened.

'What are you even doing here?' Viv said, as soon as they were out of the teashop's main room. She wore the look of a strict but kindly parent. 'If you think I'm letting you work a shift after what's happened you've got another think coming. The lovely Lars is filling in and Sam and Kirsty are back for the weekend.'

Sam was Viv's university-going son and Kirsty his girl-friend. They were both old hands at Monty's.

'They must love coming to visit.'

Viv tutted. 'Hard work is good for them.' She steered Eve to a chair. 'How are you?'

She still felt stunned – as though someone had punched her in the stomach. 'I feel so guilty. I was worried for Brenda yesterday and I tried to reach her, but not hard enough.' She filled Viv in on the previous day's developments. 'I should have kept on knocking at Sycamore Cottage at intervals. If I'd caught her—'

Viv put an arm around Eve's shoulders. 'It's no good thinking like that. You couldn't know she was in immediate danger.' She moved to make them a pot of tea.

A minute later she was pouring their drinks. 'Espresso cakes for strength? If they won't make you sick.' She frowned and put a couple on a plate, pushing it tentatively under Eve's nose as she sat down.

The smell, usually so appealing, made Eve's stomach turn. She'd have to wait a bit before embarking on them. The truth sat like a lump in her stomach. She should have been able to prevent Brenda's death. It was heart-breaking. Hopelessly, she imagined being able to turn back the clock.

No good.

She sipped her tea and tried to focus on the news she could pass on. She wanted to get the details straight in her head. She had to find out who'd done this – who'd hurt such a kind and innocent person. It was the only contribution she could make.

'What news from the police?' Viv asked.

'They already knew I was worried about Brenda, but Greg Boles never managed to reach her either.'

Viv squeezed her shoulder.

'They think she died last night, sometime between eight and eleven. I'm guessing the killer was confident the woods would be deserted – it was so cold. People's fear probably kept them indoors too.' Everyone had been jittery since the attack on Coco.

Eve leaned her elbows on the table, her head in her hands. Had Brenda been on to Kelvin? Going off with a friend for the day made Eve wonder if she'd been avoiding him. Yet it seemed to be Poppy who was on her mind when they'd spoken at the pub.

'And how was Palmer?'

'Awful as usual. He wanted to know why I'd chosen to walk to the Fairview Estate rather than round the village. He virtually implied I had something to do with the death, even though Brenda had been there overnight. He's still obsessing over the fact that Emory gave me money before he died.'

'He's such a pea-brain.'

'I know. I found it hard to focus on what he was saying. My mind kept straying to Brenda. She'd had such lot to contend with recently, what with poor Emory. And then to be saddled with a false friend like Kelvin...'

'Too true. Do you think he's guilty?'

Eve frowned. Robin had called just before she'd come out. He'd wanted to make sure she was okay, but he'd had information too. 'He claims he stayed home at Sycamore Cottage all evening, according to the gossip – from the time Brenda got back from Ipswich until this morning. But a neighbour says the house was in darkness from around eight onwards.'

'Very suspicious.'

Eve nodded, her head full of regrets. Why hadn't Brenda called her or Greg? Eve supposed she'd been tired after her trip, then distracted, maybe, by her errand or appointment in the woods – whatever it had been. And she was just the sort to decide it was too late to bother people and she'd call in the morning...

'If my conclusions are correct, Kelvin had every reason to kill Emory to stop his secret getting out and Brenda could have clicked and met the same fate. I still don't know how Kelvin got away with taking her belongings in the first place.' She closed her eyes for a moment. 'I gather he's had to vacate Sycamore Cottage but I'm sure Palmer will have told him not to go far. As far as I'm concerned, he's one of two prime suspects now.'

'Two? With a motive for both killings and the attack on Coco?'

'I guess anyone who killed Emory could have had a motive

for the other two. Emory was close to both Coco and Brenda; they probably knew things about him no one else did.'

'Okay, good point. So the second suspect is still Poppy?'

Eve nodded. 'Brenda mentioned her to me in the Cross Keys the day before yesterday. She looked worried. Something about unsuitable relationships, and how Emory was concerned. And now I think Poppy had a much stronger motive for killing Emory than I'd realised.'

Viv's blue eyes opened wide. 'What are you talking about?'

Between tentative mouthfuls of the bitter-sweet espresso cakes, Eve told Viv what she'd discovered about Poppy and Laurence's meetings with Emory at the Blue Moon, and what she'd guessed.

'Blimey,' Viv said, after she'd finished. 'You think Emory would have done that?'

'I don't *want* to think it, but he was perpetually short of money.' She'd had to remind herself that she hadn't known him well. Likeable people could be flawed. That was a pretty momentous flaw, though.

'And what about the other suspects you had for Emory's murder?' Viv said. 'Roger and Selina. Are they back in play?'

She'd never totally written them off and it was too soon to know about alibis for Brenda's murder. 'It's not impossible. I guess someone must have persuaded Brenda to meet them at the woods and that was likely someone she trusted – or at least that she didn't suspect. Roger or Selina could fit, but I don't really believe it. There are too many arguments against – assuming it's one killer.

'If it's two, that's different. Kelvin could have killed Brenda to protect his secret and Poppy could have murdered Emory in an act of revenge, then tried to silence Coco if she thought she was a threat. That's assuming my deductions about their motives are right. But it's a huge coincidence if the two deaths are unrelated. Something tells me Emory's murder led to the attacks on Coco and Brenda.'

Viv nodded.

'I'd say Kelvin's most likely. I suspect he's been involved in crime for years, which might make murder less of a leap. But it would have been odd for Brenda to meet him in the woods, given they share a house. He could have invented an excuse to get her there, I suppose. Told her he'd found something, maybe? Or that something odd was going on at the Dower House and he wanted an extra witness. He might have left Sycamore Cottage before Brenda got back from Ipswich.' Sadness gripped her again and she forced herself to focus. 'It certainly sounds as though the house was in darkness once she left. Maybe her phone records will help. Her killer might have called to set up the meeting.' But in reality, Eve doubted it would be that simple.

'Well, I hope the police come up with something concrete,' Viv said wryly. 'Half the people in here still maintain this is Dorothea Landon and Mildred Kirby's revenge on the Fultons.'

'What would they have wanted with poor Brenda?'

'Gwen Harris was saying she was in the line of fire because she worked for the descendants of Eustace Fulton, even though its apparently common knowledge that he was a killer. A few people are saying they'll refuse to talk to the police, because it would count as helping the Fultons. They think it might incur the wrath of Dorothea and Mildred's spirits.'

Eve felt tired. 'Please could I have another cup of tea?'

37

Back at Elizabeth's Cottage, Eve lit a fire and sat down on the rug with Gus. She didn't want lunch after all the cakes. Instead, she cuddled her dachshund and stared into the flames. When tears took hold, she forced herself to snap out of it. She'd got no business wallowing in self-pity. She needed to find an answer. She owed it to poor Brenda.

She had to speak to Poppy again. Eve was convinced she could get her to talk if she faced her with the guesses she'd made that morning. She called her and – after some resistance – got her to agree to a walk on the beach a little later on.

After that, she took her phone from her pocket to check her emails.

Nick's Dr Prentice at the British Museum had been in touch. She'd passed the photo of Emory's box on to a colleague who ought to be able to help. The man in question was copied in. She said she was hoping to see Nick again soon. It was a light spot on a dark day. Eve googled her. She looked friendly and sparky with clouds of dark hair; Eve could see why Nick was keen.

A moment later, Robin called.

'*Are you okay? Sorry, stupid question. Can we meet tonight? I can sneak over to yours if you like.*'

'That sounds great. What's the news from Greg?'

'*The woman who went to Ipswich with Brenda says they spent the afternoon in the cinema.*' It explained why Greg hadn't got through when he'd called. It was such tragic bad luck. '*The friend dropped her back home at seven. Her family confirm she was back with them by seven fifteen, so that ties in.*'

And the house had been in darkness by eight. It probably explained why Brenda hadn't returned Greg's call, or made contact with Eve. It looked like she'd rushed out again an hour after she was back.

'*And Roger and Selina both have alibis. They were at home with Coco at the Dower House and the chairman of the trust visited. They got chatting apparently, so he didn't leave until late.*'

'That's that then.' The alibi sounded solid.

'*They've interviewed Kelvin Brady again; told him a neighbour's confirmed Sycamore Cottage was in darkness from eight o'clock. He claims he went to bed early with a headache. He says he knew Brenda had gone out, but he had no idea she'd failed to come home. It would have been nice if they could face him with theft charges too. Greg thought your story was worth following up and by the look of it, you were right. Uniform went to talk to your man at Peggy's Curiosity Shop but the place was locked up. No answer from the number on their website either.*'

'Heck, I must have put the wind up him when I visited.' Palmer would be livid. Thoughts of omelettes and breaking eggs drifted through her mind. 'So Kelvin's free.'

'*For the time being. Greg wants to interview you about the antiques.*'

'That's something. I tried to tell Palmer but he wouldn't listen.'

'*Figures. He's checked Poppy Rice's alibi, by the way. She's still Palmer's top suspect and no one can vouch for her. Officially they were all at the hall, but they weren't in the same room and the place is cavernous. She could easily have slipped out. I might have more by the time we meet this evening. I'm looking forward to it.'*

'Me too.'

Eve hung up. The latest information left Kelvin and Poppy looking most likely. Neither of them had alibis for either of the murders or the attack on Coco.

She was noting the latest details on her spreadsheet when her ringtone sounded again and a number she didn't recognise appeared on the screen.

'Eve Mallow.'

'*It's Coco Fulton.*' The young woman tried for the same cocksure tone she'd had the last time they'd met, but a tremor ruined her performance. '*I wondered if we could meet again. Not out in the woods.*' Eve could hear the fear in her voice. '*Could you come to the Dower House? My parents are here, but maybe we could talk upstairs?*'

'Of course.' She took a deep breath. *At last.* The need to see Coco face to face had been nagging at her. She might pick up something the police had missed. 'Now?'

'*Yes. Please.*'

Eve didn't imagine she used the word often. She glanced at her watch. She had time before she was due to meet Poppy. 'I'm on my way.'

It was Roger Fulton who let Eve in. He leaned forward conspiratorially, as though they were old friends.

'Did she tell you what she wanted to talk about, Eve? Only Selina and I are very concerned. She's barely been downstairs since the attack, and she won't confide in us.'

'I'm afraid she didn't say, Roger.' It was just too tempting. 'If she mentions anything significant, I'll encourage her to share.' But not necessarily with her parents. Eve wasn't going to promise that. Selina, Roger and Coco were all behaving as though Coco was in her teens, not her late twenties. It couldn't be good for any of them.

Roger showed her to Coco's rooms. The young woman looked terrible: pale, the bruises on her neck yellowed but still shocking, her eyes wide and red as though from lack of sleep. Eve remembered the sight of her staring out of the upstairs window early that morning and wondered if she'd been there all night. Maybe she was too scared to let go.

Coco shut her sitting-room door on Roger and stood there for a full half-minute. There was silence at first, but at last came the sound of retreating footsteps.

Coco's room was expensively kitted out; she'd brought warehouse-style living into the grand old Dower House. Industrial pendant lights hung from the ceiling and the wall lights had black metal mounts and cage shades. Everything was in shades of grey or black. It jarred with the style of the house, but she could understand Coco putting her mark on her space. Maybe she'd even paid to kit it out herself, if she'd managed to save money from her bar jobs on all those gap years. The room smelled of a cloying perfume Eve didn't recognise.

Coco motioned Eve to a seat and took a pack of cigarettes from the pocket of the long, trendy jacket she was wearing.

'I'm taking advantage. Smoking indoors is sanctioned until I feel up to going outside again.' Her hand shook as she lit up. 'Do you want one?'

Eve shook her head. 'No thanks. Lovely flowers.' There was a bouquet sitting in a vase which had probably come from Rice and Fulton and clashed with Coco's aesthetic.

The young woman pulled a face. 'From my pathetic lovelorn ex. You understand. You've seen him.'

Eve hoped he saw the light and found someone else.

'Mum mentioned you've written about murder victims before Emory,' Coco said, taking a drag of her cigarette. 'And that you're known for investigating.'

Eve waved the smoke aside automatically, but turned it into a gesture to wave aside her words. She wanted to build bridges with Coco, not offend her. 'I've had a bit of luck in the past. I suppose it's inevitable that I'll occasionally stumble across something useful. I end up interviewing the same people as the police.'

Coco leaned forward, her blue eyes focused on Eve's, her hand shaking again. 'I want to know what's going on. I haven't left the house since I came home from hospital and when I ask my parents they tell me to think about something else! As if I could. The police have said nothing but they must have an idea of who attacked me. Especially after the latest murder.' She didn't mention Brenda's name, Eve noticed. 'What have you heard? I'm going crazy up here, not knowing. There must be gossip. Suspicion.'

Eve thought of the people who'd decided that Dorothea and Mildred's ghosts were at work. 'Nothing useful. But if it was Emory's killer who attacked you, they must believe you know they're guilty. Or that you have information that could lead to the truth. You don't have any idea yourself? The police can help, if you do.'

Coco shuddered so that the ash fell from her cigarette onto the rug at her feet. 'No. No idea at all.'

Eve paused. 'It might be worth giving it more thought. I know you're scared. Have you even been outside since your mom brought you back from hospital?'

Her look was hostile. 'Would you?'

'Probably not. But I'd be racking my brains to work out why I was a danger to the killer. It would be the best way to stay safe.'

Coco ground her cigarette out angrily in a minimalist black

ashtray. 'There's nothing I can tell the police or you. I'm tired now. I'd like you to go.'

Eve's irritation at being dismissed, just as easily as she was summoned, was compounded by Roger Fulton. He dogged her heels as she left the house, hoping for information.

But as her frustration subsided, uneasiness took over. That shudder of Coco's when Eve asked if she had any idea who'd attacked her. The tremor of fear.

Eve had a strong feeling that Coco wasn't just remembering the attack, but the attacker. In which case, who was she protecting, and why?

38

Eve walked back from the Dower House, picked up Gus from Elizabeth's Cottage and made straight for the beach.

Poppy hadn't been keen to come out when she'd called her, but at last she'd agreed to the meet-up. Eve had chosen a public spot for safety. The beach was rarely empty on a Saturday afternoon, even in winter. Eve had wanted somewhere that gave them privacy, but not so much that Poppy would present a threat. Guilty or not, Eve hoped she'd talk. Gus's presence might help; he tended to ease tensions. He was dashing after the ball she'd just thrown him, smart in his tartan coat. Eve was desperate to put her theory to Poppy. If she was right, the jeweller had a much stronger motive for murder than she'd previously realised. In theory, Eve could imagine her doing it. She needed to watch her eyes as they talked to judge how deep Emory's betrayal had cut. The thought made her shiver, nerves gripping her stomach, but there was another dog walker not far off, and a gaggle of teens shoving each other and laughing. Poppy couldn't try anything without a band of witnesses.

At last Eve spotted her, walking over the heath towards the beach, her red hair caught by a fierce gust of wind.

'I wanted to ask you about Emory again,' Eve said as soon as she got near. 'About the day you met him in the Blue Moon pub in Blyworth. You asked him to make contact with your mother, didn't you? It was only natural to want her approval before you married Laurence.'

She could see from Poppy's eyes that she'd got it right.

'How did you...' Her sentence trailed off and tears came. The moment she started crying, Eve's shoulders dropped and she released the breath she'd been holding. Poppy was devastated but not furious. To Eve, that said she was probably innocent.

'I'm sorry. You must have been under so much strain. Let's walk.' She indicated up the beach. 'I don't have to put any of this in Emory's obituary. It's just that I tend to stumble across unexpected information sometimes, in the course of my research.'

Poppy was hesitating. Eve reckoned she was desperate to offload. It was human nature. She'd been bottling up so much for so long.

She took a tissue from her bag and clutched it tightly as she dabbed her eyes. 'All right. But you're right – I don't want any of it to go into your article. I need to think.'

'I understand. I can use it to inform what I write without including the details, or disregard it completely if you'd prefer.' Eve didn't like glossing over the truth, but Poppy had the upper hand. If Eve didn't make the promise, she likely wouldn't tell her anyway. This way the information might at least help the murder enquiry.

'So you wanted your mother's approval before you married Laurence?' Eve had to raise her voice against the wind. 'I can understand that. I set a lot of store by what my mother says.' Eve was close to both her parents. She missed them badly. Seattle was such a long way away. 'Emory made contact with your mother when you asked?'

Their eyes met. 'That's what I thought at the time, but I didn't lie to you. You asked me if he'd ever tried to contact her when we first spoke, and I said no. That's because he never did. I know that now.' She took a juddering breath. 'It was all a pretence. But how did you know I'd asked him?'

'Various things people said. The timing of Emory's last visit here. Someone who'd seen you with him at the Blue Moon. It all came together.' She couldn't bring herself to admit the lengths she'd gone to to get at the truth. 'So Emory told you your mum gave her blessing?'

Poppy stared out at the sea, gunmetal grey. Her words were quiet when she answered. Eve had to strain to hear them. 'Yes. And I believed him.'

Eve took a deep breath. 'Did he confess, the day he died? Was that why you were upset outside Magpie Lodge?'

Poppy stifled a sob. 'That's right. I'd gone to confide in him. Laurence has been... well, our relationship isn't...' She looked up and met Eve's eyes at last. 'Our relationship isn't going well. I've been working at it, doing my utmost. Because even though I thought Mum had given us her blessing, I knew she'd been full of doubts when she was alive. I didn't want to admit defeat, having gone ahead and married Laurence anyway.' She was crying again now. 'I could always talk to Emory. He really listened and I felt I could trust him completely, but I was wrong. When I told him I thought Laurence despised me – that he was putting up with me at best – I guess the guilt got to him. After I'd poured out my heart, he admitted Laurence had asked him to intervene on his behalf – and that he'd lied about making contact with my mother.' She took a great breath. 'He didn't hold anything back. He said he'd already decided we ought to marry before Laurence approached him. He thought my mother had been overprotective and it was clear I was in love.'

She shook her head. 'He didn't seem to realise that although I was bowled over by Laurence, I wasn't actually sure. If I had been, I wouldn't have asked for Mum's approval. He just decided what was best – thought he knew. But how *could* he? He'd hardly met Laurence before that! And when Emory told Laurence he was sure my mum would give her blessing, Laurence slipped him some money. Several hundred pounds, apparently. He told Emory it was a thank-you present.

'Emory admits he should have refused it, but he'd already made up his mind. He said he saw it as helping a couple of love-birds and he couldn't deny the cash came in handy... I could see he felt wretched about it. But how could he?' She blew her nose. 'It was so... so arrogant!'

Gus was dashing alongside them, caught up in a frenzy by the wind, tail wagging, ears flapping, oblivious to their conversation.

Eve found Poppy's question impossible to answer. She'd never have believed it a week earlier when she'd been starting to get to know the man. 'It seems extraordinary. I hadn't got much beyond first impressions, but I liked him.'

'He thought he knew best,' Poppy said. 'He might have seemed laid-back – and he was in his own life. Everything slid. But he intervened when he thought someone he loved was making the wrong decision.

'At the time I was too angry to be rational. I called him a money-grubbing, heartless cheat and stormed out of the lodge in tears. But later that evening, sitting in the dark on my own at home, I realised he was probably telling the truth. He was kind. He did so many stupid things, but I never saw him being callous or ruthless. He was good-hearted but' – her eyes met Eve's – 'he could be phenomenally stupid at times. He didn't see the consequences of his actions.

'I never got the chance to apologise for what I said to him.' She sounded utterly desolate as she pushed her hair out of her eyes. 'He shouldn't have done it, but it was true about Mum being overprotective. I guess she was worried about Laurence's motives, though she never admitted it. But he wasn't the only man she'd objected to and Dad didn't raise any concerns.' She bit her lip. 'Then again, he's never been very present. He cares, deep down, but his focus is always on work, and Laurence fits right in there.'

She put her hands over her face. 'If the police discover the truth, I expect they'll arrest me. What a motive! And I was furious. But when Laurence called, I really was in the house. I let the phone go to the answerphone because I was curled up in a darkened room crying, not because I was out killing Emory. Laurence told me to say that the call had connected and we'd spoken. He didn't think they could prove it was a lie once we'd wiped the answerphone and he didn't want a scandal.' She laughed suddenly, harsh and wild. 'What a joke!

'I can't forgive *him* either, for going to Emory behind my back, and I can imagine what he thinks of me. Even if he loved me to start with the rot probably set in the moment he realised I didn't worship him enough to marry without my mother's blessing. He'll have hated that. But he went ahead in spite of it all. And that's probably because of my dad and his position.'

'You haven't had it out with him? He doesn't know Emory came clean?'

Poppy shook her head. 'I couldn't work out how to tackle it. And if I do that's it. We'll break up. I don't know how I'd cope with that. What would my father say? Laurence is his rising star.'

As Eve walked back home, Poppy's words floated in her head. She felt desperately sorry for her now she understood everything, and anxious too. It seemed she'd lost whatever confidence she'd had. Eve's anger at Laurence bubbled inside her. And she believed Poppy. Her initial fury, then hours cooling off and a miserable evening licking her wounds at the hall made sense. If she'd been angry enough to kill at any point it would surely have been when Emory had broken the news at Magpie Lodge. The idea that Poppy would digest what had happened and then coolly decide to drown Emory at Sycamore Cottage made no sense. It was time to focus on that rat in human form, Kelvin Brady.

39

Back at Elizabeth's Cottage, Eve did some supper preparation, ready for Robin's visit, then settled down to write up her notes. She was deep in thought when her mobile rang. She glanced at the screen and answered.

'Robin?'

'*I'm on my way over but I've just seen something interesting in Blind Eye Wood.*' His tone was grim. '*One Kelvin Brady, entwined in the arms of a smart-looking woman of around sixty in an expensive coat with shoulder-length blonde hair. It was all I could do not to intervene. I can't imagine this is a new relationship since Brenda died.*'

Eve felt the anger heat inside her too. 'Are they still there?'

'*Yup. I can just see them through the trees. They're about a hundred yards from Heath Lane, close to the burned oak.*' The tree had been struck by lightning, leaving it with a cleft running vertically down its trunk.

'I might approach from the other side.'

'*I'll keep watch from this end. If you need me, I'll be here. Either way, I can join you once you've done your stuff.*'

A minute later, Eve and Gus were walking through the moonlight, he in his tartan coat, she in her chocolate-brown one.

Brenda had certainly thought Kelvin was fond of her. They'd kissed – were in a relationship as far as she was concerned. But Kelvin wasn't only stealing from her, it looked as though he'd been two-timing her as well. What if he had a string of women? He might be stealing from all of them. If Brenda had found proof of that he could have killed her.

Her heart beat faster as she and Gus pounded along the pavement. The dachshund seemed to understand the urgency. He trotted along rather than pausing at his usual spots. Eve went more cautiously as she approached Heath Lane. She wanted to see the couple without being seen. If she went in all guns blazing, she'd never get the information she needed.

There was a sleek white Audi parked by the side of the road, tucked in amongst the trees. As Eve passed by, she spotted an expensive-looking black umbrella with a chestnut handle on the parcel shelf, next to a pair of men's leather gloves. If the vehicle belonged to Kelvin's lady friend, it looked like she was married. Eve had already guessed as much. Why else would they hang around in a bitterly cold wood? It was the kind of thing she and Robin were driven to, for heaven's sake. Hardly ideal. Once again the need to act like guilty lovers triggered a twinge of frustration, tight in her chest.

'There's no justice in this world,' she murmured to Gus, then put a finger to her lips. He knew that signal and gave her a tired look. She bent to stroke him before stepping quietly into the trees.

A moment later she could just pick the couple out. A shaft of moonlight penetrated the leafless trees and the woman's hair gleamed. Brenda's eager face filled Eve's mind: her delighted reaction when Eve said Kelvin seemed nice. She could understand Robin's anger; she felt a hot fierce fury in her chest too.

There wasn't much to learn from watching the pair. They

weren't talking – it was all physical – but they wouldn't be long, Eve guessed. This was no night for making love out of doors. She imagined this was a quick assignation to tide them over until something more relaxed was possible. Maybe they had to wait until her husband was away.

Sure enough, Eve was numb but not yet in pain from the cold when the couple broke up. Eve could see Kelvin's roguish grin. A warning sign if ever there was one.

Eve followed the pair as they walked to the edge of the woods; she reached the lane a little east of where they did. At the road, Kelvin gave the woman one last surreptitious kiss, laughing when she flinched and glanced over her shoulder. And then he was gone.

Eve fought the urge to chase after him. Her feelings were at boiling point, but she knew it made more sense to talk to the woman and she'd need to hurry. She did own the Audi; she was unlocking it now.

'Excuse me.' Eve caught her as she opened her door. Gus helped by gazing up at her and wagging his tail. 'I think I saw you with Kelvin Brady just now?' She ploughed on before she thought better of it. 'I'm sorry. I can imagine you might not want to hear me out, but I interviewed him and his landlady recently for an article I'm writing. I've found out quite a lot about him since then. I think you might want to know.'

'Who are you?' The woman was edging back, ready to get into her car despite Gus's appealing look. Eve wasn't really surprised. She'd do the same.

'My name's Eve Mallow. I'm writing Emory Fulton's obituary. You probably know he was killed in the house where Kelvin's been staying.'

'I don't see what that's got to do with me.' She was lowering herself into the driver's seat, the door almost closed.

'You've probably heard that Brenda Goody, Kelvin's land-lady, is dead too. She believed she and Kelvin were in an exclusive relationship and I'm convinced he was stealing from her. I think I can get proof.'

The woman had pushed the door further open again, ready to slam it, but at Eve's final words she paused.

'I just wanted to warn you. If you've noticed anything going missing recently, it might be worth considering whether Kelvin could have taken it.'

The woman's face was white in the moonlight. It took her half a minute to answer. 'I have. A gold watch I keep on the dresser. I only wear it for parties. I'd been meaning to have a thorough search. I thought it must have slipped down the back or into one of the drawers.'

Or possibly into Kelvin's pocket...

Eve had expected to meet with more resistance. For the woman to protest that Kelvin would never do such a thing. But it wasn't happening.

'You don't seem that surprised.'

The woman got out of the car again. 'It never crossed my mind that Kelvin had taken it, but I always had the impression he was a bit wild. I wasn't sure what I was dealing with, but I'm afraid that was part of the appeal. Life's not as exciting as it used to be. I was seeing him for kicks.' A regretful smile crossed her lips, but it was gone as she focused again, to be replaced by hard anger. 'If he's got that watch! It was a present from my husband. I mind about it, and he's bound to ask where it is sooner or later.' Then suddenly her eyes opened wider and her face blanched. 'What did he take from his landlady?'

'An assortment of valuable artefacts from around the world, a statue from Japan, a bronze bust from Africa and several other things. Are you all right?'

The woman's hand was shaking slightly. 'Oh no. They were in his car once when he gave me a lift. I've only just put two and two together. He said they were on loan for some exhibition a friend of his was arranging. I didn't think anything of it at the time – just that he had hidden cultural depths. I found it attractive. Intriguing. Dear God.'

That explained his gambit. It was as Eve had thought – a short-term fix. He must have planned to run out on poor Brenda before she became suspicious. Without Emory's death he might have got away with it. Maybe Brenda would have felt too sad and humiliated to speak up. But Eve imagined he'd had to delay his plans: running away with stolen goods straight after a murder wouldn't have been smart. But it was still entirely possible he'd killed Emory to keep his secret, even though the timing was terrible. He was clearly a hateful, ruthless man, and he'd have been desperate. Eve's insides knotted in fury at what he'd done.

The woman's eyes focused on Eve. 'I'm sorry, what was your name again?'

Eve repeated it. The woman held out a hand which Eve shook. 'Jemima Smithson.'

Jemima Smithson. *John Smith...*

40

Standing opposite Jemima Smithson, the thoughts Eve had been having moments earlier about Kelvin's possible guilt faded. She had a feeling she might have stumbled across his alibi for the night of Emory's death.

'You didn't meet Kelvin briefly last Sunday evening did you? Sometime after nine?' She held her breath.

The woman looked at her sharply. 'Yes. Here again.' She sighed. 'Another brief liaison. How did you know?'

'It was the night of Emory Fulton's murder. Kelvin spent most of the evening in the Cross Keys but he admits he nipped out at one point. Rumour has it, he told the police he was with someone called John Smith, an old friend whose mobile number he didn't have.'

'Ah.' Her look was sour, her mind still on the watch, Eve guessed. 'At least he had the good grace to keep me out of it.'

'You weren't with him last night as well, were you?'

Her shoulders went down. 'Yes, I was. My husband was down in London at an old school reunion. Kelvin was with me until around one. He wouldn't stay. Too scared of being caught, I suppose.'

Eve let out a long breath. So he was in the clear for Brenda's murder too. It all fitted. He'd probably told her he'd get an early night when she set out for her walk. Then off he'd gone to Jemima's for a few hours of passion. But he'd have wanted to be back at Sycamore Cottage by morning to cover his tracks. If Brenda found out he was two-timing her it would have been the end. He'd have been out of his comfy home and she'd have asked for her valuables back. Maybe he'd hoped to keep her sweet until Emory's murderer was found and he could make off without raising a manhunt.

'I don't want the police to know he was with me,' Jemima said. 'He's taken me for a fool. I don't see why I should destroy my marriage to prove his innocence.'

Eve could understand that.

'Thank you for warning me,' the woman added. 'I'll keep an eye out for the watch in the local antique shops.'

As Eve watched her drive away, Robin appeared at her elbow and was mobbed by Gus. 'Interesting discussion,' he said, bending to make a fuss of the dachshund, then standing to kiss Eve.

'You heard it all?'

He nodded. His eyes glimmering in the moonlight. 'Nice to know that particular revenue stream's been cut off. Shame she won't be going to the police, but maybe Greg can use official channels to get more out of the guy at Peggy's Curiosity Shop.'

The thought of Kelvin sweating in a police interview room was more than appealing.

Eve and Robin crossed the road to the woods on the other side. It was best to approach Elizabeth's Cottage via the estuary path, rather than through the village. If they were seen arm in arm it would set tongues wagging.

Minutes later they were walking next to the Sax, heading inland, the inky water snaking its way past them towards the sea.

'So Kelvin's out of it.'

Eve nodded. 'He has to be. Jemima Smithson alibis him for both murders. The police think Brenda died between eight and eleven on Friday night and even if they were out by a couple of hours, I can't see Brenda heading off to the Fairview Estate mid-evening then hanging around until one.'

'Nor me.' He pulled her close. 'I'm sorry; it must have been awful, finding her body. She was such a gentle soul. I hope she never discovered what a nasty piece of work Brady is.'

Eve squeezed him back. 'Me too. And I can't bear what happened to her. I have to find out who did this, Robin.'

He kissed the top of her head. 'You'll get there.'

'It's not feeling very likely right now. I'm out of suspects.' She told him about her talk with Poppy. 'It doesn't prove anything, but to me she doesn't fit. The method of killing and the timing's all wrong. It has to be someone who was utterly determined and ruthless. Anyone who was simply hurt and angry would have had to sustain that feeling until Emory was at Sycamore Cottage. I just don't see it. Anything fresh from Greg?'

'The police think Brenda probably went to her rendezvous on the back of a call from an unregistered mobile. The killer covered their tracks. Kelvin says he asked Brenda where she was going, but she said she'd tell him later. She must have set out almost immediately after the call, so she didn't have much time to confide in any case.'

'Maybe the caller told her they'd got information on Kelvin. She wouldn't have confided in him then.'

'Could be.'

'There's nothing more?'

Robin shook his head.

Eve felt she'd hit a dead end until they reached Elizabeth's Cottage and she checked her phone. An email had arrived from the British Museum about Emory's box.

Robin uncorked the bottle of wine he'd brought as Eve put the black olive and chicken casserole she'd prepared back into the oven to reheat. There was a rustic loaf of olive bread to go with it.

'So what does the email say?' Robin poured them each some of the Chianti.

Eve scanned the message. 'The upshot is that it's a game that became associated with fortune-telling and a person's destiny. It sounds akin to senet but rarer, and it was first found in ancient Egypt.' Eve felt a buzz as she remembered thinking it looked similar. 'Dr Prentice's colleague says he'd be happy to advise the police and that he could tell us more if he saw the box in person. He says it's unlikely to be original – if it were, it would date back to around 1300 BCE. But he does say it looks old and even if it's a replica it's probably very valuable. A modern-day reproduction of that quality would be worth thousands, apparently. If it's a few hundred years old, we can probably multiply that to tens or even hundreds of thousands.'

She took the glass Robin held out to her as she scanned the last of the message. 'He says its rightful owner is likely to be someone with an interest in ancient Egypt, as you'd expect.'

'Anyone spring to mind?'

For a second, her mind was blank, but then a tiny flicker of memory lit a far corner of her brain. Goosebumps rose on her arms as his eyes met hers. Wasn't that Laurence Rice's field? When his mother and Selina had been point-scoring at the fundraiser Selina had mentioned it. He was up for a post as the head of some exclusive academic society for Egyptologists and, as his father-in-law was one of the trustees, he'd probably get it.

She explained to Robin.

'So Emory might have stolen it from Laurence.' He was leaning against her worktop, his brow furrowing in concentration. 'When he visited Fairview Hall to perform the séance, perhaps?'

'It's possible. But how could he have sneaked away with it? It wasn't small. Unless Emory had a bag big enough to take it. And if he did steal it, surely Laurence would have noticed. Yet he's said nothing to the police, I presume?'

'That's right. No one has. If it's valuable, Laurence might keep it hidden away, I suppose, in which case no one might have spotted that it's missing. But then how would Emory have found it in the first place?'

Eve wrinkled her nose. 'I agree. It doesn't make sense. And how does it tie in with Emory's murder? If he was handling stolen goods, it would be a big coincidence if it didn't relate to his death.'

'Absolutely.' Robin frowned. 'Let's take it step by step. In that household, Ada and Laurence have alibis for Emory's murder. Ada was at Rice and Fulton all evening, and Laurence joined her at around eight forty-five. Assuming it's all one killer, they're out of it, whatever the truth about the box.'

Eve nodded. 'But Poppy isn't. And my assumption that she's innocent is based on her motive. She's produced surprise after surprise in this case. What if she had another reason to want Emory dead? What if Poppy stole the box?' Eve could see her doing it more easily than Emory. Her opportunity was better, and she was in the throes of addiction. She needed the cash. Eve tried to work it through in her mind. 'I could imagine her trying to sell the box, but not how it might have ended up with Emory. He had no money to buy it.'

'Could he have cottoned on to what she was up to? Maybe he took it from her to protect her, and hoped he could convince her to give it back.' He was frowning, sipping his wine. 'She could have broken into Magpie Lodge to look for it. If so, we know she never found it. After that, maybe she visited Emory at Sycamore Cottage to try to persuade him to give it back so she could sell it on. Maybe she killed Emory in a fit of fury when he refused. Or he could have tried to blackmail her. He was short of cash too.'

But Eve shook her head. 'I'm sure he wouldn't have tried to capitalise on her misery like that. And she couldn't have paid him anyway.' Eve knew she'd never rest that night. The question and the details would be tumbling in her head like tickets in a tombola. 'But he might have insisted she return it. That could have made her desperate enough to lose control.' Maybe she'd gone too far to pull back, as Robin had once suggested.

'I think I should go to the hall tomorrow,' she said. Meeting Robin's eyes, she held up a hand. 'We keep coming back to Poppy. Maybe this time it's best to get her on home territory. Having the others around might turn up the pressure. Don't worry. I'll make sure I'm not alone with her.'

41

Eve had been right – sleep was hard to come by on Saturday night. Her mind continued to wrestle with the puzzle of the box.

It made her impatient to speak with Poppy, but she ended up frustrated. The talk would have to wait until Sunday afternoon. Ada and Laurence Rice were at church that morning; Eve had seen them cross the green. Their presence meant Poppy was likely home alone, which was no good. Eve wanted a private conversation but not one where she was isolated.

Her plan was to call at the hall and ask for Poppy specifically. It was handy that she was supplying Monty's with jewellery; there were plenty of excuses she could come up with for a private talk. Chatting alone, but within earshot of the others, would be perfect.

Eve had already walked Gus down to the sea. He was now sprawled on a rug next to the radiator in the sitting room, and made no protest when she prepared to leave without him. She could relate. The rain was lashing against the ancient casement windows, the sky outside lowering.

'I won't be long.' She bent to cuddle him.

She was almost knocked sideways by the wind as she walked along the Old Toll Road. Her red umbrella just about stayed up if she pointed it into the blast, but concentration was required. Turning it sideways meant it blew inside out.

She passed Sycamore Cottage, the rain pelting down on its roof, and felt a wave of sorrow crash over her. Poor Brenda. The weather matched Eve's mood: a sort of thrashing anger, gusty like the wind. The rain came down like a torrent of tears. The birdbath Eve had spotted on her previous visit had filled with water. Rivulets ran off the snowdrops and cyclamen. Everything was battered by the fall.

As Eve walked on, a strange pricking sensation came over her: that feeling that she was missing something. Something small – possibly meaningless, but something that jarred, nonetheless.

What was it?

She couldn't trace the feeling's root but it stayed with her as she walked on. At last, she turned off towards Fairview Hall. Ordinarily she'd have taken one of the main tracks but walking amongst the trees was tempting. There was a lot more shelter from the wind and rain. She could give up the battle with the gusts and put her umbrella down for a bit. Her hat would keep her dry enough.

It meant she approached the hall via a new route and before long she found an alternative way into its grounds: a side gate in an ivy-clad brick wall. She could make for that rather than using the grand front entrance.

She'd just walked through the gate, onto Ada's land, when she caught movement, over to her left. Some distance from the hall, screened by a row of conifers, was an outbuilding: an old barn by the look of things.

Eve felt a shiver of surprise. Making her way towards it, with repeated glances over her shoulder, was Coco Fulton.

Eve stepped back against the wall so that she was hidden by

the evergreen leaves of a large viburnum. Peering round, she saw Coco take one last glance behind her and go into the barn.

What the heck was going on? She'd only seen Coco at a distance, but her body language was clear enough. She wasn't just being secretive, she was afraid too. Eve wondered if this was the first time she'd left the Dower House since she was attacked. What was compelling enough to lure her to the barn?

Eve hesitated, but her odd behaviour might mean every-thing. She couldn't carry on without finding out more.

She followed Coco, keeping amongst the conifers to avoid being seen by her or anyone else who might come along. When Eve was opposite the outbuilding, she settled down to wait.

It was a good fifteen minutes before Coco reappeared. She was wearing a beanie, which looked saturated. Underneath, her platinum-blonde hair was heavy and dripping. Whatever she was up to, it was enough to make her ignore the weather. She looked just as fearful as before, but angry now too. It was there in the way she stamped away from the building, her shoulders tense.

Eve waited ten more minutes, but no one came or went. Had Coco been due to meet someone? Or to collect something? Her actions might have nothing to do with the case. She had an alibi for both murders, and Eve was convinced the attempt on her life had been genuine. But she still couldn't let it go. She texted Robin for safety, to let him know her movements, then dashed to the barn door and opened it.

The place had two floors. Downstairs was home to machin-ery: a ride-on mower, various gardening implements – shears, a couple of pitchforks and so on. There was a portable gas heater too. It would be necessary if anyone spent any time in there. The place was freezing – a draught coming from under the doors and up above. A hayloft. Eve could see the hay. Ada Rice must keep horses. She hadn't known that.

Eve paused to check outside again and listened. Nothing. A

moment later she made for the ladder to the loft. She climbed as quickly as her calf-length coat would allow, up under the eaves. It reminded her of climbing up to the sleeping platform at Magpie Lodge.

Eve held her breath as she took in the dim scene, lit only by shafts of light reaching through a couple of air vents. Shivers of hot and cold ran over her as she tried to make sense of what she was seeing and its significance.

Someone had been using the place for more than just storing hay.

There were blankets and rugs up in the loft, along with a part-drunk bottle of brandy and a biscuit box. A battery-powered lantern stood on a bale, but Eve used her phone torch to examine the room further.

The draught came from the vents. Her heart beating fast, Eve stood on tiptoe to look out of one. She was still aware someone could come at any time, but the angle was no good. All she could see was the tops of trees and the distant chimney pots of the hall. At the far end of the loft was a hay door. That must be how they got the hay up here. With a pulley maybe, or just by hurling it up from the back of a truck.

Eve swept her phone torch around the room. In a moment she was crossing the floor to a bale next to the blankets. There was a sheet of white paper there. Handwritten. Folded over. Addressed to Laurence.

42

Eve didn't have time to hesitate. Under the circumstances, reading the note felt essential. She peered at the sloping writing.

Why won't you see me?

I won't say anything. And we're safe enough here. Poppy's the most incurious creature I've ever met. I could knock on your door and ask to see you and get away with it. Don't tell me you'd rather carry on with your dull old life, a slave to convention?

You can't avoid me forever.

She hadn't bothered to sign off, but Eve was certain it was Coco who'd left the note. It had been put there by someone who'd just walked through the rain. The paper was damp in places yet the barn was dry.

Eve's mind was poring over the implications. She'd had no inkling, yet now it made perfect sense.

Coco and Laurence had been having an affair. Coco, a future student at Bathurst and Laurence, a professor there. A professor with a lot to lose. Married to the vice chancellor's daughter, with a prestigious new role likely to come his way, so long as he kept his father-in-law sweet.

And Coco was his volatile lover. Or had been, before something had made Laurence pull back.

The solution came to her instantly. Emory. Emory, who'd been pretty sure he was Coco's father. Emory, who'd exchanged angry words with Laurence after the séance at Fairview Hall.

Laurence had told Poppy that Emory had been concerned for her and he'd got angry with him for interfering, but that had been a lie.

Emory had found out Coco was having an affair with an older man. A married man in a position of power at Bathurst. He must have hated it. He'd tried to persuade Coco to study elsewhere, or to take more time out. Go travelling. Get away from Laurence. But his pleas had fallen on deaf ears. Of course, Coco had said he was bossy. Eve bet she got a kick out of the affair; *she* wasn't going to walk away. She had nothing to lose.

But Laurence's position was entirely different. He must have been terrified when Emory confronted him. His entire future and reputation were on the line. Emory stood between him and safety. Eve didn't understand how he could have been at Sycamore Cottage at the right time, but his motive was huge. And Coco would protect him, of course. If she genuinely hadn't seen her attacker, she probably couldn't accept that it had been him. It might explain why she'd been so anxious to quiz Eve about the police enquiry. She'd want to believe in his innocence, but she must be worried.

Eve turned to reverse down the ladder from the loft, feeling her way carefully. She was shaking.

How had Emory found out about the affair? Eve looked at the barn. It was hardly the most comfortable of meeting places, rather like Magpie Lodge. But one had a heater, and the other a wood burner. And they were both nice and private. Or at least, Magpie Lodge had been, until Emory had moved in.

Goosebumps crawled their way along her arms.

What if they'd been meeting at Magpie Lodge originally? It was far from romantic, but it wouldn't have seemed so bad when the weather was warmer, and Coco might have got a kick from sneaking around, under her parents' noses. Maybe she and Laurence had played the ancient Egyptian game there, and Emory had found it and recognised it for what it was. The academic at the British Museum had said it was used for fortune-telling. It was his area.

Eve was almost at ground level when she realised she'd left her umbrella on one of the hay bales. She badly wanted to get out, but it would be obvious someone had stumbled across Coco and Laurence's secret if she left it where it was. That could be dangerous...

Her palms were clammy as she began to climb the ladder again.

She needed to focus on getting safe, but her mind ran on; she couldn't stop it. Once Emory realised the fortune-telling game came from Egypt, she bet he'd made the link with Laurence. He was bound to know what the man did. Poppy had probably referred to it at some time or other; she was his goddaughter after all. He'd have guessed Laurence had been in the lodge. And who with. It was bound to be one of the Fultons: only they had access to the key, and only Coco had suddenly decided to go to university, with an inexplicable preference for conventional Bathurst.

It explained so much.

Maybe it was Laurence or Coco who'd broken into Magpie Lodge to try to steal the game back. Using the key was no longer an option; Emory had it. The sticking plaster on Coco's arm with its 'Don't ask' pop-art wording flashed into Eve's mind. Eve hadn't wanted to pander to her. Had decided not to ask. But maybe she should have. Perhaps Coco had acquired her injury climbing through Emory's window. Moira's words came back to her: Coco had been away when Emory turned up and he'd arrived with little warning, according to Angie. She'd probably had no chance to take her parents' key and retrieve the box beforehand.

If Eve was right, the game hadn't been where Coco and Laurence had left it. Emory had hidden it, so she'd gone home empty-handed.

Eve grabbed her umbrella then turned to go back down again.

This was no good. Laurence had a cast-iron alibi for Emory's murder, just like Coco. But even as she said it, Eve thought of Coco's ex-boyfriend. The one she'd invited over, at such a convenient time. Just why had she done that? She clearly despised him. She hadn't bothered trying to hide it. And now it was clear she was hooked on Laurence.

Eve shivered. In that moment, she knew she'd got it wrong. Laurence wasn't guilty. You only had to consider Coco's note to see that. Emory had confronted him – given him an ultimatum most likely: break off the relationship or face the consequences. And he'd made his choice. Turned his back on Coco, ready to move on. She must have been livid. It was she who'd been left out in the cold. She who would have been looking for a solution. And retribution.

But if the time of death was correct then—

'May I ask what you're doing here?'

Eve almost fell off the ladder in fright. She was only four rungs off the ground, but that didn't help. She turned to look into the eyes of Ada Rice.

Who was armed with a pitchfork.

43

'Climb back up.'

Eve had no doubt Ada would use the pitchfork if she needed to. The look in her eyes was terrifying. Utter focus without any hint of weakness.

'Go on!'

Ada followed at a distance, the pitchfork set to impale Eve if she fell. Eve was climbing one-handed. She was tempted to drop the umbrella but it was the only thing she had to defend herself. In the end, she threw it ahead of her.

'Coco killed Emory Fulton.' Eve didn't know why she said it. To surprise Ada maybe, in the hope of putting her off balance. She had to do something to shake that look of control. 'She gave herself an alibi. The time of death must be wrong.'

It was the only thing that made sense. How had she done it? Eve's right hand shook as she gripped the ladder, her teeth chattering from cold and shock.

'Of course she did. To think that a son of mine should choose to have an affair with such an arrogant, selfish little madam.'

Eve glanced behind her and saw Ada Rice was shaking too,

with anger. Selina and Emory's affair filled her mind. Coco had likely killed her dad.

Eve's skin crawled. 'You knew. You went to see her at the Dower House. It was you who tried to strangle her.' It all fitted. Selina had dropped in at Rice and Fulton the morning of the attack. Ada knew she was in town and probably that she needed to hang around for Roger. She must have dashed over to Saxford after Selina left, guessing the coast would be clear.

'Coco told Laurence. Laurence told me. Can you imagine if it got out? An affair with a murderer? His career would be in ruins.'

Eve's mouth was too dry to reply, but she was lost for words anyway. Terror and horror combining to rob her of coherent thoughts.

'Yes, I went to see Coco. To tell her she must leave the country and never come back. Give up her university place. Never see Laurence again. But she was angry. No remorse, no fear. Arrogant! She said she'd killed Emory to protect Laurence and enable their affair to continue. She acted as though she deserved a reward. She'd been furious with Emory when he told her she must end the relationship. He said the same to Laurence. Coco was sure Emory would tell her parents if she didn't give up her place at Bathurst. She didn't kill to protect Laurence, but for her own selfish reasons. She knew their affair would be over for good if word got out. Laurence would never have forgiven her. That's what she couldn't stand.'

Eve had reached the loft again now. When she glanced over her shoulder she realised Ada was no longer following her. She was almost back at ground level, the pitchfork held high, ready to attack if Eve tried to follow.

A second later, she was on firm ground and pulling the ladder away.

Eve had no means of escape. Her heart was racing. She felt like she could hardly breathe. What was Ada planning? She looked around at the dry hay and felt her legs shake. There was no way Ada would let her survive, given what she knew.

She had to keep her talking. 'You're as bad as Coco is now.'

'I lost control. She deserved it.' The pitchfork shook in Ada's hands. 'If only her parents hadn't come back when they did. But she's in no position to tell. With more time I might have another go. Make it look like an accident.'

Eve's palms were clammy but she tried to keep her voice steady. 'You killed Brenda too.' It couldn't have been Coco. She'd been home all evening. The Fultons had had a caller who'd confirmed it.

'I asked her to come and speak with me privately up at the hall, but I intercepted her in the woods. I pretended I was planning a surprise round-the-world trip for Laurence and Poppy's anniversary and asked if I could pay her to organise it.'

'She came at such short notice...'

Ada gave a thin smile. 'I explained I was snatching the moment because they'd gone out and it was all a great secret. I didn't entirely trust her, though. Urgency was part of the plan. I gave her no time to chat, and she was just as eager as I'd hoped. Everyone always said she loved her work as a travel agent.' Her tone was entirely dispassionate.

'But why?'

'She was starting to put two and two together. I realised that when I overheard your conversation in the ladies at the Cross Keys.'

'But she was talking about Poppy.'

Ada shook her head, her cold blue eyes on Eve's. 'She said she was *thinking* about Poppy, and about how young women get involved in the most unsuitable relationships. And then she said it *reminded* her of something Emory said. Something else. Something that worried him. Some passing comment about Coco, I'm quite sure. If I'd arrived a minute later, she'd have told you.'

Eve remembered Brenda's words. The way she'd said her theory didn't fit the facts. Because she assumed Coco must be innocent, after she'd been attacked?

'I did what I had to do,' Ada went on. 'And what was Brenda's life compared with Laurence's?'

Fear and anger were doing battle inside Eve, adrenaline still making her shake.

'So Emory didn't really die after nine.'

'Evidently not, though how that little witch arranged it I don't know.'

The air suddenly went out of Eve. 'I think I do.' How bizarre for the mist to clear in that terrible moment of danger. She'd got it: the reason something had jarred outside Sycamore Cottage. It was the birdbath.

'Before the weather froze we had days of rain. It poured for most of the day of the fundraiser, just as it had all week. And then it froze. The birdbath in Brenda's garden *ought* to have been full to the brim with ice when I interviewed her about Emory, but it wasn't. There was just a very shallow layer.'

Brenda's description of the crime scene came back to her. She'd mentioned a caddy over her bath. Eve's parents owned something similar. It had a central mesh basket, but to either side of it, where it stretched to hook over the tub, it was more open. You couldn't balance a phone there; it would fall straight through. But not if it was resting on something solid, wide enough to span the open wire structure.

'I think there was a block of ice in the birdbath, with a shallow layer of water underneath. My bet is that Coco managed to lever it out and balance Emory's phone on it, above the bath caddy. He was already dead, but his call to the horoscope line – one I'll bet Coco made – cut out when the ice melted and the phone fell into the water. It wasn't waterproof.' He'd probably left it in his trouser pocket or somewhere. Coco would have known what sort he had. They'd spent a lot of time together.

Eve's legs were still shaking, but through the fear came sorrow. The thought of the time Emory had spent with a young woman who was likely his daughter.

And why hadn't Brenda's description of the caddy struck Eve before? The picture she'd created had been vivid. Memorable. She'd mentioned Emory's body, and the water splashed on the floor. But she'd remembered everything else being peaceful. *So normal,* she'd said. *The bath caddy across the tub, the fluffy towels on the heated rail...* There was no way the caddy should have been in place like that. Poor Emory would have thrashed about like crazy and knocked it into the bath most likely, or at least skew-whiff. Coco had put it back carefully for her own convenience. Then back home she'd come in from her 'cigarette walk', calmly spoken to her parents and then entertained her all-too-willing ex, while the ice melted back at Sycamore Cottage, creating her false alibi. She'd known Brenda and Kelvin wouldn't be back for hours. They were bound to stay for Jo's birthday fireworks at the pub. The neatly arranged bath caddy hadn't caught the police's attention, but even that fitted. When Brenda saw what had happened she'd dashed to Emory and tried to pull him out of the water, then slipped and dropped him. That had probably knocked the caddy aside, making the scene fit the struggle that had taken place.

'What happens now?' Eve cursed the tremor in her voice.

'No one knows about Laurence's affair, Coco's guilt, or mine, and I intend to keep it that way. But I can certainly make *your* death look like an accident.' She smiled. 'There's a lot of gossip about you in the village. Everyone knows you stick your nose into other people's business. When your remains are found they'll accept that you were here investigating. I have a feeling you suspected Poppy. They'll think you came to look for clues and turned on the gas heater because it was so cold. I'll make sure it's nice and close to the ladder and the old petrol mower. The whole place will go up nicely. I shall be cross that you were trespassing, but of course very sorry that you're dead. I don't anticipate any trouble from Inspector Palmer.'

She lit the heater, took a rag, poured petrol onto it and tied it round the second from bottom rung of the ladder. As she put the ladder back in place again, the fumes caught at Eve's throat.

She could have climbed down, but Ada still held the pitch-fork. A second later the rag was on fire with the next rung already catching.

44

It would be useless to call 999. The fire brigade would never get to her in time. Yet still she reached for her phone automatically. What she saw on the screen removed all hope. Her text to Robin hadn't sent. For a microsecond she stood staring at the alert. She had no coverage and in her haste to explore she hadn't waited long enough to see the message fail. No wonder Ada hadn't tried to take her phone from her. She must know there was no signal here.

Eve rushed to the hayloft door but it was stuck fast. Down below, she could hear flames crackling. If the petrol mower went up...

Where the heck was the door fastened? At last she found it. A latch, quite high up. She managed to lift it and in a second she had the door open, the cold air hitting her. More oxygen for the fire. And there down below was Ada, watching her, the pitchfork in hand. Eve might make the jump – possibly without breaking anything – if Ada wasn't blocking her escape. As it was, she'd likely be impaled.

She went to one of the vents in the roof and tried to bash it open with her umbrella. After three hard thrusts it came loose but there was nowhere near enough room for her to climb out. Uselessly she thrust the umbrella through and opened it. It wasn't much good as signals went but it was red. If there was anyone in the vicinity they might spot it. But it wouldn't be in time.

Yet at that moment Eve heard someone calling Ada's name. A woman. Poppy?

Ada paused, torn. The fire wasn't yet visible from outside the barn, Eve guessed. If she allowed Poppy to approach, there was every chance the place would go up in flames before her eyes. At last Ada drove the pitchfork handle into the sodden ground, the tines pointing up towards Eve, and rushed away.

Eve swallowed. The fire had reached the loft. It was now or never. She'd have to jump and miss the pitchfork. She turned to face the interior again and pressed herself to one side of the door, as far away from the fork as she could, but there was barely any leeway. Her hands shaking, arms feeling weak, she lowered herself down, feet first, fingers slipping. She'd never been so scared.

The flames were rushing towards her. How could fire travel that fast?

Eve dropped.

45

Eve missed the spikes, but she landed badly. Excruciating pain shot through her ankle. She pulled herself up using the pitchfork and managed to wrench it from the ground, but it was too heavy to use as a weapon in her current state. Too cumbersome for a crutch too. Her umbrella stuck out of the top of the barn uselessly. It would have been perfect to lean on.

How long would it be before Ada got rid of Poppy and came back? Poppy or Laurence might see the smoke and come to investigate, but only if they happened to be facing in that direction and paying attention. Eve's only hope was to get away, but she could barely walk. She felt like sitting down and clutching her ankle or crawling. Survival meant coping with the pain. She limped forwards in the direction of the gate in the wall. It seemed to take forever.

Eve was only just through it, still far from the road, when she looked back and saw Ada had reappeared. Fear robbed her of breath. It was like a nightmare. Ada was back by the barn, looking to left and right. Eve should have left the pitchfork stuck in the ground. She'd made her escape obvious and Ada would spot her and catch her in no time.

As Eve pulled her mobile from her pocket, she watched Ada snatch up the fork again. There was still no coverage, but you could do more with a phone than make a call.

She fiddled with the settings, then threw it with all her might, through a clearing in the trees, in the direction of the track that led to Magpie Lodge.

In seconds, Ada was through the gate. Eve lay flat on her stomach behind a thicket of holly trees. An instant later the alarm she'd set went off. She'd changed the tone to sound like an incoming call. Unless Ada was supremely confident that none of the mobile networks functioned there, she'd hopefully take the bait. She wouldn't want Eve picking up and telling her story.

Eve didn't dare look straight away, but almost immediately she heard running feet. Peering from behind the holly, she saw Ada's retreating figure. She took a deep juddering breath, trying to control both her breathing and the pain. Thank goodness Eve had learned how to throw better after hours of practice on the beach with Gus.

With every ounce of strength she had left, she hobbled back the way she'd come as fast as she possibly could. But even as she went, she heard sirens. By the time she reached the main track a police patrol car was driving towards her. A second one followed. The first carried on at speed towards Fairview Hall but the second – containing DC Olivia Dawkins – pulled up. In seconds she was being helped inside, and moments later an ambulance was called. The pain was so intense she might be hallucinating, but in the distance she thought she could see Robin too, standing, his hand raised.

46

Eve was in the sitting room at Elizabeth's Cottage, her feet up on one of the couches, one ankle tightly wrapped in bandages. The hospital had let her go the night before after treating her for shock and a bad sprain.

'I can't believe you didn't break it.' Viv was sitting on the couch opposite. There were offerings from Monty's on the coffee table between them: iced fruit and peel cakes, red velvet sponges with vanilla frosting and, of course, some of the sloe-gin spice cakes. ('For strength and healing,' Viv said.)

It was six o'clock, so they were having Prosecco too.

'It's to celebrate you not being dead,' Viv explained. 'No need for me to advertise for a new business manager for Monty's.' Gus did a funny little skip at her words, sensing the festive aura.

'Gee, thanks. So glad I didn't put you out.' Eve had the urge to joke about it too. It made it easier to discuss. It would take a while for the bad dreams to stop. She'd woken repeatedly in the night in a cold sweat, but Robin had stayed with her and Gus had been on hand. Two sources of comfort and Viv was another. 'Thanks for sorting out the rota for walking Gus. You're one in a million.'

Viv had been in to air him before work, and lovely Lars had obliged later in the day. Viv said she'd got it all worked out until Eve could manage.

Viv smiled with just a hint of smugness. 'You see, I can do scheduling and stuff too. There was a slight hiccup this morning when— But don't you worry about that. We'll be fine until you're back.'

Eve took a deep breath and resisted the urge to press her for details. One thing at a time...

'So what I don't get is, how come the police were already on their way?' Viv asked. There hadn't been time for a full debrief earlier, so there were crucial details to fill in.

Eve sipped her drink, the fizz tickling her nose. 'It was all down to Poppy. Her and Coco.'

'Coco?'

'I could see from the note she left in the barn that Laurence had spurned her. My assumption is that Emory threatened to reveal their affair unless he stopped seeing her. I'll bet that's what they talked about in private, the evening of the séance. It was the day after the break-in at Magpie Lodge. I think Emory somehow clicked Coco was responsible. Maybe he could smell her perfume in the air.' Eve remembered noticing its cloying scent when she'd visited her. 'Or perhaps he'd already had his suspicions about her and Laurence. At that point, it looks like he became sure. He started to research other universities for her, and places that might tempt her to go off travelling again.'

'So he spoke to both Coco and Laurence, telling them to end the affair, and Laurence caved?'

Eve nodded. 'That's my guess. There was no way he'd risk his career. And of course, once she told him she'd killed Emory it was the final straw. I'd love to think it was a moral reaction but if it had been, he'd have told the police. He was only bothered about saving his skin.

'As for Coco, her note made it clear she was running out of patience. She wrote something like, *Poppy's the most incurious creature I've ever known. I could knock on your door and ask to see you and get away with it.* It turns out that's just what she did next. She looked angry when she left the barn. She'd become militant and she has no limits.

'When Coco called at the hall it was Laurence who answered the door but as it happened Ada was in earshot and of course, she knew the threat that Coco posed. Anyway, it turned out Poppy wasn't as incurious as Coco thought. She'd heard the door go too, and was just upstairs, out of sight. She heard every word Coco said. Ada eavesdropped as well; she had no idea Poppy was listening in.'

'Blimey. That sounds like an explosive situation.'

Eve reached for a sloe gin spice cake. They really were powerfully effective, especially alongside the Prosecco. 'Absolutely. Ada was peering into the hall from a doorway. Poppy could see her when she looked down from the galleried landing. She'd moved round so there was no chance Laurence would catch sight of her.'

Viv prepared to tuck into a red velvet cupcake. 'What did Coco say?'

'Accused Laurence of being a coward for putting their affair on hold, even though she'd seen to it that Emory couldn't give them away. Told him how brave she'd been and how scared she was. Didn't he realise it was his mother who'd tried to kill her? And that she must have killed Brenda too, to silence her. And so it went on. Coco stormed off, telling Laurence to keep an eye on Ada. She didn't want to be followed. But Poppy said Laurence didn't move. When she shifted so she could see him again he was standing there as though he was transfixed.'

'He didn't know his mother was a murderer?' Viv seemed to have forgotten about her cake. That was saying something.

'Seems not. Even if he suspected he must have blanked it. Poppy says she saw Ada disappear back towards the sitting room, and her gut told her she might try to kill Coco again. Laurence went through to the back of the house, but Poppy followed Ada, only to find she'd disappeared and the French windows were unlocked. Poppy paused to call the police, which held her up a bit, what with all the explanations. But after that she went outside to look for Ada. She said she thought she'd be safe enough if she was within earshot of the house. She kept calling her name. She was hoping it would stop her trying to kill Coco again. She wouldn't risk it with a possible witness close at hand. Meanwhile, Ada made her way towards the barn. Evidently, she'd discovered the love nest and thought she'd find Coco there, but instead she found me.'

Viv leaned forward and gripped Eve's hand for a moment. 'Talk about being in the wrong place at the wrong time. I'm so glad you're okay. And that was brave of Poppy. Pretty noble too, considering she'd just heard her husband had been sleeping with Coco. And that Coco was a murderer.'

'I know. She's made of sterner stuff than she realises. She came to visit me earlier today and told me she'd acted on instinct. She saved my life.'

'To Poppy,' Viv said, raising her glass as Eve echoed her. 'She must be going through an awful time.'

Eve nodded. 'Ada's been arrested of course, and Laurence has been taken in too – for withholding information. He's in serious trouble. Poppy says their marriage is over. No surprises there. And it's weird maybe, but she seems to have a new sense of purpose. She's going to get help for her addiction. I know it'll be a fight, but I think she might have turned a corner. She's talking about settling locally. She confided in her dad after the drama yesterday and he's going to help her. Poppy says she's always been fond of Suffolk – she associates it with her grand-mother – and there's a good market for her jewellery. The tourists in summer will help.' Eve shook her head. 'Her constant lying made me think she was guilty, but I think I understand it now. I guess it became habitual because of her gambling. I imagine she'd have kicked the habit if it hadn't been for Laurence being such a rotten husband. He robbed her of her self-esteem. Even when she knew he'd asked Emory to lie for him she clung on. She didn't feel able to cope on her own, but I think she's feeling her strength now.'

'Good for her. She'll be so much better off without him. Any other news?'

'It's no consolation, but I think Kelvin's about to get his comeuppance. I reported my suspicions to the police, and I hear they've got CCTV from Little Millmarsh, showing him entering Peggy's Curiosity Shop. It'll give them some leverage when they go to question the proprietor. I suspect there will be more to find out through his old employer. What's the betting things went missing from the homes of their clients, too?'

Viv's fizz was down on the table. 'He's a complete and utter boil on the backside of humanity.'

'You said it. There's no evidence that Brenda ever found him out.' It was only a tiny crumb of comfort. The thought of seeing Kelvin behind bars was another one.

47

Robin had been a regular visitor during Eve's convalescence, sneaking along the estuary path with baskets of food, bottles of wine and news from Greg Boles. All the same, it was several days before the loose ends of the case wove together.

Just over a week after Eve's ordeal, Robin was sitting opposite her at the kitchen table with Gus at their feet. They had steaming platefuls of coq au vin in front of them. He was an excellent cook.

'So Kelvin's under arrest?'

Robin nodded. 'The proprietor of Peggy's Curiosity Shop admitted he'd sold the bronze when Greg faced him with the CCTV footage. He claims he bought it in good faith.'

'Hmm.'

'Quite. And your hunch was correct – Kelvin had been stealing from the houses he visited for work. The company paid compensation and swept it under the carpet. There's a full-scale investigation going on.'

'That's very pleasing.' At least there was one satisfactory outcome from this awful business. But so much pain too.

Robin took her hand and squeezed it. 'You were right about

the ice from the birdbath as well. Turns out it was a good thick layer, with water below, so I guess it wasn't too hard to extract. Coco had taken a small crowbar with her in case she needed to force a window to get in, so she used that to lever it out. She saw the birdbath as she was about to leave and realised she could alibi herself.'

It all made sense. The liquid water underneath would have frozen again quickly, explaining the shallow layer of ice Eve had seen when she'd visited Brenda.

'Greg says she seemed proud of what she'd done,' Robin went on. 'Your input helped the police to frame their questions. Poppy had heard her confessing to the murder, so Coco knew there was no point in clamming up; but when she realised she was confirming a theory, she was furious. She couldn't stand that someone had guessed what she'd done.'

'I can imagine that. So she was all set to break in to Sycamore Cottage if she needed to. Did she go there intending to kill?'

Robin nodded, his face sober. 'She was quite clear about that. In her eyes, Emory's "unreasonable" behaviour gave her a perfect right to remove him.' He shook his head. 'She thought she'd be able to carry on as before. That Laurence's rejection was only temporary and that he'd come to his senses. After Ada's attack, she was busy making plans to go up to London, ahead of her start at Bathurst. She's got a friend down there who lives in a posh gated estate. She reckoned she'd be out of Ada's reach, ready to reunite with Laurence at the end of his sabbatical.'

'I wonder what Ada would have done if she'd gone. She told me she'd have another go at finishing Coco off if she could make it look like an accident.'

'Greg says she's refusing to comment, but my bet is she'd have left it. She clearly hates Coco and would happily see her dead, but trying again would have been a risk and they were in a state of mutually assured destruction. I doubt Coco would have told. Though she is a loose cannon.'

'She sounds completely delusional.'

'Greg says she's frightening. No sign of empathy at all.'

'It's just how she struck me. I should have made more of it, but her alibi seemed solid. That was another clue, of course. Why call an ex whom she clearly despised? And I could have clicked about the shallow layer of ice in the birdbath the moment I visited Sycamore Cottage. I noticed it; it just didn't occur to me that it made no sense. Even Coco's background makes her a good fit; Selina mentioned her diving and rock climbing when she travelled. She must have plenty of upper body strength. Poor Emory. That was crucial when it came to drowning him.'

'Hindsight's a wonderful thing. It was hard to see a motive.'

Eve nodded. 'But I could have got there much sooner. I knew Coco was going to Bathurst, even though it's a bastion of tradition and she's the sort to rage against the machine. And there was handsome Laurence, a professor at that very institution, whose marriage was on the rocks. And when I first found the box at Magpie Lodge it reminded me of senet, an ancient Egyptian game. I was on the right track. I could have made the link with Laurence then, but I didn't.' So many missed opportunities. If only she'd done better... 'I might have saved Brenda.'

But Robin shook his head, clutching her hand more tightly. 'Not with Ada involved, too. It was a tangled web.'

In the days that followed, Eve heard more about the fallout from the Magpie Lodge affair.

Moira had been round and sat and chatted for two hours straight while her husband minded the store. She brought the news that Selina and Roger Fulton were divorcing. Selina was moving away. Rice and Fulton was already up for sale and

Moira had it on good authority that she intended to set up a new business in the south-west. She didn't mention Dale Buckingham, which meant the affair hadn't come out. If Moira didn't know, no one did. Eve was glad for Dale's wife, though she couldn't help hoping the man would get his comeuppance one day.

As for Roger, he'd discovered that there was a question mark over Coco's parentage and had insisted on a DNA test to prove they weren't father and daughter. Only it turned out she had been his after all.

He'd resigned from the Blyworth and Villages Charitable Trust and discontinued his partnership in the legal firm he'd established. He was said to be looking for a new job – possibly down in anonymous London. The Dower House already had an estate agent's board up. It wouldn't stay in the family after all. There was no one left to leave it to.

As for Laurence Rice, he'd been in the process of applying for an Ivy League university post when the police charged him with perverting the course of justice. He'd hoped to be off as soon as his stewardship of the exclusive society for Egyptologists had been confirmed. It was an international organisation, so the move to the States wouldn't have been a problem. Eve imagined he'd been eager to leave Coco, Ada and Poppy behind. His plans were in tatters now, of course. He was on bail, facing a prison sentence. He'd been sacked from Bathurst and his applications to the US university and the learned society had been rejected. Moira had heard Fairview Hall was to be sold, just like the Dower House.

Later that day, Eve reread the opening of the obituary she'd written for Emory. It was ready to send off.

Emory Edgar Fulton – author, spiritualist and ghost hunter

Emory Fulton, well known for the 'Haunted' book series, including the bestsellers *Haunted England* and *Haunted Wales*, was killed in Suffolk on Sunday 17 January. A woman has been arrested for his murder.

Emory was one of two siblings, brought up by conventional parents in the shadow of Fairview Hall. The grand home was once the Fultons' family seat, but Emory's father was forced to break up the estate and sell off land, leaving the family in the Dower House. It was still a palatial home, with sizeable grounds, but perhaps Emory's father felt the family's status ebbing away.

As Emory grew up, his parents compared him unfavourably with his older brother, Roger. While Roger worked hard and passed exams, Emory would sneak down the garden to look at wildlife or find a quiet corner in which to sit and write a ghost story. His parents fretted over his lack of progress, but in some areas, Emory was soaring ahead. He quickly discovered his talent with an audience. He was a showman, excellent at storytelling, and charming with it, sought after at school fundraisers where he drew in crowds who hung on his words. He was popular with friends and loyal to them. From the height of his fame to his lowest ebb, he never failed to send his former childminder regular postcards, ensuring they stayed in touch.

In his heyday, he wrote a host of bestselling books about Britain's most haunted buildings and made countless appearances on television. His light-hearted and gregarious nature led him to enjoy other benefits that went with fame too:

parties, high living and a string of admirers. Instead of keeping his life balanced, his career started to suffer. He ran out of ideas for new books and his drinking became a problem. It was this situation which led Emory to a career change: from working for a distant audience, who read his books and watched him on television, to one sitting opposite him as he told fortunes and conducted séances. The switch presented him with new opportunities, but it came with some downsides. Guided by his sympathetic nature, it's clear he edited or even invented some of the supernatural messages he delivered. All the evidence suggests his aim was to help his clients, but it was a high-risk strategy. Leaving aside issues of honesty, everything depended on Emory's ability to judge what was best for his clients. Good-hearted though he was, it's clear from his business dealings, including a disastrous hotel venture, that he frequently failed to predict the consequences of his actions. He abided by his own moral code, but that wasn't enough to protect everyone he tried to help. That said, he was a well-liked man with legions of fans. He remained generous to the end, giving some of his earnings to children's charities and attempting to repay his debts. His death leaves the world a less colourful place.

Eve wished she'd known him for longer. She wondered how convinced he'd been that Coco was his daughter, but something told her it wouldn't have mattered. He'd sensed she'd lost her way. He'd have wanted to help her either as a daughter or a niece. Or even if he'd just met her as a fellow traveller on the road.

At that moment, Gus leaped up and dashed towards the front door. He must have heard something. Eve walked slowly to catch him up. Her limp was much better now, her ankle less painful. She'd got off lightly, but her close call still made her breathless each time she thought of it.

Opening up, she found Robin on the step. He leaned in to kiss her and she caught her breath, automatically looking up and down the lane. Sylvia and Daphne were her only neighbours, and they knew about her secret relationship, but other villagers used the road as a shortcut to the estuary.

Robin's eyes met hers. 'I've come to hassle you. I remember you saying you'd have the obit done by lunchtime.'

Eve glanced at her watch. It was just after two.

'Finished?'

She nodded.

'I thought you might need taking out of yourself. Do you fancy a walk along the estuary?' He grinned. 'You can lean on me if you like. Gus looks keen.'

Her dachshund was bouncing around like crazy.

Eve hesitated. 'Do you think someone might see us together?'

He gave her a half smile. 'What about if we only go as far as the track to Ferry Lane? I've parked my van there, right at the end. I was thinking the three of us could sneak away in it. Head up the coast. Blow away the cobwebs. Eat out where no one knows us.'

It sounded like heaven. 'You don't think it's too risky?'

He took her hands. 'I think events can remind you that some risks are worth taking.'

'Well, put like that...'

Eve fetched her coat.

A LETTER FROM CLARE

Dear reader,

Thank you so much for reading *Mystery at Magpie Lodge*. I do hope you had fun puzzling over the clues! If you'd like to keep up to date with all my latest releases, you can sign up at the following link. Your email address will never be shared, and you can unsubscribe at any time.

www.bookouture.com/clare-chase

I got the idea for this book after stumbling across an article about a tumbledown dwelling, which inspired Magpie Lodge. It had been clad in black corrugated metal but the shell of the building inside had been preserved in its ruined state, complete with warped timber, dead ivy and crumbling plasterwork. The pictures were wonderfully creepy, and I wondered what it would be like to live there, who might wind up in such a place and why. The story spun out from there.

If you have time, I'd love it if you were able to write a review of *Mystery at Magpie Lodge*. Feedback is really valuable, and it also makes a huge difference in helping new readers discover my books for the first time. Alternatively, if you'd like to contact me personally, you can reach me via my website, Facebook page, Twitter or Instagram. It's always great to hear from readers.

Again, thank you so much for deciding to spend some time

reading *Mystery at Magpie Lodge*. I'm looking forward to sharing my next book with you very soon.

With all best wishes,

Clare x

www.clarechase.com

 facebook.com/ClareChaseAuthor

twitter.com/ClareChase_

instagram.com/clarechaseauthor

ACKNOWLEDGEMENTS

Much love and thanks as ever to Charlie, George and Ros for the useful suggestions, feedback on random ideas and the cheerleading! Love and thanks also to Mum and Dad, Phil and Jenny, David and Pat, Warty, Andrea, Jen, the Westfield gang, Margaret, Shelly, Mark, my Andrewes relations and a whole bunch of family and friends.

And as always, crucially, I'm hugely grateful to my brilliant editor Ruth Tross for her invaluable insights. It's a joy to be able to work with her. I'm also indebted to Noelle Holten for her superhuman promo work and to Alex Holmes, Fraser Crichton and Liz Hatherell for their expert input. Sending thanks too to Tash Webber for her wonderful cover designs, as well as to Peta Nightingale, Kim Nash and everyone involved in editing, book production and sales at Bookouture. It's a privilege to be published and promoted by such a skilled and friendly team.

Thanks also to the wonderful Bookouture authors and other writers for their friendship and support. And a huge thank you to the hard-working and generous book bloggers and reviewers who take the time to pass on their thoughts about my work. I know it's a massive job. I really do appreciate it.

And finally, but importantly, thanks to you, the reader, for buying or borrowing this book!

Printed in Great Britain
by Amazon

46553731R00169